THE AMATEUR

A NOVEL BY

Robert Littell

SIMON AND SCHUSTER · New York

1   3   5   7   9   10   8   6   4   2

Library of Congress Cataloging in Publication Data

Littell, Robert, date.   35367
The amateur.

I.   Title.
PS3562.I7827A8   813'.54   80-29630

ISBN 0-671-41873-4

thiS booK IS dedicAted
to tHE GraNdpaReNts
LeOn anD syD littElL
anD
their GranDchIlDreN
jonATHaN octOber And
jeSsE AuGuST lItTelL

pro•fes•sion•al \prə-'fesh-ən-əl\ *n.* someone who thinks that if something is worth doing, it is worth doing well

am•a•teur \ 'am-ə-tər, ə-chər \ *n.* someone who thinks that if something is worth doing, it may be worth doing badly

FOREWORD

CHARLIE HELLER'S name is not exactly a household word in America. Still, enough people are aware of what he did (without necessarily associating it with his name) to make a book on the subject worthwhile. Heller himself cannot write it. When he joined the Central Intelligence Agency nine years ago next month, he signed the usual contract stipulating that the CIA had the right to review anything its employees wrote. The Supreme Court, in its inscrutable wisdom, subsequently upheld this clause. It goes without saying, a book by Heller would never have slipped through Byzantium's (to use Heller's pet name for the Agency) sticky fingers. Which is what brings me to the subject. I don't say Heller himself put me up to it, though he did seem familiar, in the one conversation we had, with my "fictional" accounts of the American defector Lewinter and, later, of the Soviet defector Kulakov. In any case, I am not bound by an American version of the Official Secrets Act, especially since I am presenting Heller's story, which I pieced together from various sources, in a "fic-

9

tional" framework. I am not required to submit my manuscript to anyone for prepublication review (and emasculation). And the fact of publication puts the people at the CIA at a decided disadvantage; they could sue me for giving away trade secrets, but that would only confirm that I had secrets to give away. One sees their problem; one can even sympathize with it. Almost.

For the record, then, this is a novel; all of the characters in the book are fictitious, and any resemblance to actual persons, living or dead . . . et cetera, et cetera. In the end, even Heller may be a figment of my imagination. My written request to the CIA, under the provisions of the Freedom of Information Act, for his dossier brought this straight-faced response: "No person by that name has been, or is currently, employed by the CIA."

Which is as good a note as any to start the story on.

R.L.
Grasse, France
August 1980

THE AMATEUR

CHAPTER
ONE

PLOWING toward retirement like an icebreaker, the lady Consul General half raised her right hand and asked in a voice ideally suited to recorded announcements, "Do you swear or affirm that you have told the truth, the whole truth and nothing but the truth?" Without waiting for a reply, she slapped the consulate stamp down on the signature, scratched her own initials alongside and slid the application for a new passport through the window to the dignified old gentleman with the homburg set squarely on his head. "Cashier's window, second floor, with twelve U.S. dollars or the equivalent in German currency," she intoned. And looking past the gentleman as if he had simply ceased to exist, she called out, "Next."

Next was a young couple, Americans also from the look of them, the boy fussing nervously with the knot of his tie, the girl all smiles and pimples. "We're interested in matrimony," the boy explained timidly. The girl had a better grasp of details. "We want to get married. To each other. Today if possible. Tomorrow at the latest."

The lady Consul General, who always referred to her own husband as her "future ex," unlimbered the Oscar Wilde line she had squirreled away for occasions like this. "Bigamy," she stage-whispered to the pool secretary typing away behind her, "is having one spouse too many. Monogamy is the same. Ha!" She saluted the couple with raised eyebrows. "Passports."

Across the reception room at the consulate bulletin board, two young men with fresh beards and worn knapsacks studied the index cards pinned up by people looking for rides or passengers. "Here's a Munich–Stuttgart," one said.

"Look at the date," the other replied. "It left last week."

Above the bulletin board hung a printed poster showing an American GI and a German soldier (wearing the helmet the world knows and loves) linking arms against the menace from the East—a Russian bear. With a mischievous glint in his eye, one of the bearded young men produced a knife-sharpened pencil and scribbled in the margin of the poster, "Man has a quick forgettery," and then signed it, "Carl Sandburg."

"Listen up, Carl Sandburg," drawled the Marine guard who had wandered over from his post at the front door. He was a corporal with a polished sharpshooter's medal lost on the expanse of his breast. His right hand rested casually on the flap of his whiter-than-white holster. "Defacing government property is against the rules of the consulate, and the law of the land."

"My name's not Carl Sandburg," corrected the bearded young man.

"Don't much care what your name is," retorted the Marine, deadly serious. He indicated the poster with his chin. "Erase it."

"Erase it? You're kidding?" The bearded young man looked at the Marine, then at his friend, then back at the Marine. "You're not kidding."

The Marine confirmed that he was not kidding. "You wrote it, you erase it."

The Consul General closed the passports she was examining with a bureaucratic snap. "Better do as he says," she called over.

"It's only a poster," the girl with the pimples pointed out to no one in particular.

A very striking woman in her late twenties, wearing a bright red sweater and pleated blue jeans under an old Burberry that had seen more than its share of rain, glanced up from the post-card she was writing. Everyone in the reception room seemed to be choosing sides, so she thought she would too. "Reminds me of when they got Arlo Guthrie for littering," she teased the Marine, and added, "Writing graffiti is not an extraditable offense." Then, unaccountably, she smiled at the Consul General and the young couple contemplating marriage and the old gentleman with the homburg squarely on his head and the Marine and the two young men with beards. (Later, when they spoke to the television reporters, everyone would comment on her smile—how soft and natural it was, how it flashed on at the most unlikely moments, how it seemed to physically warm the person at whom it was directed.)

The Marine, suddenly indecisive, turned to the Consul General for marching orders. She pursed her lips and reached for the telephone and thought better of it and started to say something, but her words were drowned out by the explosion.

Six plastic charges, placed on the street side, blew the heavy metal fire door, with the words EMERGENCY EXIT ONLY barely legible in faded red, off its hinges.

Unrelated details. Fragments. Figments (of imagination?): the electric wall clock falling to the floor with a crash and not breaking; a grenade rolling up to the feet of the Marine and not exploding; Carl Sandburg opening his mouth to scream and no sound coming out; the burglar alarm ringing insistently, like a distant telephone, and then stopping abruptly, as if someone had answered it; the young couple instinctively grabbing back their passports and trying to hide behind them.

And the terrorists. Most of all the terrorists. They appeared out of the smoke and swirling dust like a medieval apparition, masked genies summoned up for the denouement of a passion play, Hieronymus Bosch's nightmarish vision of the guardians of hell.

It seemed as if there were at least a dozen of them, but there were actually three: two men and a woman wearing gogglelike Army surplus gas masks, pitching Dutch A-17 tear gas grenades ahead of them, brandishing Uzi submachine guns with folding

15

metal stocks and forty-shot clips taped back to back for quick loading. They grunted and yelled obscenities and called to each other in Spanish and German phrases that had no verbs, or sense.

"From behind you—"

"Without hands—"

"Not three, not four—"

"Almost, almost—"

Firing from the hip, the woman terrorist shot out the consulate's bank-type security camera mounted on the wall, then turned on the screaming, milling people and herded them into a corner under the official color photograph of President Nixon. The Marine guard, his mouth hanging open, spittle running down his clean-shaven jaw, backed against the wall with his hands stretched as high over his head as he could get them. The Consul General, catatonic, stared out from her window at the smoke and the confusion and the unbroken electric wall clock on the floor and focused on the muzzle of a submachine gun and understood what she was looking at—and began to scream long, endless siren screams that left no room for ordinary breathing.

The two male terrorists threw off their gas masks as they raced up the steps to the second floor. The one who appeared to be the leader and spoke in German flushed a very frightened civilian security guard from behind a hall desk and made him lie face down on the threadbare carpet which the consulate had been trying to have replaced for years. The security guard, convinced that he was about to be shot in the back of the neck, started rolling his head from side to side and moaning, "Hail, Mary, full of grace," over and over. Hard as he tried, he couldn't remember the next line.

The door to one of the offices was double locked. Inside, the Counselor for Commercial Affairs (actually a CIA man who was running a string of prostitutes targeted against East German businessmen) was on the phone to his desk officer in Washington. "I'm afraid you're going to have to wake up several of our betters," he said with supreme calmness. "The consulate is in the process of being attacked."

"I thought you said 'attacked,' " said the desk man.

"I did say 'attacked,' " confirmed the Counselor.

"Burn your papers," shouted the desk man.

"Not to panic," the Counselor assured him. "The fire is already going in my wastebasket."

In the hallway, the Spanish-speaking terrorist covered the hostages while his German companion studied the locked door. He stepped back, shot out the locks with two quick bursts from his Uzi, then pushed the door in with his foot. When he spotted the fire in the wastebasket and the Counselor for Commercial Affairs calmly feeding in more papers, he sneered, "You must be the local CIA man." Gesturing with his Uzi, he ordered him to join the others in the hall.

Seventeen minutes after the fire door was blown off its hinges, the Consul General and the Counselor for Commercial Affairs—an Uzi trained on their spines—unfurled a large hand-sewn Palestinian flag from the small balcony on the second floor of the consulate. The first German police cars had already blocked both ends of the street leading to the consulate; armored personnel carriers, jeeps, trucks, even a tank would take up positions ringing the consulate before the hour was out. A local newspaper photographer, working with an old Leica and a 135-millimeter lens that he had bought on time and was still paying for, snapped the balcony just as the flag was unfurled. It was a photograph that would appear in hundreds of newspapers around the world the next day.

"We'll be famous tomorrow," the lady Consul General quipped nervously in German as she stepped back into the consulate.

"If there is a tomorrow," snapped the female terrorist in German. She started to laugh and then the laugh turned into a hacking cough that racked her body, but her Uzi never wavered from the hostages, all of whom had been crowded into the large corner office on the second floor.

"Didn't anyone ever teach you to cover your mouth when you cough?" the Counselor for Commercial Affairs taunted her in English. He was testing to see if she could speak something besides German.

The female terrorist slowly brought the muzzle of her gun to bear on the Counselor. "How would you like me to shoot out your kneecaps?" she asked in excellent English. Her finger tightened on the trigger. "Answer, or I will do it!"

The Counselor only stared at her.

"Don't," the striking American woman said quietly. She was standing next to the Counselor. "It's not . . . necessary." She looked the female terrorist in the eye—and smiled at her.

The female terrorist hesitated, and turned away.

In the far corner of the room, away from the window (and out of sight of the snipers who lay on their stomachs on roofs across the street), the terrorist leader spoke into the telephone. "You are to free the two Palestinian freedom fighters you are holding in your prisons. You are to make a plane available for me and my comrades." He listened for a moment, then raised his voice. "We permit no bargaining. This is not a negotiation. You have one hour. If you haven't agreed to our terms by then . . ." He realized he was yelling and lowered his voice. "If you haven't agreed to our terms, we will begin to execute our hostages, one every hour. Their fate depends on you. Their blood will be on your hands."

In the chancellery in Bonn the storm raged. Footsteps resounded through the long marble corridors of power, minor government functionaries scurried in all directions, small armies of temporary secretaries manned "crisis" phones and responded to stock questions with stock answers, armed guards held the mob of reporters at bay, television crews set up their lights and cameras for the fifteen-second interviews they would jostle each other to get.

Inside, in the holy of holies, it was the eye of the storm. Eight men and two women sat around a felt-covered table, smoking, talking in restrained voices, scanning contingency plans, weighing options or just staring off into space trying not to think about the unthinkable. A brown telephone purred once and a man in civilian clothes, with one sleeve pinned neatly back at the elbow, snatched up the receiver. He listened for a long moment, then meticulously thanked the caller for the information and hung up.

"Well?" demanded the Chancellor from the far end of the table. He sat with his head propped up in his hands, anguishing over the decision that had to be made in the end by him. Slowly, almost painfully, he lifted his head. His eyes, heavy with worry, settled on the one-armed civilian.

"That was the Central Intelligence Agency's chief of station," the one-armed man said. "He is offering us his reading of the situation—a reading, for what it's worth, which has been cleared with the Director of Central Intelligence in Washington and represents the official American line."

"The Americans," said one of the women at the table, "have a line on everything."

The Chancellor made a visible effort to keep his tone neutral. "And what is this official American line?" he inquired.

The one-armed civilian declined to look the Chancellor in the eyes. "They have concluded that the terrorists are not bluffing," he reported. "And they warn against an upsurge of anti-German feeling on the highest levels of government if, as a result of miscalculation, any American lives are lost."

"They want us to give in to the terrorists!" exclaimed a man in a general's uniform.

"They have a way of treating us like schoolchildren," complained the second woman. Several others around the table nodded in agreement.

The Chancellor looked at the general. "To get away from the Americans for a moment"—his facial expression made it evident that this was easier said than done—"why don't you lay out the options from the military point of view."

The general selected his words carefully; if things went badly, *if people were killed,* he would want the record to show that he had been prudent to a fault. "Everything depends on whether we believe the threat," he said. "If we don't believe it, we should simply sit it out. Time is on our side. The longer this drags on, the better the terrorists will come to know their hostages, the less likely it is that they will kill any of them."

"And if we believe the threat?" asked the Chancellor.

"If we believe it," said the general, "we must either give in to their demands or storm the consulate."

"Militarily speaking, what will happen if we storm the building?"

All eyes were on the general. "There are, of course, no guarantees," he said. "The troops, as you know, are specially selected and well trained. We have lowered microphones down the consulate chimney and located the room where the hostages are being held. We can fill the building with smoke in a matter of seconds. We can create a diversion—sheer noise is often effective in situations like this. We can put our people into the second floor in minutes. But it only takes one grenade . . . one burst from an automatic weapon." The general shrugged. "The line between a dramatic rescue operation and a catastrophe is a very fine one."

For a long moment no one spoke. The Chancellor's head sank back into his hands. He breathed heavily through his nostrils, distorting his facial muscles to suck in air. "Everything," he said softly—he seemed to be speaking to himself—"everything depends on whether we believe the threat."

The people around the table read and reread the transcript of the telephone conversation with the terrorist leader. Someone suggested it might help to actually hear it. Equipment was set up and the tape was played several times. The voice of the terrorist leader filled the conference room: "This is not a negotiation. . . . Their blood will be on your hands."

A psychiatrist who had worked closely with the police on kidnappings explicated the text. "Here, right here, he begins to raise his voice, to lose control," the psychiatrist explained. He squinted at the tape recorder, concentrating on the voice coming from it. "Now he pauses for an instant, right here, and reasserts his control, and goes on again in a more or less normal voice. Here you hear how calm he has suddenly become?" The psychiatrist shook his head and arched his brows and removed his eyeglasses and massaged the corners of his eyes with a thumb and third finger. "One can never be a hundred per cent certain, but if I had to make a judgment based on nothing more than the sound of his voice, I would guess that he has thought it all out very carefully, that he is a very logical fellow, that from the point of view of logic, killing a hostage is the first thing you threaten but the last thing you do, because once you've done it, there is no turning back. If he had screamed out the threat, if he had ranted and raved a bit, I would be more worried than I am."

They kicked it back and forth for another fifteen minutes. Finally, with time running out on them, the Chancellor did what he was paid to do—he *decided.* "They're bluffing," he concluded. "We must play for time." And.in an undertone charged with resentment, he added, "Hell will freeze over before I let the Americans dictate our policy toward terrorism!"

The Venetian blinds had been lowered and partially drawn in the corner room on the second floor of the consulate, projecting slanting zebra stripes of sunlight onto the walls and furniture. The hostages, twelve men and six women, sat on the floor with their backs to the wall, or in the few available chairs, facing the female terrorist, who presided over them like a schoolmistress, from a high stool, her Uzi cradled lovingly in her arms. Several of the hostages held lighted cigarettes, and the smoke twisted and danced above their heads in the bars of sunlight. The Spanish-speaking terrorist came into the room, checked his wristwatch, shrugged and with elaborate Latin politeness began collecting passports or identity cards in a State Department mail sack. As soon as he left, there was a buzz of conversation, but the female terrorist brought her submachine gun to bear on the hostages and the talk instantly subsided.

In the hallway the Spanish-speaking terrorist emptied the contents of the sack onto a desk, and the terrorist leader began examining the passports and identity cards, sorting them into two piles as he went along. When he finished, there were five passports in one pile, the rest in the other. The leader picked up the five and read off the names: "Hillel Rothenberg, Samuel Steiner, Sarah Diamond, Nathan Goldstein, Morris Cohen. There are several others who might qualify, but there's no doubt about these."

"Consider the possibility that we are rushing things," suggested the Spanish-speaking terrorist. He was visibly uneasy and kept glancing out a side window that overlooked a garden. "They need time to convene the government, time to discuss our demands—"

The terrorist leader turned on him savagely. "We agreed on a course of action before we began," he reminded his companion. His voice was pitched low, but was intense; he almost stuttered in an effort to get the words out rapidly. "Everyone threatens, but no one succeeds, because they don't believe the threat. Time is against us. By tonight we will call the hostages by their names. By tomorrow we will know which ones have children and crippled mothers. No! We must demonstrate to the authorities that we mean what we say. There is no other way."

The Spanish speaker reluctantly accepted this. The leader fanned the five passports as if they were cards and held them out. "Pick one."

The other man regarded the passports, and then looked up at the leader. "I will do whatever has to be done," he whispered, "but do not oblige me to be the one who picks."

The leader withdrew the passports. "For some," he told his companion, "the selection is the hardest part." He glanced toward the door of the corner room and smiled coldly. "She will pick for us."

The leader went into the corner room with the zebra stripes of sunlight and held out the five passports to the female terrorist. "The hour is up," he said in German. "Take one." The Spanish speaker lingered at the door, curious to see what she would do.

Without a trace of hesitation, she reached out and picked the middle passport and handed it back to the leader. He looked at the cover. It was an American passport. He opened it and called out the name. "Sarah Diamond."

The Counselor for Consular Affairs, who was based in the Bonn embassy and was only visiting the Munich consulate, climbed to his feet. He was a rail-thin man in his early fifties who brushed his hair back over his bald spot. "I vigorously protest against the singling out . . ." His voice faltered. He swallowed nervously, unable to go on.

"You can't do this," the lady Consul General mumbled weakly. "For the love of God . . ."

"I have been through this kind of thing before," announced the old gentleman with the homburg. "At Auschwitz." He looked directly at the terrorist leader. When he spoke, his voice trembled. "You are the son of your father. You are a barbarian."

The leader ignored him. "Sarah Diamond," he called again.

In the back, near the wall, the striking young American woman got shakily to her feet. She was trying to smile—and, astonishingly, almost succeeding. "What is it you want?" she asked in a husky voice.

22

"You are Jewish," said the female terrorist. It wasn't a question but an accusation.

All the hostages turned toward the American woman. The Counselor for Consular Affairs caught her eye and prompted her with a quick shake of his head. She looked around uncertainly.

"Surely you know if you are Jewish or not?" taunted the female terrorist.

"Yes, I know."

"And are you?" demanded the terrorist leader.

Sarah took a breath. "Yes," she said. "I am Jewish." And she smiled at the hostages around her.

Several of the women began to weep.

The terrorist leader said to Sarah, "You are instructed to come with me."

The old gentleman with the homburg started forward. The female terrorist brought her gun to bear on him. The American woman smiled at the old gentleman, smiled through mists forming in her eyes. Then she stepped away from the other hostages and followed the terrorist leader out the door.

Unrelated details. Fragments. Figments (of fear?): the front door of the consulate squeaked when it opened; "They're coming out," someone yelled in a high-pitched voice; the single tank parked down the street (the Germans didn't bring in more because their treads ruined the asphalt) lurched forward and lazily swiveled its turret around until the cannon pointed directly at the open door; Sarah Diamond came into view; a rain so fine it passed for mist was falling; she raised her face to it as she would have to the sun if there had been a sun; the terrorist leader stood right behind her, obscenely close, his left hand gripping her tightly around the chest, his right hand holding an Egyptian nine-millimeter Parabellum pressed to her skull; overhead the colors were running in the hand-dyed Palestinian flag hanging limply from the second-floor balcony.

There was an audible sucking in of breath from the hundreds of soldiers ringing the consulate. Then a stillness so profound it felt as if time were standing still.

A television cameraman, kneeling behind the fender of a

parked jeep, zoomed in on the face of the American woman. Over his earphones came the annoyed voice of his unit director. "For Christ's sake, hold on her face, will you. Your hand is *shaking.*"

The cameraman steadied the camera on the fender.

The American woman, savoring the softness of the rain, tried to smile, but she couldn't locate the muscles that did the work. She made a conscious effort to transport herself in time and space to a *noisier* place. But she felt the man's body against hers, and his arm across her breasts, and the point of his pistol against her skull, and she lost control. Silent tears streamed down her face. She looked out pleadingly and saw that nobody could help her. She clenched her fists and shut her eyes. Her knees started to buckle.

The pistol cracked and snapped back in recoil. The American woman collapsed like a rag doll on the consulate doorstep. The terrorist leader darted back inside and slammed shut the door; the sharp, dry thunderlike sound of the door slamming accounted for many people saying there had been two shots.

Down the street, inside the television trailer, the television director stared at the small monitoring screens. "What happened to the girl?" he whispered into the microphone to the cameraman in the street.

It was a moment before the cameraman, who had filmed more than his share of births and deaths, could bring himself to reply. Finally he said, "She blew away."

The terrorist leader took the phone from the Spanish speaker and talked quietly into it. "One every hour," he said. Then he handed the phone back to the Spanish speaker, who placed it softly on the cradle.

Twelve minutes before the second deadline, a bus with the shades drawn over every window pulled up in front of the consulate. The Spanish speaker sauntered out past the body of the American woman and circled the bus once. Then he climbed inside and frisked the driver. Walking backward, the muzzle of his Uzi pointing down, his finger on the trigger, he returned to the consulate.

They came out shortly after, the three terrorists forming the nucleus, the seventeen remaining hostages tightly packed around them so that it was impossible for snipers working with telescopic sights to get a clear shot. The group, looking like a formless centipede, with some people walking backward, some forward, some sideways, quickly covered the short distance between the front door and the bus, and an instant later they were inside. The terrorists crouched in the aisle, their Uzis moving nervously in every direction. The hostages sat in the seats. The bus started up, rolled past police barriers that had been pulled back and, sand-wiched between several police cars with wailing sirens, headed for the airport.

At the airport the curtained bus raced through an open door in the chain link fence and pulled up alongside a parked Luft-hansa Boeing. The two freed Palestinian terrorists, smiling hap-pily and flashing the V for victory sign, waited at the top of the portable staircase, just inside the plane's door. The female terror-ist mounted the steps, shook hands with the freed Palestinians and ducked in to inspect the plane. Then she returned to the bus. Again surrounded by the hostages, the three terrorists scrambled aboard the Boeing. The Spanish speaker embraced the two freed Palestinians. Just before the door closed, he glanced over his shoulder and taunted the world with a fist raised in triumph.

CHAPTER
TWO

THE inflated rubber tube gripping Heller's chest made it difficult for him to breathe.

"Have you had any contact with a government or intelligence representative of a foreign country?" the operator asked. He was a Company man, soft-spoken, crew-cut, wearing a three-piece suit with a government-issue pinstripe. His gestures and comments were delivered in exquisite slow motion. Earlier, watching him set up his black box, Heller had been reminded of the hour hand of a clock.

"Could you, eh, loosen this a bit?" Heller inquired.

The operator, with the name (according to the laminated identification tag pinned to his jacket) of John G. MacMaster, leaned forward and hooked a finger over the rubber tube to see how tight it was. He slowly shook his head. "That's about as loose as I can rig it and still get a reliable reading on your breathing rhythm," he explained. He glanced at his yellow legal pad. "Have you had any contact with a government or intelligence representative of a foreign country?"

Heller breathed deeply; his ribs strained against the inflated rubber tube. "No."

The three styluses in the black box on the table behind Heller scratched away—a sound so absolutely expected that it seemed part of the silence.

There was a long wait while MacMaster analyzed Heller's trace. Finally: "Have you ever indulged in any homosexual activity?"

Heller studied the blood pressure cuff on his arm and the electrodes held against his palm by springs stretched across the back of his hand. "I still prefer girls," he said. The Mona Lisa–like smile for which he was more or less famous crept over his face. He was thinking of one girl in particular. "Change that to 'girl' in the singular," he added.

The operator said, "You have to answer with a simple yes or no. Do you want me to repeat the question?"

"Have I ever indulged in any homosexual activity? No. No homosexual activity."

Heller had been "fluttered" (from the Company cryptonym for the lie detector test, LCFLUTTER) before: once when he joined Byzantium eight years before, then at roughly eighteen-month intervals, part of a program of periodic checks to insure that the Company had not been penetrated by what everyone politely referred to as "the opposition." Heller was fluttered more often than usual (secretaries, for instance, were fluttered every four or five years) because of the nature of his work. He was one of a handful of men assigned to Division D of the Clandestine Service, a tiny "higher than top secret" unit that engaged in cryptography (making ciphers) and cryptanalysis (breaking them) that the Company considered too sensitive to put into the hands of the National Security Agency at Fort Meade, Maryland, the principal cryptology organization of the intelligence community.

"Have you used Company computers or facilities," asked MacMaster, "for anything other than Company projects?"

"No," Heller answered immediately. He tried to get a look at his wristwatch. Fluttering had already killed most of the morning.

MacMaster deflated the rubber tube around Heller's chest. "You seem to be having a bit of difficulty with that last one," he commented, studying the trace. "Is there anything you want to clarify in order to narrow the question?"

Heller shook his head. Then it came to him. "Ah, yes, there is a project." He laughed at his own stupidity. "I have permission from the Deputy Director Plans. I'm using my computer to search for ciphers in Shakespeare's plays."

MacMaster, the indefatigable detective relentlessly tracking his subject through the twists and turns of memory, nodded patiently. "If I phrase the question, 'Have you used Company computers or facilities for anything other than Company projects, with the exception of an approved project to search for ciphers in Shakespeare's plays?' you could then answer no?"

"Yes."

MacMaster reinflated the rubber tube around Heller's chest. "Have you used Company computers or facilities for anything other than Company projects, with the exception of an approved project to search for ciphers in Shakespeare's plays?"

"No."

The styluses scratched across the paper. There was another wait as the operator studied the trace.

"Here's the last question. Have you ever stolen government property?"

"No."

Heller thought he detected a snicker from the operator.

"Maybe," offered MacMaster, "I'd better phrase that one more narrowly." He spoke with his usual excruciating slowness. "Have you ever stolen government property other than pens, pencils, Scotch tape and clerical objects?"

"No," said Heller, trying to mask his annoyance.

"That's better," declared MacMaster, hovering over the trace.

As Heller was being unplugged from the black box, he remarked casually, "I hear Technical Services Division has come up with something that's going to put you guys out of business."

"If you're talking about voice prints or rapid eyelid movements—"

"It's not that," said Heller with a straight face. "It's something the Clandestine boys picked up in Taiwan. Apparently the Chinese used it for centuries to test if someone was telling the truth."

MacMaster's face distorted with worry. "My God, we haven't heard a word about this."

"You know how the Technical Services people are," observed Heller. "They probably didn't want to alarm you guys at fluttering." He slipped into his suit jacket and started for the door.

"What's this new device?" stammered MacMaster.

Heller turned back at the door. He hesitated, as if he was considering whether MacMaster had a need to know. "I suppose I can tell you," he said finally. "You're bound to find out about it sooner or later. It's rice powder."

"Rice powder?" moaned MacMaster.

"Rice powder," insisted Heller. "You put a spoonful in the subject's mouth and ask him to spit it out. If he's lying, his salivary glands dry up and the rice powder comes out dry. The system's mobile, cheap, and it's supposed to be a hundred per cent accurate too. The Chinese swear by it!"

Heller just had time to cash a personal check at the Company credit union before it closed, then he headed down to the cafeteria for a quick bite with his best friend, Paul Slater. Heller's laminated identification card, with a color photograph that had captured the first faint hint of his Mona Lisa smile, was checked by the uniformed security guard at the door. Slater, a middle-aged man prematurely gray and suffering from the human equivalent of metal fatigue, had saved a seat for him at a corner table.

"Got a cigarette?" demanded Heller.

"I thought you gave up smoking," said Slater. He lifted the whole wheat bread to examine the tuna fish underneath.

"I did," explained Heller. "But I didn't give up temptation."

Slater came up with a cigarette for Heller, who passed it under his nose several times as if it were a fine cigar with an aroma to be savored. Then he reluctantly returned it to Slater.

Someone at the next table raised his voice. "The fact of the matter is the Company is *not* an equal opportunity employer," he argued. Heads turned in his direction. "Look around you," he continued, gesturing excitedly with his fork. "How many blacks do you see?"

Slater leaned toward Heller. "It's the house liberal," he commented. "Every house needs one. Hey, how was your ayem?"

"My morning, by Charlie Heller," said Heller. "It was a total, unmitigated waste. Down the drain." He made a face. "I was fluttered."

"Mine was wasted too," commiserated Slater. "One of the boys in my shop was operated on for a double hernia. I had to stay in the operating room to make sure he didn't spill any secrets under the Sodium Pentothal."

"Did he?" inquired Heller. "Spill any secrets?"

"Yeah," confided Slater. "He mumbled something about how the world was divided between those who say icebox and those who say refrigerator!"

Later, over chocolate chip cookies and coffee, Heller asked his friend how things were going in his shop. Slater was one of a handful of Company crateologists—specialists in determining the contents of crates from their shapes. It was Slater, in fact, who first spotted the medium range ballistic missiles going into Cuba in huge wooden crates on the decks of Soviet ships, a discovery that led to stepped-up U-2 flights over the island and eventually, the confrontation known as the Cuban missile crisis.

"Take a guess what the Russkies just delivered to New Delhi," challenged Slater.

"I'll bite."

"The Clandestine boys produced some blurred photos taken at the airport," explained Slater. "They showed wooden boxes, roughly as big as this table, being off-loaded from a Russian plane. What made the locals jittery was they thought they spotted armed guards accompanying the freight."

"So what was it?" asked Heller, swiping a chocolate chip cookie from Slater's plate. "Guidance systems for SAM missiles? Night sights for the T-fifty-four tanks? Wire-guided armor-piercing anti-tank rockets?"

"Condoms!" exclaimed Slater triumphantly. "The configuration of the crate matched the shape of crates used by a condom factory in Alma-Ata." Slater lowered his voice to a whisper. "I hear our people are going to put pinholes in them—give the Russians a bad name around town."

30

"Another triumph for crateology.". Heller laughed. "Where will it end?"

They stacked their trays and headed upstairs. "Put one over on the wife yesterday," recounted Slater modestly. "It was our wedding anniversary. When I got home, I found a long, thin two-ply grade B cardboard box with heat-sealed seams on my dinner plate. Without even opening it, I announced what was in it."

"They must think you have X-ray vision," quipped Heller. "What was it?"

"Three long-stemmed yellow roses."

"How could you tell?"

"Simple," explained Slater, all innocence. "It's a family joke. The wife always gives me roses. This was my twenty-second wedding anniversary, and my twenty-second batch of roses."

On his way back to Division D Heller was buttonholed in the hallway by a China watcher, a woman who spoke fluent Mandarin with a French accent (she had studied it at the Sorbonne). She had gone through "basic training" at the Farm at Camp Peary, Virginia, with Heller eight years before when they were both raw recruits. "You've got to see this to believe it," she gushed, backing Heller against a wall with her abundant bosom, waving a scrap of paper before his eyes with "Top Secret" stamped in red across the top. "It's Mao Tse-tung's astral theme. He was born three-thirty in the afternoon, twenty-six December 1893, in Hunan Province. That makes him a Capricorn ascendant. In fact, to really get a handle on his character, you have to come to grips with one particular detail—he's a Capricorn-Scorpio. Mars and Uranus were in that last sign, and these two planets were especially powerful there."

"I'm not sure you should be telling me this," Heller suggested politely.

The China watcher, suddenly cautious, took a step backward, put on her eyeglasses, which hung from a gold string around her neck, and peered at Heller's security clearance printed in red letters around the edge of his laminated identification card. "You're cleared as high as the Director—top secret, eyes only, atomic."

Heller looked up and down the hall to make sure they

couldn't be overheard. "Have you ever come across something called the Chinese tea syndrome?" he asked in a low voice.

"The Chinese tea syndrome?" she repeated in a whisper. She had known Heller over the years; was familiar with his penchant for teasing, though his teasing often had an edge to it; with him you could never be sure what the darting humorous glances from behind his ever slipping eyeglasses were meant to convey. "Actually, I'm not familiar with it," she admitted. "Is it Nationalist or Mainland?"

Heller cleared his throat in embarrassment. "I thought so." He studied *her* security clearance and shrugged. "I'm sorry. I shouldn't have told you as much as I have." And he turned and started down the corridor, a slow Mona Lisa–like smile spreading across his features.

Heller's identification card was checked and rechecked by guards at several turnstiles. He found the security procedures maddening at times. He was often on a first-name basis with the guards who went through the motions of meticulously comparing the photograph on his ID card with his face. Actually, anything that slowed Heller down tended to infuriate him. He went through life at a fast pace, almost as if he thought that the simple act of hurrying would solve most, if not all, of his problems. Now he arrived at his own door feeling frustrated at how much time he had wasted getting there. He attacked the cipher lock, to which he alone held the combination. (It was also printed on an index card in the office safe of his immediate superior, the assistant to the Deputy Director Plans, responsible for Divison D.) Heller dialed the letters until they spelled out the word "elbow." The door flew open. He spun the dials, erasing the code word, and charged in.

Heller created, and later deciphered, one-time pad ciphers, the single most secure form of coded communication in existence. The security stemmed from the fact that the ciphers were never (as their name indicated) used more than once, and only two people in the world held the key: the sender, who burned his copy as soon as a message was enciphered (the keys were coated with potassium permanganate and ignited at the slightest heat), and Heller at the receiving end, tucked safely away in the heart of the most security-conscious building in America.

The great bulk of enciphering and deciphering was ordinarily done by the National Security Agency, the vast complex at Fort Meade, Maryland. There were certain messages, however, that the Company considered too secret to let out of its own hands, even to the supersecret National Security Agency (which, unlike the CIA, was known to have been "penetrated" by the "opposition"). These dealt mainly with communication between the Company and its clandestine "assets" in various corners of the world. Which is why the Company maintained its own cryptology capability, albeit a small one, Division D of the Clandestine Service. And within Division D it was Heller alone who dealt with one-time pad communications.

To make an already sure system even more secure, Heller had devised a signature system for each one-time pad. It consisted of inserting "nulls" at prearranged intervals in the message, and switching from a straight one-for-one substitution system to a more complicated two-for-one system (two letters in a cipher equal one letter in the plain text) on every fifth word. The result not only guaranteed the utter absence of any discernible pattern, but it also eliminated the possibility that the cipher could be used by the opposition even if it managed to get its hands on the sender's key, because there would be no way of knowing from the key alone that the originator of the message was supposed to switch on every fifth word to a two-for-one system.

Because he handled incredibly secret material, Heller was obliged to take extraordinary precautions in his workroom. He routinely deposited the cartridge typewriter ribbon, along with any odd scraps of paper in view, in his office safe every time he left the room, even if it was only to go to the toilet down the hall. Heller's three-million-dollar computer, an IBM 7090 capable of performing 229,000 additions every second, held in its memory bank the keys to all the one-time pads he had created, and the plain text of the messages that had been sent using those keys. The computer itself could only be activated by a code word, which Heller alone knew. (Though again, as a precaution against his being run over by a car, the word was written on a card and stored in the safe of his immediate superior.) When Heller deciphered a one-time pad message, he typed up a single copy (a tedious process, since he never got beyond the hunt and peck method) and hand-delivered the plain language text to the Deputy Director Plans, the boss of the Clandestine Service. Even the cleaning of Heller's workroom was governed by iron-clad security rules. Every Thursday evening between 5 and 6 P.M. a black cleaning lady (who held a security clearance) was permitted to mop the floor and dust the furniture and the computer—under the watchful, if embarrassed, gaze of Heller.

On the occasional night when Heller worked late (usually on his Shakespeare project; he was using his computer to see if there were, as many people have claimed, ciphers in Shakespeare's plays proving that someone other than Shakespeare was the real author), an armed security guard was assigned to "baby sit" in the hallway in front of his door.

Cryptology had been Heller's passion as far back as he could remember. In the seventh grade he was already breaking ciphers devised by cheap cipher rings that came in breakfast cereal boxes. By the time he was in high school he had mastered thirty shorthand systems, including Gabelsberger, Schrey, Stolze-Schrey, Marti, Brockaway, Duployé, Sloan-Duployan and Orillana. While he was still an undergraduate at Yale, he was dissecting language phonetically, phonemically, grammatically, logically, semantically, historically, statistically and comparatively. He was drawn to ciphers—more accurately, drawn *into* them—because they nourished something deep inside him: a sense of spiraling into the core of language, of stripping away layers of confusion to get at some nugget buried beneath. And, of course, there was the added advantage that it was something he did *alone,* submerged in his own thoughts, following his own instincts. Struggling to work out a cipher, he lost the sense of his own identity, and only found it again when he triumphed over the encipherer, when the pieces fell into place and he came out of the gibberish with a clear text.

Heller had always been a loner. When he was ten and spending a miserable summer in "group activities" at a camp in upstate New York, he wrote on one of his obligatory daily postcards, "Dear Mommy, here everyone goes around in twos. I go around in ones." He was still going around in ones when, in his senior year at Yale, he published a paper in the *Kenyon Review* on the cipher system used by Samuel Pepys in his famous diaries. Pepys, Heller concluded, had employed a modified form of the system invented by the poet Thomas Skelton in 1641, which Heller had already deciphered.

It was Heller's paper on Pepys, in fact, which brought him to the attention of the Company head hunters. A professor at Yale on retainer with the CIA sounded him out and reported back to Washington that Heller didn't much care whom he worked for as long as it involved cryptology. And so in short order he wound up at the fortresslike building in Langley, eight miles from his favorite Chinese restaurant in downtown Washington, complaining like everyone else about the air conditioning system which never functioned properly because the Company had refused to tell the subcontractor who installed it how many people worked in the building.

Heller, twenty-nine and three-quarters (he was fond of fractions and used them whenever he decently could), impeccably shabby with his rolled-up shirt sleeves and knotted laces on his scuffed Clark boots, pushed his eyeglasses back up along his nose with a delicate forefinger and knocked once on the door of the Deputy Director Plans.

There was an almost imperceptible buzzing sound—faint evidence of electricity in the immediate vicinity of the lock!—and the door clicked open. Heller smiled over his shoulder at the secretary responsible for the flow of electricity and hurried in.

The Deputy Director Plans, a tall, ripe, soft-spoken Southerner named Turner Rutledge, was there, along with his assistant, a thin, gloomy former field man named Mudd, and—to Heller's surprise—Paul Slater, his friend from crateology.

"What are you doing here, Paul?" Heller asked pleasantly. Without waiting for an explanation, he handed the single typewritten sheet he carried in a metal file folder to Rutledge. "I figured out the Inquiline message," Heller offered. "It wasn't too difficult. He had the signature cipher right, so we know it's Inquiline and not the Russians who are originating. But he messed up the transposition." Heller launched into a brief technical description of the agent's enciphering error. Nobody interrupted.

Heller had been working on the Inquiline message off and on for several days. It had been improperly enciphered by the Company's agent in Prague who ran Operation Inquiline. This was the fourth or fifth time the agent, who had never received formal enciphering training, had made an enciphering error. Each time Heller, with a little help from his IBM 7090, figured out the mistake and broke the one-time cipher so that it was again readable. In the course of straightening things out, Heller had come to know something about Inquiline—a Company operation that brought in each week several dozen personal letters addressed to Russian soldiers stationed in Czechoslovakia. It seems that the Russians were not issued toilet paper, with the result that those who relieved themselves in the fields around their bases wound up using anything that came to hand—and this turned out, often enough to attract the Company's attention, to be letters they had in their pockets. Inquiline's field hands scoured the area around the Soviet bases, collected the letters and brought them to Inquiline in Prague, who sent them westward hidden under sheets of newspapers on the bottoms of cages of guinea fowl exported to France. From France, the letters were sent on to Langley, where a special room had been set aside to "launder" them, a process that involved removing human as well as bird droppings. Then the letters, smelling suspiciously of Ajax, were translated and studied for whatever tidbits on troop movements or command changes or morale they contained.

"Actually," said Turner Rutledge, scanning the Inquiline message that Heller had handed him—it announced the departure to France of another shipment of guinea fowl, and requested the Company supply him with Italian earplugs to block out the sound of low-flying planes and a copy of an Indian cookbook—"actually, that's not why I asked you up."

Normally Rutledge would have greeted the deciphering of the message with a measured amount of enthusiasm. He tended to look at things the way he must have regarded the first fish he ever hooked: delighted to have it, but willing to graciously throw it back if for reasons beyond his control (its size, his schedule) he couldn't dine on it. Now, however, he seemed uncommonly ill at ease. He glanced uncomfortably at Mudd, whom office wits had dubbed the "Shadow" because he invariably turned up right behind Rutledge. The Shadow seldom spoke, but when he did come up with something to say, he said it with God-given authority, *ex cathedra,* as if nothing had ever been said before on the subject. He and Rutledge both looked at the world as if it were *mechanical,* something to be taken apart, tinkered with and put back together so that it worked *more smoothly.* For once, Mudd too appeared out of character. He opened his mouth, then snapped it shut and looked expectantly at Slater.

"If it's about the ribbon I left in the typewriter last weekend," Heller said, looking from one to the other, trying to put them out of their misery, "I can explain that." (Rutledge, a stickler for security, had made an unscheduled tour of his precincts on Sunday and greeted his underlings Monday morning with a written list of their transgressions.) "It was a new ribbon, and I'd only used it for some Shakespeare work."

"It's not about the ribbon," remarked Rutledge.

Suddenly Heller wheeled on Slater. "What *are* you doing here, Paul?"

Slater said softly, "It's about Sarah."

Mudd said, "We thought Paul here, being your friend . . ." He let the sentence trail off.

"What about Sarah?" Heller spoke directly to Slater.

Slater couldn't bring himself to reply. He turned away to stare out a window.

"For God's sake, what about Sarah?" repeated Heller. His voice had become raw, like a saw biting into wood.

The Deputy Director Plans cleared his throat. "There was a terrorist attack on the American consulate in Munich this morning. They wanted the Germans to release two Palestinians they had in jail. They threatened to"—Rutledge moistened his lips—"to shoot one hostage every hour until their demands were met. The Germans thought they were bluffing."

The intercom on Rutledge's desk buzzed. He slammed down a lever with his fist and said, "I told you not to interrupt me." He looked up again at Heller. "The Germans were wrong. The terrorists weren't bluffing. At the end of the first hour, they picked out one hostage at random and shot . . . her." Rutledge fortified himself with a deep breath. "It was Sarah." He took another deep breath, and then a third. "She's dead."

37

Heller backed slowly away from the desk. He appeared to brace himself, as if he expected an enormous wave to wash over him.

"I want you to know," Rutledge mumbled, "how much we sympathize with you. Naturally, if there's anything at all we can do . . ."

Rutledge continued talking, but Heller no longer heard his voice. The words of condolence lapped against him. And then it hit him—the *sense* of what Rutledge had told him struck against him, washed over him, drowned him in agony, in grief. "Sarah," he moaned. And he turned away and reached out like a blind man and located the wall and began beating his head against it—short, savage, methodical strokes that jarred his brain until he no longer knew where he was or who he was or why he was suddenly trying to kill himself.

CHAPTER
THREE

HELLER was graced with the rare ability to experience something one day and view it with a certain (almost satiric) detachment the next. At times it didn't even take that long; at times Heller had the uncomfortable feeling of being both the participant and the observer simultaneously.

Which is how he felt as he waited with his crateologist friend, Slater, for the coffin to be off-loaded from the Air Force Boeing. Heller's head throbbed from the beating it had taken two days before, but the rest of him regarded the proceedings with the clinical eye of someone watching from the sidelines. He admired the dexterity of the forklift as it wheeled toward the plain wooden coffin resting on the lip of the baggage compartment. To Heller, it seemed as if the whole thing was a bad joke—but someone else's bad joke!

"Try to guess what's in the box," Heller instructed Slater, who shifted his weight nervously from foot to foot on the cold tarmac. "It's made of knotted pine—"

"Stop it, Charlie." Slater rested a hand on his arm.

"It looks to me as if it's been put together with nails, as opposed to screws or glue," Heller plunged on, roughly shaking off Slater's hand. "It's long and narrow, about the size of—"

"For Christ's sake, you're not making things easier!"

"About the size of a human body. Hey, I think I've stumbled on something. A human body! I'll bet anything there's a human body in the box, female probably, judging from the ease with which the crewmen lifted it. The configuration of the crate matches the shape of crates used to transport lifeless human female bodies in Germany."

An old Ford delivery van in mint condition, its chrome glistening like ice in the sunlight, backed toward the forklift and pulled up. The driver, a thick-set man in his late sixties or early seventies, with noticeably strong arms and shoulders, came around and opened the rear doors. He pushed aside the spare tire and a tin of motor oil and a toolbox to make room for the coffin. Then he turned back to wait for the forklift.

Heller went up to him. "I'm Charlie Heller," he said.

The old man accepted this with a noncommittal nod. "I recognize you from your photo." Neither man offered his hand. "Here," said the old man, who was Sarah Diamond's father, "you can help me."

Together, Diamond and Heller lifted the coffin off the forklift. It was heavier than Heller expected; for the first time in his life he understood the deeper meaning of the expression "dead weight." Two workmen in overalls started to reach for the coffin, one on either side. Slater took a step forward too. The father, who looked ill at ease in his brown zipper sweater and greenish winter suit jacket, raised his bushy eyebrows; the look was enough to stop the workmen and Slater in their tracks. "Kindly don't touch," Diamond said. The words were spoken quietly, but it was an unmistakable order just the same. Then Diamond nodded to Heller, and they carried the coffin the few paces to the van and slid it into the rear compartment.

An Air Force officer armed with a clipboard approached Heller. Somehow he managed to walk without producing the sound of footsteps. "Could I trouble you for a small signature?" he whispered. He uncapped a ball-point pen and offered it to Heller.

Diamond reached over and plucked the clipboard out of the officer's hand. There was neither politeness nor lack of it in the gesture. "I'm the father," he informed the officer. "I'm the signer." He produced an old Parker and with an immigrant's respect for bureaucratic forms, carefully sought out the appropriate space and signed his full name. His signature, perfected in a Polish "gymnasium" before the First World War, was legibly written, with long, thick, stiffly slanted, evenly spaced letters untainted by curlicues or elaborations. The signature, in fact, was very much the mirror image of the man—straightforward, dignified, serviceable. If Heller, watching from the relative safety of the sidelines, could read anything into the signature, or the man, it was this: The fact that there was evil and suffering in the world did not come as news to him.

"Mr. Heller." The father beckoned Heller with a thick forefinger. "I don't care one way or the other—"

A giant Air Force Globemaster at the end of the runway revved up, drowning out the father's voice. He waited stoically until the plane had taken off and began again. "I don't care one way or the other, but you are welcome to come with me in the truck."

Heller noticed that the old man spoke with a vague East European accent, a slight slurring of words, as if they were liquid instead of solid, as if they had no beginnings or endings.

"I'd like that." Heller said. He turned to shake hands with Slater. "A ride in the countryside's just what the doctor ordered," he told his friend. "Take my mind off my lack of troubles."

Heller climbed in on the passenger's side. The father took off his suit jacket and folded it carefully on the coffin, then climbed in behind the wheel. Diamond was methodical to a fault. He removed his wristwatch and hooked it, face outward, over the directional bar. Then he noted the mileage reading on a scrap of paper; he had tallied the mileage coming down, and would continually glance at the scrap of paper on the way back to see how far he had to go. It was his theory that a long trip was easier if you knew at any given moment how much of it was behind you, and how much ahead.

They drove north, not talking for hours on end, each absorbed in his own thoughts. Once, just outside of Philadelphia, the van went over a bump and the coffin in the back jumped. Heller imagined Sarah's body being banged around inside and winced, but Diamond only said, "She's stone dead. She don't feel nothing."

Conversation between them, the little there was of it, tended to be strained fragments that skidded off in any direction and never seemed to reach any logical conclusion. "She told me all about you, Mr. Heller," Diamond said at one point. They were driving past oil refineries in New Jersey that filled the air with a thick tarlike odor.

"I'd feel more comfortable if you'd call me Charlie," Heller said.

"I feel more comfortable with mister," insisted Diamond. He had the knack of saying things directly without being rude. He kept his eyes fixed on the highway. He wore thick glasses that distorted his eyes and made them appear smaller. Once, at a gas station, he removed his glasses and wiped them with a very large white handkerchief, and Heller saw his eyes without the glasses for the first time. They were cold and light gray, like stainless steel. "She said you were some kind of genius . . . mathematics . . . something like that," ventured Diamond.

"I work with ciphers for the government," Heller started to explain, but Diamond, pursuing his own trend of thought, went right on.

"She told me you could beat a computer at chess. I suppose there aren't many who can beat a computer at chess, are there, Mr. Heller?"

"Anybody who plays well," said Heller, "can outfox a computer."

Heller stared out the side window, thinking of the time he had tried to teach Sarah to play chess. She had listened intently to his explanation, then laughingly pushed her men around in a way that showed she had absorbed very little of what he had said. The more illogical her move, the more she laughed, until finally, with tears streaming down her cheeks, she had ringed Heller's king with a cluster of pawns and announced, "Checkmate—now I get

42

to fuck the king," and then landed on top of him and smothered him with her desire.

They left the turnpike for gasoline, and Diamond decided that he needed new windshield wipers, so they drove up to the garage. It took several minutes to get the mechanic's attention, and several more while he hunted through the stockroom for a pair that would fit on the old Ford. Heller sat in the van waiting. Diamond paced back and forth across his field of vision, then came around to the passenger's side and signaled for Heller to roll down his window.

"She collected stamps," he said. "Did you know that?" He put the question with an intense earnestness, as if his life depended on the answer.

Heller shook his head. It came as news to him that she had collected stamps.

Diamond seemed pleased to know some detail that Heller didn't know. He rubbed it in. "Red stamps."

"Red stamps?"

"She was crazy for red. Didn't you never notice how she wore so much red in her clothes? Red scarves. Red shirts. Red blue jeans."

Heller hadn't noticed; he never had time to. They had met eleven months before; had slept together almost immediately; had quickly realized that their lives were linked; had decided on marriage just before she left for Germany on a photographic assignment for *National Geographic*. In all their time together, Heller had never discovered that she collected stamps, or that she had a thing about the color red. He knew she was Jewish. But it had never occurred to him that if her life depended on it, she would admit it.

Diamond pulled in at a roadside diner in New Jersey for lunch. Heller settled into a seat at the counter and kept glancing over his shoulder at the van, visible through the window, as if he were afraid someone would run off with it; run off with her. Diamond, attacking a number four club special, talked with his mouth full.

"Revolutions don't change nothing," he argued. Heller couldn't remember what they had been talking about that had prompted him to say this. "They just rearrange things. Sometimes"—Diamond sucked at some food caught between his teeth and signaled with his forefinger for the bill—"sometimes they create moral codes that are maybe better than the ones they replaced, but most of the time the *before* and the *after* look to me like the same lady."

"I see you're a devout optimist," put in Heller, but the old man only ranted on, almost as if he were talking to himself.

"An optimist is somebody who don't know enough!" People within earshot turned their heads, but Diamond couldn't have cared less. "Me, I know more than enough. I seen a lot. I been to places"—he thrust out his wrist; Heller caught sight of faded bluish numbers tattooed on the soft white underside and thought for an instant they were the key to a combination lock, and then it dawned on him what they were without his ever having seen anything like it before—"places, sonny boy, where sunrises and sunsets were not everyday occurrences, but genuine, certifiable God-given miracles." And the old man shook his head and announced in a quivering voice, "Me too, I'm stone dead. I don't feel nothing also." And he abruptly departed for the men's room to hide the fact that he was lying.

Heller bought a pack of cigarettes at a vending machine and tore it open and stuck one in his mouth. He actually lit a match and brought it teasingly close to the cigarette before he considered he had sufficiently tested himself and threw the cigarette and the pack away.

In an alcove near the front door, two teenage girls giggled hysterically as they watched an Astro-Flash computer print out the horoscope of one of them. "Now all you have to do is find a tall, dark, unmarried Capricorn!" laughed one of the girls.

Diamond, coming up behind Heller, asked, "You believe in those things?"

"Computers or horoscopes?" Heller asked, but the old man was no longer interested in the answer to his own question, and Heller didn't press it on him.

Heller spelled the old man at the wheel, and Diamond dozed fitfully in the passenger seat, his head on his jacket, which he had neatly folded and wedged against the window. He woke with a start south of Hartford, looked out his window, checked the mileage and said, apropos of nothing, "It was that son of a bitch Freud who took us off the hook—told us we're not responsible for what we do. If you ask me, it's exactly the kind of thing you shouldn't say even if it's maybe true. But who asks me?" With a bitter snarl, he added, "Nobody is who asks me."

They left the turnpike and headed into the rolling countryside on two-lane back roads that had no white line down the middle and no shoulders. They crossed old bridges with gold-lettered historical markers at both ends, and woods full of trees without leaves, and deer crossings that seemed unlikely places for deer to cross, and abandoned vegetable stands, and a roadside store with MORNINGSIDE FLOWERS hand-lettered over the door. And then the road narrowed to one lane and they came to the Jewish cemetery in the middle of an S-curve, with its wrought-iron Star of David over the entrance.

They pulled up at the gate, and the old man jumped out to open it. Heller drove the delivery van into the cemetery, and Diamond swung the gate closed behind him. Waiting for the old man, Heller stared off at the sea of gravestones stretching away to the trees, and the trees stretching away to the town behind. He didn't even know the name of the town. They were late, he thought. They had missed autumn by several weeks; the colors now were muted, quieter, earthier, faded—as if mixed with too much water, too little pigment.

Diamond seemed to know the cemetery like the palm of his hand. "Left here, left again," he directed Heller down the dirt paths with the exaggerated arm movements of a traffic cop, then leaped out and, using hand signals, had him back the van to an open grave.

Several of the cemetery workmen digging nearby dropped their shovels and came over to help with the coffin, but Diamond waved them off. (Heller had the impression that the old man would have waved them off even if he hadn't been there to help.) Together they carried the coffin to the edge of the grave. Together they placed long canvas straps under it and slowly lowered

45

it into the hole. Heller's end slipped several inches. The old man looked up sharply and let his own end down until the coffin was again level, and then they lowered together until it touched bottom.

And then it was over. Diamond stared at the pine box for a long time, his face contorted with thoughts that Heller could only guess at. Finally the old man looked up, looked across the fault at Heller. "You can't say I didn't warn her," he mumbled.

A small plane flew low over the cemetery on its way to a nearby runway. Heller waited until it had passed. "Warn her?" he asked, searching for a logical thread in a conversation that was bound not to have one; they were both a little bit crazy. "Why do you speak now about warning her?"

"If I told her once," groaned the old man—he removed his glasses and started to wipe them with his white handkerchief, and Heller could see tears forming in his eyes—"I told her a thousand times. What idealism is is an ideal. What it isn't is a formula for everyday survival. If only she had denied it. If only . . ."

He fitted his eyeglasses back on, carefully hooking them first over one ear, then the other. "I know something about everyday survival. I'm the world's living expert. Lot of good it did me. Want to know the story of my life in two words, sonny boy?" He looked down at the coffin with a breaking heart. "In two words!" He was screaming now. "Almost! Over! And for this I thank every day the God I don't believe in."

Heller would never have accepted Diamond's half-hearted invitation (extended out of . . . what? Politeness? curiosity? desperation? force of habit?) to sleep over if he had known where he would have to spend the night. For the only room available was Sarah's bedroom.

Sarah's bedroom: under a slanting roof, so that Heller could only stand up at one end of it; an old tarnished brass bed with a high school yearbook under one leg to make it level, and an ugly Chinese doll propped up on the pillows; cobwebs in the corners, but no sign of spiders; a shelf full of books that a teenage girl might read; a collection of *National Geographic*s; an old Philco phonograph and a dozen or so long-playing records—Brandenburgs, Villa Lobos's *Bachianas Brasileiras,* several Mozart sonatas that she had especially loved, that sort of thing.

Sleep was out of the question. Heller sat on the bed fully dressed, legs crossed, trying to figure out new palindromes— words or phrases that are the same whether you read them forward or backward. Toward midnight he came up with "rotator." He got "Was it a cat I saw" sometime after his wristwatch stopped, which was at two-seventeen. In his stocking feet, Heller tiptoed down the stairs. He had a sudden craving for a glass of warm milk. The house was engulfed in a darkness that was beyond the mere absence of light; in a silence that was beyond the absence of noise. As he approached the kitchen, he noticed a ribbon of light seeping under the door. It was a swinging door, and Heller inched it open with his fingertips. The old man was slumped over the kitchen table, his head buried in his hands, his body racked by silent sobs.

Quietly, Heller let the door swing closed and returned to the torture of Sarah's chamber.

In the end he dozed off. When he woke up, his knees drawn up toward his chin, his limbs stiff and cold, someone had thrown a quilt over his body. There was a tiny basin in a corner of the room and a red toothbrush—Sarah's toothbrush! Heller washed his teeth with it, and went in search of Diamond.

He found him at the rolltop desk, surrounded by mountains of pamphlets, in the bay-windowed front room that served as his office; the old man presided over a small scatter-brained mail order business that advertised in the back pages of odd magazines printed on cheap paper and sold cures for acne, obesity, insomnia, bunions, backaches, stammering, blushing, piles, fat thighs, flat feet and baldness, to name a few. There were also schemes for increasing your height or intelligence, developing your breasts or memory, giving up drinking or nail biting, playing the guitar like Segovia in three easy lessons or speaking Swahili like a native in seven weeks.

Every weekday morning the postman would arrive with a pile of envelopes. Diamond slit them open with a knife he had "borrowed" from a Howard Johnson, removed the dollars or coins Scotch-taped to a card, or the stamps or money orders, copied off the sender's address in his straightforward, dignified, serviceable

47

handwriting on a plain manila envelope and inserted the appropriate pamphlet.

Heller leafed through some of the pamphlets while the old man finished up the morning's mail. "If it interests you, be my guest," Diamond offered, systematically licking with his large pink tongue the flaps of the envelopes and then pressing them closed with the heel of his hand.

"I ought to be starting back," Heller remarked as Diamond led him to the kitchen.

"I phoned up for you this morning," Diamond said. "There's a train direct. You don't have to change at New York. It leaves Hartford at four. I'll drive you in."

"I don't want to put you to trouble," Heller said.

"Put me to trouble," the old man challenged. "It won't change nothing."

Diamond whipped up some hamburgers and fried onions by way of lunch, and only discovered Heller was a vegetarian when he set the plate in front of him and saw him hesitate. Heller insisted he wasn't really hungry, but the old man snatched away the hamburger and started to beat eggs for an omelet. "Eggs here been in warehouses for months," Diamond said. "Sometimes the eggs don't taste even like eggs. The people who sell these things, they think I don't care if eggs taste like eggs. They're wrong. I care."

After lunch they cleared away the dishes and set up a worn folding board and played chess on the kitchen table until it was time to leave. Heller, playing white, moved his queen's pawn—an opening that usually produced slow, cerebral "closed" games as subtle as spiderwebs.

At one point Diamond pushed forward a bishop with the tip of his index finger. "Check." His eyes remained fixed on the game. "What will you do now?" he asked Heller.

Heller replied thoughtfully, "I'll move my king."

"I don't mean with the game," Diamond snapped. "I mean with your life?"

Heller was suddenly defensive. "What do you expect me to do?"

"I never expect nothing from no one," rasped the old man irritably. "From long experience, I got the opposite of great ex-

pectations. I got minuscule expectations. I got in fact no expectations." His tone softened; he waved a hand in vague apology. "I
was just curious what you are going to do, was all."

"I don't know what I'm going to do," Heller whispered. The
thin thread with which he had held himself together seemed to
unravel as he spoke. And then the last strand snapped. Suddenly
the bad joke he had been laughing at from the sidelines was *his*
bad joke. Tears spilled from his eyes. Blinded, he pushed aside
the chess pieces with the back of his hand. "I can't cope . . . The
idea . . . the idea makes me sick. . . . It makes me want to . . .
melt."

Diamond pulled a thick wallet from his back pocket and produced a snapshot from one of its compartments. He propped it
up on the table against the king so that Heller could see it. Heller
wiped his eyes with the back of his sleeve and looked.

The photograph was sepia-colored and brittle at the edges.
It showed Diamond, younger, stronger, wearing corduroy knick-
ers and a thick turtleneck sweater. He had his arm over the shoulder of a short woman with short wavy hair. There were two little
girls in the picture too, one in front of each parent. Diamond and
his lady regarded the camera solemnly; the girls had all to do to
keep from laughing.

"Which one is Sarah?" Heller asked in a barely audible voice.

The old man shook his head. "No one is Sarah. This was
taken before the war. Sarah was born after the war. This"—he
picked up the photograph and studied it—"this was taken in Po-
land, in the mountains near Zakopane." He started absently to
replace the photo in his wallet. "I lost my first wife . . . my first
family . . . two beautiful little girlies . . . in the war . . . in the
camps." He looked up at Heller; he was coming to the point. "I
thought for a long time the loss would kill me. But I survived."

Heller asked, "How?" as if it were a crime to have survived.
His eyes bored into Diamond's. Was this why he had been invited
to his home? Because the old man had something important to
tell him?

"To survive the death of people close to you," Diamond lectured, "you need ritual. In the camps there was no possibility of
ritual—no corpses, no funerals, no sending or receiving condo-
lences. So I created a ritual appropriate to the situation in which

49

I found myself." The lids closed over his eyes and he summoned up a vision. "I spent three years tracking the doctor who sent them to the gas."

There was a terrible stillness in the kitchen. Heller hardly dared to breathe. A painful knot was forming in his chest. "Did you find him?" he whispered.

"I found him, yes." The old man's eyes were still closed.

"And?" When Diamond didn't answer, Heller asked, "What did you do when you found him?"

Diamond opened his eyes and held out both hands, palms up. "I created one last ritual. With these hands I strangled him."

After a moment Heller said, "It didn't bring them back from the dead."

The old man shook his head impatiently; Heller had missed the point. "It brought *me* back from the dead!"

CHAPTER
FOUR

THEY sat around in small groups talking quietly about "trade-craft" or trading stories they had picked up on the Georgetown cocktail circuit the night before. Rutledge, the Deputy Director Plans, off by himself in the front row of the projection room, used the opportunity to read through a National Intelligence estimate that was being prepared for the Company's principal client, the President, on Soviet oil production and reserves; it was the Company's considered conclusion that the Russian production would peak this year or next at twelve million barrels a day, and could drop off in the mid-1980s by as much as a third—a shortfall that would oblige Moscow to compete on the open market for Middle Eastern oil.

Rutledge found the report long-winded and the grammar awkward (he cringed inwardly every time he came across a paragraph that began with "Being that . . ."), and he scrawled almost illegible notes in the margin as if he were an English professor marking an undergraduate thesis.

Several rows behind, Rutledge's shadow, Mudd, leafed through a stack of photographs taken by an automatic camera installed in the ceiling of a New York hotel. The photographs showed a Polish diplomat assigned to the United Nations Secretariat making love to a fourteen-year-old prostitute whom the Company had arranged for him to bed down with.

The telephone in the console next to Rutledge purred once. He picked up the receiver. "He's on his way up," a voice said.

Rutledge turned to the others in the projection room. "He's coming up," he repeated.

The laughter subsided. The faces took on serious, studied expressions.

Heller arrived several minutes later. Rutledge stood up and smiled and offered his hand and motioned him into the imitation leather seat next to his own in the front row. Then he dialed the number seven on the phone and told the person who answered, "We'll begin now."

The house lights dimmed. In the back row an agent from the Company's photo identification section leaned toward the man next to him, a German area specialist attached to a Deputy Director Intelligence regional team, and whispered, "Who's the guy with Rutledge?"

"He works in Rutledge's Division D," the German specialist explained. "Makes and breaks one-time pads, I think." He tapped a finger against his skull. "An egghead. He had something to do with the girl who was killed."

The first frames flickered on, in black and white, without a sound track, eerily silent, eerily slow, almost as if they had been filmed under water. The clip, taken by the consulate's wall-mounted security camera fitted with a wide-angle lens, showed the reception room just as the fire door was blown off its hinges. The wall clock, jarred from its mounting by the explosion, fell to the floor without breaking. The Marine with the polished sharpshooter's medal on his uniform stared in disbelief at the smoke grenade that rolled up to his feet and failed to explode. One of the bearded hikers opened his mouth to scream. Smoke from the explosion and smoke grenades filled the room, swirling up as if it were being sucked in by the camera. The terrorists, wearing gas masks with gogglelike eyepieces, appeared out of the smoke, rolling grenades ahead of them, herding the hostages into a corner with excited gestures of their submachine guns. Suddenly the female terrorist caught sight of the camera on the wall, swiveled toward it and, firing from the hip, shot it out. Heller instinctively ducked in his seat to avoid the bullets that killed the camera. Then the screen flickered white, and a slide came on showing the female terrorist in a police mug shot, full face and profile.

The house lights came up halfway.

The Chief of Section Identification blew into a hand microphone to see if it was alive. Glancing occasionally at a file card he obviously knew by heart, speaking in a dry, almost metallic voice, he began to read the curriculum vitae of the female terrorist. "Her real name is Gretchen Franke. Twenty-seven years old. German mother, Cuban father. She kept her mother's name. Raised in Germany, in Stuttgart, actually. She was on the fringes of the Baader-Meinhof gang when she first attracted the attention of the German authorities. In 1970 she was arrested in connection with several bombings—that was when this mug shot was taken. She was said to be an expert on explosives, and there was some suggestion that she picked up her expertise in a KGB training camp in Central Asia, though this has never been confirmed. While she was awaiting trial in Germany, she was transferred to a TB sanatorium. She suffered from a chronic cough—"

"Still does," piped up the Company man who had been in the Munich consulate under the guise of a Counselor for Commercial Affairs. "And she doesn't cover her mouth when she coughs."

There was an appreciative chuckle from several corners of the room.

"She *suffers* from a chronic cough," continued the briefer. "She escaped from the sanatorium by jumping from a second-story window. After that she disappeared for two and a half years, presumably into the Middle East. She surfaced again in our consulate in Munich."

"She's quite a dish," commented Rutledge.

"She's very hard," agreed the Company man who had been face to face with her in Munich. He said it with a certain amount of professional admiration. "It was she, you know, who picked out the passport of the victim. She never hesitated. No trace of emotion. She might have been picking a card out of a deck for all the feeling she displayed. I don't doubt for a moment she would have pulled the trigger herself if she had been ordered to."

Heller said, "Can I ask a question?"

"Of course," Rutledge assured him. "Ask away."

"The fire door," Heller said thoughtfully. "It was blown off its hinges . . ."

The Shadow said, "There were six plastic charges placed on the street side. Three opposite the hinges, two opposite the locks, one opposite the bolt."

"How did they know exactly where to put the charges?" inquired Heller. The question hung in the air.

Rutledge cleared his throat. "If you're suggesting that someone inside the consulate supplied the terrorists with the measurements of the door—"

"There's absolutely no evidence to support that," insisted the Shadow. His voice betrayed a certain edginess; it wasn't the business of someone in ciphers to get involved in operational details. Mudd had been against inviting Heller to the briefing to begin with, but Rutledge had insisted, as a matter of in-house courtesy; it was Heller's fiancée who had been killed, Rutledge had reasoned, and that gave him certain prerogatives.

"I wasn't suggesting anything," Heller defended himself. "I was only asking."

Rutledge said, "They could have gotten the placement of the hinges and locks and the bolt in any of a dozen different ways. One of the terrorists or an accomplice could have visited the consulate for information or visas and snapped a photograph of the door."

Rutledge reached for the phone. Heller said, "Please, just a moment." He stared at the mug shot on the screen, stared *into* it, attracted to tiny details: the coarse texture of the girl's skin, the receding chin that marred her profile, the thick eyebrows, the corner of her mouth that seemed to turn up, the nostrils that seemed to flare in— What? Defiance? Anger? Boredom?

Finally Heller nodded, and Rutledge spoke softly into the phone. "Roll the airport footage," he instructed the projectionist.

Gretchen disappeared and the screen turned bright white, like a slate wiped clean.

The next sequence had been shot by a German police photographer using a very powerful telephoto lens and filming from the roof of an airport building opposite the parked Boeing. The bus with curtains drawn over all of its windows pulled up to the Boeing. The two freed Palestinians, smiling and flashing the V for victory sign, waited just inside the door of the plane. The hostages, with the three terrorists hidden in their midst, poured from the bus and raced up the steps of the ramp into the plane. The nameless photographer on the roof reached out with his zoom lens, reached into the milling hostages, frantically trying to capture the face of one of the terrorists. Just when it seemed he would not succeed, just as the last handful of hostages pushed through the door into the plane, one figure among them glanced quickly over his shoulder and raised his fist in triumph. The camera, grateful for the opportunity, zoomed in on his face, and the image, which filled the screen of the projection room, froze.

"That," announced the Chief of Section Identification into his hand microphone, "is the second terrorist. Nobody knows his real name. Or his nationality for that matter. He's known in terrorist circles as Juan Antonio, which suggests Latin origins. He looks to be in his mid-thirties. He's a killer, no mistake about it. He shot a Turkish policeman in the face at point-blank range two years ago during a raid in Cyprus. He was known to be in Bolivia with Che Guevara's group when Guevara was captured and, eh, eliminated. Juan Antonio was believed to be the lover of the mysterious Tania, the lone female in Guevara's band. After Guevara's death Juan Antonio disappeared for seven years, though there were rumors, never pinned down, that he was involved in various terrorist activities in Germany and Italy and even Ireland. He turned up in Beirut in the late sixties as a bodyguard for one of the important Palestinian leaders, then dropped out of sight again. Except for the affair in Cyprus, the next time we hear of him is here, in Munich."

The German specialist in the back row said, "Tania, you will no doubt remember, was an East German national with proven connections to the Soviet KGB. We have reason to believe that Juan Antonio's ultimate loyalty, like Tania's, is to Moscow also."

Juan Antonio's picture faded from the screen.

The overhead lights started to come on. Heller turned to Rutledge. "What about the leader? What about the one who pulled the trigger?"

Rutledge, embarrassed, said, "We didn't think you'd want to see the clip we have on him."

"You're wrong," Heller said quietly.

Rutledge looked him in the eye. "I would like to dissuade you if I can."

Heller shook his head. He had come this far; he would go the last mile.

Rutledge shrugged. "Roll the third clip," he said into the phone. Several of the agents in the back rows squirmed in their seats; they knew what was coming.

The house lights dimmed. The screen turned bright white again, then filled with the image of the front door of the consulate, filmed in living color by the television camera down the street. The door opened. Sarah Diamond came into view. The terrorist leader was partly hidden behind her, pressed up against her, his left hand around her breasts, his right holding a pistol to her brain.

Barely breathing, his rib cage pressing in on his lungs, Heller sank into his seat. His facial muscles distorted the way a test pilot's are pushed back during rapid acceleration. He felt as if he was being forced against the back of the chair by gravity—or grief.

On the screen the television camera, steadied on the fender of a jeep, zoomed in on Sarah. She raised her face to the rain that was so fine it passed for mist. She tried to smile, then swallowed and looked out pleadingly at the troops and armored cars filling the streets. And then she lost control. Tears streamed down her cheeks. She closed her eyes. The terrorist behind her seemed to be holding her up. The pistol pressed to her head snapped back —and Sarah disappeared from the screen. It was almost as if they had used trick photography. One instant she was there, the next she wasn't.

The camera, as if stunned at her sudden disappearance, moved the few inches to the face of the terrorist leader, who was already ducking back into the consulate, and froze. His face filled the screen.

For a moment no one said anything. Then the Chief of Section Identification started speaking into the hand microphone. His voice was toneless, that of a supply clerk reading a list of spare parts.

"This is Horst Schiller. Age thirty-three. German, obviously. He first caught our attention when he surfaced at the London School of Economics. He was a brilliant student, and the London station chief put him down as a possible candidate for recruitment. Before an approach could be made, Schiller transferred to Patrice Lumumba University in Moscow. He spent three years there and roomed with a man who is known to hold the rank of major in the KGB. There is very little doubt in anyone's mind, but very little proof to support it, that Schiller works, ultimately, for the KGB. In any case, after his stint at Patrice Lumumba, Schiller disappeared into the Fatah camps in Lebanon. He's been involved in three hijackings. He was spotted with the Baader-Meinhof crowd at one point. He's been reported in Ireland, in Portugal, in Iran. And, of course, in our consulate in Munich. He had never personally killed anyone before that we know of. The Munich raid gives him a new dimension—that of a cold-blooded killer totally committed to international terrorism. The raid established him as one of the most important terrorist leaders in the world."

Rutledge helped himself to a second bourbon and branch water. The Shadow, Mudd, poured himself another glass of Coca-Cola. Rutledge's secretary, a fresh-faced young girl from a small town in Virginia (the Company generally recruited its secretaries from small towns, on the theory that they were less "politicized" than their big-city sisters), handed Heller a cup of coffee, then smilingly held out the sugar bowl. Heller took two lumps, and then a third. He thanked her and absently stirred his coffee until the secretary left the office. Then he looked up at Rutledge, who seemed very at home in his soft leather swivel chair. "What do you mean, nothing?" Heller asked. He was making an effort to control himself. "How is it possible, nothing?"

Mudd bridled. "The briefing was extended as a courtesy—"

Rutledge cut him off with a wave of his hand. "Believe me, Heller, we understand how you feel. If I were in your shoes, I'd react the same way. But you have to take into consideration the hard realities of the situation."

The Shadow said, "They have ties to the KGB. That's where they get their funds and weapons. Schiller was even educated in Moscow—"

"I must be missing something," Heller interrupted. He stopped stirring his coffee. "They're supposed to be terrorists, but they have ties to the KGB. Why don't you discredit them at least? Spread the word around."

"We've thought of that, of course," Mudd murmured in a distinctly superior tone. His patience was wearing thin. "Anything we can say against them only strengthens their position with the different terrorist groups."

"It's like giving them a letter of recommendation," Rutledge explained. He shook his head. "Besides, they don't make any bones about their contacts with the Russians. They claim that they are using Moscow to further their ends."

Heller sipped his coffee. "Where are they? Physically, I mean?"

Rutledge and the Shadow exchanged looks. It was Rutledge who responded. "Where we can't get at them," he said grudgingly. "In Czechoslovakia."

"For rest and relaxation," added Mudd, "until their next terrorist raid."

"Wait a second," Heller groaned in astonishment. "Do I have this right? You even know where they are, and you still won't do anything?"

Mudd leaped to his feet. "Not won't. *Can't.*"

"Request extradition," pleaded Heller. "Bring charges. They're murderers."

Both Rutledge and the Shadow were silent.

Heller persisted. "If you can't get them legally, why don't you have some of your people go in and kill them before they come out and murder more innocent people." And he added bitterly, "You do this sort of thing occasionally, don't you?"

Rutledge set his bourbon down on his desk blotter and stood up. Mudd turned his back on Heller and stared out the window. "We want you to know, Heller," Rutledge said, "that all of us in the Company share your sense of loss. Why don't you take a week or two off. With pay, it goes without saying. Time—that's what you need. Time."

Heller's crateologist friend, Slater, phoned up at closing time. "If you try for a hundred years, you'll never guess what the Russkie freighter off-loaded day before yesterday in Haiphong," he challenged.

"Give me a hint," demanded Heller.

"It was about the size of one of those old-fashioned steamer trunks," offered Slater. "Four-ply cardboard, reinforced by latitudinal and longitudinal metal bands. It had the word 'fragile' hand-lettered, in Russian naturally, on every side, and black arrows, also hand-drawn, to indicate which side was up."

"I pass," said Heller.

"You haven't tried," complained Slater.

"I still give up," insisted Heller.

"Crystal vodka glasses!" Slater announced triumphantly. "From a factory near Minsk. The handwriting on the cardboard matches the handwriting specimens in our files."

"What would happen," Heller asked, "if the Russians wised up to the fact that we have a crateology section, and started shipping hand grenades, say, in condom crates just to throw you guys off?"

"Bite your tongue," snapped Slater. "Listen, Charlie, how about joining me and Sandy for dinner tonight? We're trying out a new Mexican restaurant that just opened in the neighborhood."

"Thanks," said Heller, "but I think I'd better hang in here for a few more hours. I have some loose ends I want to tie up."

Heller phoned up the housekeepers to say he would be staying after school, and in short order a night guard, one of the baby-sitting contingent, had knocked three times to indicate he had installed himself in a chair outside the door.

For several hours Heller fiddled dutifully, if absentmindedly, with a new signature system for his one-time pads (the old signature system had been in use for almost a year, and he felt it was time to change). His office was long and narrow, with the computer at one end, partitioned off from the main space

59

with a Plexiglas window designed to cut down noise and keep the computer as dust-free as possible. The walls were windowless and painted deck gray; bits and pieces of paper, with words printed in capital letters, and dashes for the letters that were missing, were Scotch-taped to the walls, to the Plexiglas partition, even to the office safe in the corner.

Heller himself worked at a large metal table which held his typewriter, a framed photograph of Sarah, more index cards with parts of words written on them in capital letters, an old chess-board with ivory pieces (a birthday present from Sarah) and several thick dictionaries. Hanging on the wall over the work table, at eye level, was the present Heller had received from the other cryptologists in Section D on the day he was officially posted to the unit. ("To remind you how far we've come," the note accompanying the gift had read.) It was a framed copy of Secretary of State Henry Stimson's remark when he closed down the cryptanalytical section of the State Department before World War II: "Gentlemen do not read each other's mail."

Eventually Heller's mind began to wander. In a desperate effort to keep his thoughts off the one thing that drew them like an electro-magnet, he concentrated on palindromes and in short order came up with "Poor Dan in a droop," which wasn't nearly as elegant as his all-time favorite ("Lewd I did live, evil did I dwel") but would do for the moment. He keyed his computer and retrieved the doggerel on Shakespeare's tomb; Heller had long been attracted to the odd nature of the capital and lower-case letters in the verse, and he was using the computer to see if it didn't represent some sort of biliteral or triliteral cipher based on the difference in typefaces. He studied the doggerel, searching for a logical starting point.

Good Frend for Iesus SAKE forbeare
To diGG TE Dust Enclo-Ased H E. Re.

Blese be TE Man T spares TEs Stones
              Y
And curst be He T moves my Bones.
             Y

On a hunch, Heller decided to try out the cipher invented by Francis Bacon. He keyed his computer and retrieved it.

aaaaa STANDS FOR	A	abaaa STANDS FOR	I,J	baaaa STANDS FOR	R		
aaaab	B	abaab	K	baaab	S		
aaaba	C	ababa	L	baaba	T		
aaabb	D	ababb	M	baabb	U,V		
aabaa	E	abbaa	N	babaa	W		
aabab	F	abbab	O	babab	X		
aabba	G	abbba	P	babba	Y		
aabbb	H	abbbb	Q	babbb	Z		

For the system to be used as Bacon intended, all the capital letters in the doggerel must be converted into "b"s, and all the lower-case letters in the doggerel into "a"s. Working on his blackboard, Heller set out the doggerel in five-letter groups and reduced each doggerel letter to an "a" or a "b." Then he consulted the cipher key to find the appropriate plain text letter, and added that underneath.

GoodF	rendf	orIes	usSAK	Eforb	eareT	odiGG
baaab	aaaaa	aabaa	aabbb	baaaa	aaaab	aaabb
S	A	E	H	R	B	D

T(h)EDu	stEnc	loAse	dHERe	Blese	beT(h)E	Man^T_Ys
babba	aabaa	aabaa	abbba	baaaa	aabab	baaba
Y	E	E	P	R	F	T

pares	T(h)EsS	tones	Andcu	rstbe	He^T_Ymo	vesmy	Bones
aaaaa	b a bab	aaaaa	baaaa	aaaaa	babaa	aaaaa	baaaa
A	X	A	R	A	W	A	R

The plain text result, SAEHRBDYEEPRFTAXARAWAR, seemed like gibberish. Heller punched the plain text letters into his computer and instructed it to scan them for any of the following names: Shakespeare in any of its many spellings, Francis Bacon (the inventor of this particular cipher), Christopher Marlowe, Edward de Vere, Robert Burton, Anthony Sherley, Roger Manners, Walter Raleigh, Robert Cecil, William Stanley, Edward Dyer, Daniel Defoe and an Italian (who may have been the secretary to Shakespeare's patron, the Earl of Southampton) named Michele Agnolo Florio—in short, each person who at one time or another has been touted as the real author of Shakespeare's plays, and would be likely to signal that authorship by planting his name in cipher in a conspicuous place.

The computer tapes whirred for several seconds, and then the printout started up. Heller's pulse quickened; instead of its usual "No cipher detected," the computer appeared to have come up with something. He read the printout as it ran through his fingers.

The computer suggested that the letters could be set out this way:

SAEHR

BDYE	EP
RFTA	XA
RAWAR	

The letters above and to the right of the line, arranged in a different order, would produce the word "Shaxpeare"!

Heller shook his head in disgust. A cipher, to be valid, had to be unambiguous; two decipherers using the same key and working independently must be able to come up with the same "clear" text. Without a computer scanning millions of possibilities, there was clearly no way a potential decipherer could have figured out how to arrange the letters so that the word "Shaxpeare" could be retrieved. On top of that, why in the world would Shakespeare have hidden his own name in cipher in a doggerel composed for *his* tomb? It simply didn't make sense.

Heller glanced at the clock. It was past nine. He carefully removed his typewriter ribbon, collected all the cards and pieces of paper taped around the room and deposited them in his office safe.

And reluctantly called it a night.

Heller saw it in the image thrown back at him by the darkened store windows: he was walking wounded. There was an unmistakable sag to his shoulders, a leadlike heaviness to his movements, an expression on his face that was normally associated with physical pain. He felt as if he had lost a limb on the operating table. Half the time he knew it was gone, sawed off by some surgeon with a professional smile, wrapped in plastic and discreetly disposed of with the garbage. The rest of the time he was so sure the leg was still there that he would reach out to touch it. And gasp in horror when he rediscovered the truth. The emptiness. The absence.

It was gone! She was gone! There was nothing to be done about it. Nothing. Except to try not to reach out and touch something that wasn't there. He had to re-educate himself, the way they did with amputees; he had to teach himself to live with the emptiness, to walk as if there were no wound.

Which was easier said than done.

There were symptoms. One night he would wake up shaking like a leaf. The next he would wake up sweating with a fever. Vague fears that Heller couldn't quite put his finger on oppressed him; for the first time in his life he started hoarding food, filling his shelves with a variety of canned goods and bottled water. He was hungry most of the time, but eating didn't seem to help. His own voice sounded strange to his ear, as if it came from a great distance, as if it were the echo of something that went before. Sirens sent chills up his spine. An elevator starting up aroused sheer terror. Dark corners seemed alive with menace. The first thing Heller did when he arrived at his apartment on the top floor of a restored Federalist house on Cherry Hill Lane, a narrow brick street between M Street and the Chesapeake and Ohio Canal, was to turn on every light he could put his hands on. Overheads. Table lamps. Naked bulbs in closets. The small neon over the bathroom mirror that flickered in a Morse-like pattern. He even left the refrigerator door ajar so the tiny bulb would remain lit.

It helped. But not much.

Heller fried some eggs, opened a bottle of Portuguese wine and set out the food on a small round antique table just off the tiny kitchenette. He ate without appetite, more out of habit than hunger, all the while reading and rereading the postcard propped up against the wine bottle. He had discovered it in his mailbox on the way up to his apartment. "Dear heart," it began. Heller allowed his eyes to linger over the words; in his head he could recreate Sarah's voice, gently husky, saying, "Dear heart, dear heart," over and over. "I don't want to travel again without you," she had written. "We'll do everything together. We'll live together. And when there's no more point in that, we'll die together." Then she had scribbled a poem that they both loved:

Western wind, when wilt thou blow,
That the small rain down can rain?
Christ, that my love were in my arms
And I in my bed again.

And she had underlined the word "bed" and signed the card, "Your comrade in arms, Sarah."

My comrade in arms, Sarah, Heller reminded himself, doesn't exist anymore; she has disappeared from the face of the earth. She's been blown away like a leaf. She's become a figment of my imagination. I create her when I think of her. I kill her again when I try to ease the pain and think of something else.

Heller pushed away his eggs. But not the wine. A light snow was falling; enormous crystals swirled in silent eddies past the window. After a while Heller opened the latch and reached out to capture a crystal. Several landed in his palm, but they melted instantly.

Heller left the window open, let the cold night air stream through the apartment to breathe life back into it. A paper napkin flew off the table. Doors banged shut. The window shade flapped against the panes. On Heller's desk wedding invitations —"Sarah Diamond and Charles Heller invite you to share with them . . ."—were lifted one by one on the current and blown across the room.

Heller lunged for the stack of invitations, gripped it with both hands and tried desperately to summon up Sarah's smile. But it evaded him. The harder he tried, the further she seemed to slip from his memory. In panic, he turned to the open window and lifted his face to the snowflakes the way Sarah had lifted hers to the sun when there was no sun. Still nothing came.

"Where is the why?" Heller cried in agony, and he flung the wedding invitations out the window and watched them drift down with the crystals of snow into the dark emptiness below.

CHAPTER
FIVE

THE snow had melted on contact with the earth. There was no trace of it as Heller turned off the highway the next morning at the innocent-looking BUREAU OF PUBLIC ROADS marker and drove the last stretch that led to Byzantium, located on a wooded 125-acre tract eight miles from downtown Washington. He parked his car in the vast staff lot, presented his credentials at the main entrance, then made his way past the oil portrait of General Donovan, the Company's spiritual father, and the inscription on the marble wall that read, AND YE SHALL KNOW THE TRUTH, AND THE TRUTH SHALL MAKE YOU FREE.

Heller believed in truth. What was the art of cryptanalysis if not an attempt to get at the plain text under the surface; to get, in fact, at the truth? With a certain grim determination—after eight years of working for Byzantium, Heller felt as if he were putting the Company to the acid test—he decided to go over the head of his boss, the Deputy Director Plans. Surely there were others who worked for the Company, decent men who would be outraged at the idea of three terrorists living safely in the sanctuary of Czechoslovakia; and surely the Company, more than any other institution in Washington, had the wherewithal to set matters straight.

Heller got in to see the Deputy Director Intelligence, a man named Cole, easily enough. Cole had worked for years in the Clandestine Service and had dealt directly with Heller on a number of occasions when he was running agents into Iran and, later, Egypt. A tall, handsome bachelor with Eastern Establishment roots and a personal fortune inherited from his mother's side of the family, Cole was meticulous to a fault; office scuttlebut had it that he never went out in public without first having his shoelaces ironed.

Cole put aside his incoming folder and listened patiently to Heller until he ran out of things to say. He shook his head sympathetically, offered Heller a cigar, lit one himself when Heller declined, sucked thoughtfully at it for several minutes before he spoke; he had a reputation for carefully weighing his words, like a peasant at a market measuring out a precise amount of rice. Not a grain too few. Not a grain too many.

"I run an analytical shop, not a spy shop," Cole said finally. "We collect electronic intercepts from Soviet space launches, lists of dignitaries at the opening of a new factory near Leningrad, the signature cavitations from the propellers of Russian submarines"—he unconsciously ticked off the items on his fingers—"marriage announcements and rumors on who wasn't invited to the wedding, weather reports, production statistics, pictures of the Politburo members at the Bolshoi, photographs of launching pads taken from sixteen nautical miles up in the sky by planes flying at three times the speed of sound. That's the sort of thing we do. We pool the information we collect and codify it and then pore over it for months in the absolutely religious conviction that if you look at something long enough a pattern will emerge and the pieces will fall into place." Cole exhaled a cloud of cigar smoke; for a moment his head disappeared from view behind it. "The days of clandestine ops, of spies, are drawing to a close. Rutledge and his shadow are living on borrowed time. I'm genuinely sorry about what happened— you know me well enough to know I mean that, Heller—but terrorists, Czechoslovakia"—Cole shrugged—"it's just not my cup of tea."

Wandering back through the corridors toward his own neck of Byzantium's woods, Heller passed the Deputy Director Central Intelligence, a clandestine alumnus who had made a name for himself during the Vietnam years running a private war in Laos with only a handful of Americans and tens of thousands of mercenary tribesmen.

"I heard about what happened, of course," said the DDCI. He kept glancing at his wristwatch as Heller made his pitch, so he talked quickly.

"We know who they are," Heller summed up, speaking passionately. His throat was dry; his voice was hoarse. "We know where they are. Surely there's something the Company—"

"Send me a memorandum on it," the DDCI instructed Heller. "I'll see what I can do." Before Heller could say a word, the DDCI joined two senior officials passing in the hall. As Heller looked after them, one of the officials said something and the DDCI burst out laughing.

Over meat loaf and mashed potatoes in the cafeteria, Heller's crateologist friend, Slater, listened to what had happened. "You're out of your skull," he lectured Heller. "Rutledge will hear about this. He won't sit still for one of his people going over his head."

"What are they going to do," Heller asked lightly, "take my computer away from me?" He patted his jacket pockets and was annoyed to find them empty. "Do you have a cigarette?"

"You don't smoke," Slater said gloomily.

"I smoked once," said Heller. "I may smoke again."

Slater said, "Listen, Charlie, back off. These are not the kind of people you want as enemies."

Heller shook his head stubbornly. "There's still someone I haven't tried."

Slater studied his friend carefully. "If you pull something like that," he warned, "don't count on me for lunch anymore. I've got a family to support. Where else can I get a job with the narrow talents I've developed here?"

"There are job offers for crateologists in the help wanted columns every day," Heller said.

"Crateologists, as in packing crates," protested Slater, "not crateologists as in discovering what's in them by their shapes." And he added seriously, "Don't do it, Charlie. This is a civilized place as long as you keep the wrappings on. Don't stir up the dogs."

But Heller was determined; he owed it to Sarah; he owed it to himself! He made his way (thanks to the clearance coded onto his identification card) to Byzantium's holy of holies, a corner suite of offices on the seventh floor of the building with the letters DCI stenciled unobtrusively on the swinging frosted-glass doors.

The atmosphere reminded Heller of a doctor's waiting room. Several senior staffers carrying thick file folders sat around on comfortable couches talking in undertones. Just inside the swinging doors, planted like an early-warning system, sat the appointments secretary for the Director Central Intelligence. She was a scrubbed middle-aged cold warrior who made no pretense about being pleasant.

"Yes?" She looked up at Heller suspiciously.

Heller bent over her desk and quietly told her who he was and in very general terms why he wanted to see the DCI.

The secretary pursed her lips to hide her lack of interest, flipped open her appointment book (a top secret document that was stored in a safe at the close of every workday) and began searching for a free slot for Heller.

"I appreciate this very much," Heller told her. It was turning out to be easier than he thought.

"I can give you twenty minutes in"—she flipped over a page, checked something, then went back to the previous page—"in five weeks."

"Five weeks!" Heller said out loud. The senior staffers scattered around the couches stirred uncomfortably. Heller bent over the desk again and lowered his voice. "You don't seem to understand. This is a very urgent matter."

The secretary spotted something on another page. Grudgingly she offered, "I can squeeze you in here, but you can only have ten minutes." She looked up at Heller. "Four weeks from tomorrow."

Heller slowly straightened. "Is that your final offer?" he asked in a loud voice.

The secretary regarded him impassively. "There's no need to get sarcastic. The Director is a very busy man."

The senior staffers looked from one to the other as if they were following a Ping-Pong match.

The secretary said, "Do you want the appointment or don't you?"

Without a word, Heller backed through the swinging doors, then turned on his heel and left.

Sarah had changed his life, brought into it an orderliness, a tidiness, a sense of sequence. Days had a beginning, a middle and an end; things occurred one after the other. Without Sarah, they seemed to blend into each other. Everyday life became episodic, and Heller was hard put to remember if something had taken place *before* or *after* something else. Take the latest garbled message from Inquiline. For the life of him, Heller couldn't remember if he had straightened it out before or after he had seen the Company psychiatrist. It must have been before, because it was Rutledge who had given him the doctor's name and address. Yes, it must have been before.

The Inquiline message had been easy enough to deal with. Heller activated his computer, brought up the appropriate one-time key and set about finding out where Inquiline had gone wrong during the enciphering. The basic technique that Heller used was frequency analysis. He knew, from his statistical analysis of language, that there was a 12 per cent chance that any given letter would be an "e," and an 8 per cent chance it would be a "t." "H" owed most of its frequency to its appearance in the word "the." A quarter of any text was likely to be made up of the following words: "the, of, and, to, a, in, that, it, is, I."

Heller knew too that the word "Inquiline" itself would be in the message somewhere. Working on cross-ruled graph paper, he concentrated on retrieving the three "i"s in Inquiline. He soon found them, and in short order glimpsed the skeleton of a pattern in a few scattered letters. After that, it was only a question of time before he discovered the enciphering error: Inquiline had simply included too many "nulls," letters that mean absolutely nothing and are put in the message to confuse a would-be cipher breaker.

An hour and three-quarters after he started, Heller had un-raveled the plain text announcing the delivery of a new batch of guinea fowl to Paris the following week. The message thanked the Company for the earplugs and the Indian cookbook, commenting that the book was "better late than not at all." (The phrase threw Heller off the track for a full half hour; he was expecting "better late than never," and had to backtrack several times before he realized that Inquiline, who was Czech but was enciphering in English, had simply gotten the cliché wrong.) Inquiline went on to ask the Company to include a pair of waterproof boots, size seven, in the next shipment of ciphers, as the river that he lived alongside of was overflowing its banks again.

Inquiline, Heller noted to himself, had small feet for a man.

The request was touchingly phrased, considering it was in cipher: "Apologize inappropriateness but is it within realm of possibility . . ." Heller knew the drill. Somewhere, deep in the bowels of the Langley complex, an agent assigned to the procurement section of the Technical Services Division—someone who normally dealt with cigarette-lighter cameras or fountain-pen recorders or poisoned cigars—would fill out a form in triplicate requesting $14.75 in cash to purchase a pair of watertight boots, size seven. He would justify the expense in the place provided on the form with a brief description of the item to be purchased and the comment "Not manufactured by the Company" to account for having to go outside for it. Rutledge would sign the chit, and one pair of watertight boots, with all markings that might indicate their origin removed, purchased secretly with laundered, un-traceable funds that never come under Congressional scrutiny, would soon be on its way to Prague.

Heller remembered that Rutledge seemed to have other things on his mind when he brought him the deciphered Inqui-line message. "I hear," Rutledge said icily, "that you've been knocking your head against a stone wall."

Heller acknowledged as much.

"You know how things work around here," Rutledge contin-ued. "There's a chain of command. You report to me. I report to the Deputy Director Central Intelligence. The Deputy Director reports to the Director. The Director reports to God."

"I banged my head against the wall," Heller explained lamely, "for the same reason anyone bangs his head against a wall —it feels so goddamn good when you stop."

"Then you've stopped?"

Heller's voice was barely audible. "I've stopped, yes."

Rutledge scribbled a name and address on a scrap of paper. "In case you feel the urge to start again . . ." He handed it to Heller. "I'm taking into account the fact that you've had a . . . shock. If you're going to have a nervous breakdown, I'll send you to a place where you can have it comfortably. If you need some time off to pull yourself together, I'll authorize that too. Just shape up, Heller."

"Who's Dr. Bennett?" asked Heller, glancing at the card Rutledge had given him.

"Bennett is a Company psychiatrist. He's cleared up to top secret, eyes only. He's even fluttered every now and then. If you need professional help, you can go to him." Rutledge put a hand on Heller's shoulder as he steered him toward the door. "You're an extremely valuable asset to us. But there's a limit to the value of any asset. Do we understand each other?"

"We understand each other," Heller reassured him. But in his heart of hearts, he was less than 100 per cent sure.

Rutledge acted as if nothing had happened when their paths crossed later in the day—or was it the following day?—at the office pour, a cocktail party to honor one of the Clandestine Service's surreptitious entry people, an old-timer who had started picking locks for the OSS during World War II. Several dozen guests—mostly pretty secretaries and the operatives from the Technical Services Division, plus a sprinkling of topside hands— stood around in small groups sipping flat California champagne (it had been opened too far in advance) from paper cups. The lock man, whose name was Carr, was showing off a gold watch that Rutledge had presented to him. "Thirty-five years." Carr beamed. "It's solid gold. Eighteen-karat."

One of the secretaries, a bleached blonde, asked, "Anybody know what a karat is?"

Heller, working on his fourth cup of champagne, raised his

hand as if he were in school. "The karat's what we use when the stick doesn't work," he said brightly.

No one within earshot seemed very amused, except the secretary who had posed the question. "That's awful cute," she said, edging closer to Heller, letting her breast brush against his arm.

Slater came up behind Heller and whispered, "I think you've had enough."

"Pass me a cigarette," ordered Heller.

"You don't smoke," Slater reminded him.

"I should," mumbled Heller. "I should smoke, and drink, and use dirty language, and fuck teenage girls."

"My name's Cassandra," the blond secretary told Heller. "My friends call me Casey." She cocked her head coquettishly. "How come we've never met before?"

"We don't go around in the same circles," said Heller.

"What circles do *you* go around in?" asked Casey.

Heller smiled bitterly. "Vicious circles."

Across the room Rutledge said to Carr, "Things must have changed some since you first got into the business."

"Changed! Oh my, yes. I'll say they've changed. When I started out, we used to pick off the combinations listening to the tumblers with stethoscopes." He mimicked a doctor listening to a heartbeat. "Nowadays we have devices so sensitive we can hear the tumblers dropping from another room. If you ask me, there's no such thing as a safe safe anymore."

Heller plucked another cup of champagne from a tray. Casey smiled into his face and asked him what he did in the Company. "I'm a persuader," Heller whispered.

"What's a persuader?" asked Casey.

Slater tugged at Heller's sleeve, but Heller shook him off. "Leave me be." To the girl he said, "It's like this. The Company asks someone to do it a favor, right. But the someone whom the Company asks doesn't want to do this favor." Heller blinked several times to clear his blurred vision. "Which is where I come in. I *persuade* the someone in question that it's in his interests to do us this favor."

"You make them an offer they can't refuse." The girl giggled. "I saw the movie."

"Charlie, come on," begged Slater.

72

"I offer them money. I offer them recognition. I offer them girls. I offer them boys." Heller recited his list very seriously. "If that doesn't turn the trick, I persuade them in other ways."

The secretary regarded Heller with wide eyes. "What other ways?"

"What's your clearance?" inquired Heller, squinting down at her identity tag.

"I'm good for anything up to top secret."

"I suppose there's no harm . . . I persuade them by telling them what *won't* happen to their wives or children if they do the favor."

"You're putting me on," said the girl. "The Company doesn't do things like that."

"You think so?"

"I think so," she said, but it was evident that she wasn't sure either way.

Heller invited himself back to the girl's apartment. They passed Rutledge on the way out, surrounded by young women, regaling them with stories he reserved for secretaries and senators. ". . . so we urinated in the snow," he was telling them. "It's an old trick. The urine throws the dogs off, you see. By the time they picked up the trail, we were across the border and well on our way . . ."

They made love on an unmade bed, on sheets that smelled of mildew, in the pitch dark, with noisy rock music playing on the phonograph until the record failed to eject and the needle scratched round and round in the end grooves.

"Don't . . . rush . . . so," the girl whispered in Heller's ear. "Slow . . . down." Her pubic hair was wiry and moist, and *unfamiliar*. She squirmed under him and uttered throaty little cries that seemed to have nothing in common with spontaneity. She made him hard with her hand, and he tried to thrust into her, but he lost his erection. He rolled over on his back, exhausted from the effort, despairing of success, bewildered by the strange combination of desire and lack of it that seemed to grip him. "Don't . . . worry," the girl said soothingly. She worked the precincts inside his ear with the tip of her tongue, and made him hard with her mouth, and straddled him and pushed him inside her and set off on a rocking, rhythmic search for her orgasm. "Oh . . . that's . . . *good*," she moaned, quickening the pace, moistening her lips, caressing her own breasts, forgetting Heller completely, until suddenly he came off in one quick unsatisfactory spasm.

"Fuck," she whined. "Couldn't you hold off another minute?"

No beginnings. No middles. No ends. Things blended into one another. For some reason, Heller thought the dinner with Slater and his wife, Sandy, took place the day after the cocktail party, though it was actually several days later. Another man from crateology was also there, along with his wife, and an older official who ran the Company's running history program under which retiring agents were invited to spend a year or two at full pay writing their memoirs (which, since the Company owned them, were unpublishable commercially).

The evening started off well enough. Sandy passed around a tray of open sandwiches that she had defrosted for the occasion, and Slater amused everyone with shoptalk. "There were an even hundred of them," he recounted, "each one six meters long, narrow, wrapped in Fiberglas and tied with number five marine cord. They were obviously light, because when they were off-loaded, two men could easily carry one of the packages to the waiting trucks."

"Was anything written on the package?" asked Sandy.

"We made enlargements of the label," acknowledged Slater. "The word 'inspected' was printed in Russian, followed by the initials of someone whom we presumed did the inspecting."

"Doesn't give you much to go on," reflected the wife of the other crateologist.

"Too light to be tank cannons," commented the man from the history program.

"And too long," noted Heller.

"Did it have something to do with radar?" asked Sandy.

"Or the SAM missile system," guessed the wife of the other crateologist.

"I know what was in them," announced Heller. "Lances for a jousting tournament."

74

Everyone laughed. "Actually, you're not far off," said Slater. "They were aluminum flagpoles, manufactured in Armenia and sent to Cuba for the opening of the non-aligned conference. The Cubans wanted to surround the conference hall with flagpoles!"

"Flagpoles?" said Sandy.

"Flagpoles," said Slater.

They drifted through dinner, with Heller eating less and drinking more than usual, and the history program man describing his tour as station chief in Mexico City some years back. At ten-thirty, the crateology couple and the history man left. Heller lingered behind. He sat quietly in a corner nursing a nightcap, a concoction made up of half cognac, half Grand Marnier.

"What's the matter?" asked Sandy. Slater had gone to check the children.

"Nothing's the matter."

"Yes it is."

Heller said, "You talk about everything but."

Sandy sat down on the arm of his chair. "We thought you'd want to forget."

"I don't want to forget," Heller cried passionately. "I want to remember."

Sandy burst into tears. "You don't have a monopoly on grieving," she sobbed. "For God's sake, you're not the only one who misses her."

"I'm the only one," Heller told her quietly, "who will die without her."

"Do you really think you'll die without her?" inquired Bennett, the psychiatrist who was cleared for top secret, eyes only.

Heller considered the question. "I think something in me has died, yes."

Bennett, an extremely thin man who had a curious way of talking to patients without looking at them, accepted this with pursed lips. "It doesn't cheapen your grief," he said carefully, "to point out that you're not the first person in the world to lose someone very close, and feel like this. Time will make your sense of loss . . . less painful."

Heller said, "That's what I'm afraid of."

"That's normal for someone in your situation too," noted Bennett. "Your feelings toward the young lady you lost are intense. You're afraid these feelings will become less intense as time goes on. You tend to see that as a betrayal of the person. All of this is especially pertinent in the case of someone who has died violently, and before her time."

"Why don't you look at me when you talk to me?" Heller suddenly asked.

The doctor glanced up sharply. "I hadn't noticed that I wasn't."

Heller asked the doctor if he had a cigarette. Bennett said he preferred it if his patients didn't smoke in his office.

"I don't want to smoke," Heller started to explain, then breathed deeply in frustration. "Never mind." He swiveled in his seat toward the wall covered in floor-to-ceiling shelves and inspected the books. They all had impressively long titles. There were no paperbacks. Sarah had loved paperbacks. She never went anywhere without one tucked into her shoulder bag. She called it her security paperback.

Heller swiveled back toward Bennett and caught him glancing at his wristwatch. "You're telling me things I already know," he told the psychiatrist.

"Confirming things you may feel, letting you know that those feelings are absolutely normal for someone in your position, that's one of the ways I can help you." Bennett leaned his elbows on his desk, which was covered with framed photographs of his family. "What about dreams?" he asked.

"What about dreams?"

"Do you have any recurring dreams you want to tell me about?"

Heller nodded. "I've had one dream off and on for the last seven, eight years. In my dream, I'm obliged to carry an enormous sack of pebbles down a beach strewn with pebbles. The only way I can discard one from my sack and make it lighter is if I find a pebble on the beach that exactly matches one in my sack. Then I can throw them both into the sea."

Bennett seemed genuinely interested. "You work in ciphers," he noted, reading Heller's dossier on his desk. "That's a wonderful dream for someone who breaks ciphers—matching pebbles,

76

matching words. Do you mind if I use that sometime in an article?"

Heller was amused. "No, I don't mind. Do you pay royalties on dreams?"

"When's the last time you had that dream?" asked Bennett.

Heller raised his eyes to the ceiling thoughtfully. "One night last week. After I slept . . . after I slept with a young woman. In the dream, I actually found a pebble on the beach that matched one in my sack. I turned to throw them both into the sea, but the sea had disappeared. As far as the eye could see, there were mud flats with the skeletons of ships, whales, hundreds of dead fish . . ."

After a moment Bennett said, "Do you ever fantasize about the terrorists who killed your lady?"

"Why do you ask?" Heller demanded defensively.

"It would be curious if you didn't," Bennett reassured him.

"I sometimes think," Heller admitted carefully, "that it would be a great pleasure to . . . strangle them."

Bennett smiled pleasantly. "When you fantasize about killing the terrorists, do you feel—for the lack of another word—*better?*"

"What do you mean, better?"

"Calmer. Do you feel calmer? Do you feel ready to get on with your life?"

Heller nodded.

Bennett referred to his notes. "Have you ever spoken to anyone in the Company about the terrorists?"

Heller admitted he had. "I tried to persuade them"—he smiled in spite of himself at the word "persuade"—"persuade them to do something about the . . . situation."

There was a soft knock at the door, the secretary's discreet way of signaling the end of the forty-five-minute session.

"What was the reaction?" Bennett wanted to know.

Heller said, "They seemed to think it was out of the question."

Bennett stood up. "Pity," he said mildly. "From a medical point of view, revenge is very therapeutic."

CHAPTER SIX

AT first the sound was an integral part of the dream. Then the dream slipped away, and he was left with the ringing—shrill, not-to-be-denied. Heller, suddenly awake, plucked the phone from its cradle. It seemed like the only way to deal with the noise.

On the other end, the caller began to explain himself.

"How'd you get my number?" Heller asked carefully.

The caller sidestepped the question. "I'm sorry if I woke you," he said. "My name's Molton. Frank Molton. I was wondering—"

The name clicked. "You're the Molton who wrote those articles . . ."

There was an embarrassed laugh from Molton. "That's me."

Heller said, "Some of the agents you exposed may wind up with their throats cut."

"I never named a single name"—Molton defended himself earnestly—"that wasn't already known to everyone in the world except the American taxpayer who foots the bill. Listen, Mr. Heller, the reason I phoned—"

"How *did* you get my number?" Heller repeated the question. Molton hesitated. "I'd rather not say. I heard you were engaged to the woman who was killed in the raid on the Munich consulate. I heard you worked for the Company. I thought you might have become disillusioned—"

Heller snapped, "The Company didn't kill her." Then he remembered the drill. "Listen, Mr. Molton, whoever told you I worked for the Company told you wrong. I work for the National Security Agency at Fort Meade. Repairing cigarette vending machines. If you want to interview me, for whatever reason, you have to phone up the public affairs officer and put in a written request. If he's okay, and we both know he won't be, you can come on up and talk to me. I'll even let you take some photographs of me working—stacking cigarettes in the vending machines."

"Don't hang up," Molton pleaded urgently. "I know whom you work for, but that doesn't matter. All I want is for you to remember me if you ever change your mind. You know which newspaper I'm at. You can always reach me here in New York."

"I won't change my mind," Heller said.

"Incidentally," Molton added, "you're required by Company regulations to report this conversation to your departmental security officer. In case you don't know, his name is Howard. George C. Howard. His extension at Langley is 6107."

"Son of a bitch," fumed Howard. "I'd give half my pension to get my hands on the guy who gave out my extension. That's classified information."

"What do I do if he phones up again?" asked Heller.

"You tell him to fuck off," raged Howard. "Son of a bitch."

"And you waltzed up and reported it to the security officer?" Slater asked in astonishment.

Heller toyed gloomily with his franks and beans. "That's what you're supposed to do," he said defensively.

"Of course you're *supposed* to do it," Slater reproached him in a harsh whisper. "But that doesn't mean you actually go ahead and do it. Dummy. The fact that Molton *thought* you'd talk to him isn't going to do your career any good. They're probably reviewing your fitness report right now, wondering if this Molton character knows something about you that they don't."

"I didn't give him the time of day," Heller insisted sullenly.

"I believe you," declared Slater, "but will they believe you?"

Rutledge beat about the bush for a decent interval. When he finally came to the point, he made it sound like an afterthought. "By the way, we thought we'd take you off one-time pads for a while," he announced smoothly.

Heller asked, "What will I be working on?"

"Everyone in the Company thinks he can come up with a new unbreakable cipher system," Rutledge explained, absently leafing through papers on his desk. "We have quite a backlog of these things gathering dust. We'd like you to look through them, see if there are really any fresh cipher ideas floating around that we could make use of. You never know."

"You never know," Heller agreed without enthusiasm.

"It'll mean you'll have to give up your room and your computer," Rutledge went on. "Whoever takes over one-time pads will need the keys in your computer, and there's no sense programming another one."

"No sense at all," Heller conceded.

"So it's settled," Rutledge summed up jovially.

"Was there any doubt it would be?" asked Heller innocently.

The advantage to Heller's new office was that it had a window. The disadvantage was that the window looked out over the parking lot.

"You get used to it," confided the man who shared the office with Heller. His name was Bob something-or-other and he was preparing a master table of tides in Soviet coastal zones; he'd been working on it for fourteen months, and the end was nowhere in sight.

Heller deposited the three dozen or so folders he had been given on a desk, dusted them off with a cloth and attacked the first. An assistant code officer serving in the American embassy in Brazil had invented what he claimed was an unbreakable cipher involving a tetrasect shuffling of parts and encipherment in transposed order. In his accompanying letter, the officer offered to sell the cipher system to the government for a mere $10,000. The code officer also enclosed a message enciphered using the system he claimed to have invented, and challenged anyone to break it.

Heller sharpened a pencil and started in. Working on the principle of the high and low frequency of certain letters, he soon recovered the word "cipher." Then he bogged down, and only got going again by the simple expedient of free associating. He stared out the window at the cars in the parking lot until his mind was a blank. Then he said aloud the word "cipher" and the first word that came into his head afterward—"system." It fitted. Other pieces fell into place. He soon had the word before "cipher," which was "this," and part of the last word, which was "cipherable."

Forty-five minutes later, he had recovered the full message: "This cipher system is absolutely undecipherable."

Heller copied off the plain text under the "unbreakable" cipher, scrawled the word "amateur" on the Company form stapled to the suggestion, placed everything in a brown interoffice envelope and turned to the second folder with another "unbreakable" cipher suggestion in it.

It was dark when Heller checked out of the building, a process that involved showing his identification tag to one of the guards behind the desk near the main door. The guard dialed Heller's number on his computer terminal, and Heller's photograph appeared on a small color television screen. Satisfied, the guard nodded.

Heller, his mind wandering, his eyes unable to focus, didn't react.

The guard said, "You can leave now."

"Oh, sorry." Heller turned away. He walked past several workmen in white overalls decorating a large Christmas tree and made his way out the main door. A sharp gust of wind hit him. He lowered his head and pulled up the collar of his sheepskin coat and headed for the parking lot, vaguely worried about starting his car in this cold; he had meant to have the points and plugs checked, but he had never gotten around to it. Halfway down the fourth row, Heller came to where he thought he had left his Pinto —but it wasn't there. He looked around, puzzled. His car was nowhere in sight. "I could have sworn . . . ," he muttered to himself, rising on tiptoes and looking over the roofs to see if he could spot the distinctive yellow of his car.

In the end it took him twenty minutes of trudging around, his hands burrowing deep into the pockets of his jacket, before he found his Pinto. It was just where he had parked it eight hours before—on the west side of the lot, not the east. The experience left him chilled to his bones, and shaken and depressed.

As soon as he got home, Heller sank into a hot bath, then proceeded to drink himself into a pleasant stupor. He woke up on the living-room couch at two or three in the morning, shaking like a leaf and sweating profusely. As usual, all the lights in the apartment were on. He pulled a blanket over himself and turned toward the wall and tried to sleep, but the memory of the light lurked behind his lids and kept him up. He stumbled to the tiny bathroom, groped in the medicine chest for a thermometer, sat on the edge of the bathtub and held it under his tongue for what he thought was three minutes. When he took it out, it read 102. He swallowed two homeopathic aspirins and climbed between the sheets of his bed.

Heller phoned in sick in the morning. The Company promptly dispatched one of its own GP's, who peered at Heller's throat, listened to his heart and lungs, tapped a small rubber hammer against his bony knees and announced that the flu he was suffering from was not terminal.

The fever raged for two days and then began to subside, leaving Heller weak and washed out, as if he had been tossed up on a tide. Slater phoned every morning, and his wife, Sandy, came by in the afternoons with chicken broth and cooked vegetables and homemade applesauce. She straightened his sheets and puffed up his pillows and propped Heller against them and spoon-fed him until he felt strong enough to eat by himself. By the fourth day he was out of bed and working on a new palindrome—"Madam, I'm Adam." The doctor stopped by again on the weekend, looked and listened in all the appropriate places and pronounced Heller hale, if not exactly hearty. "How's your appetite?" he inquired. Heller acknowledged it was returning. "Any trouble sleeping?"

In fact, the only time Heller had slept well was at the height of the fever. Once it had subsided, he returned to what had become for him normal—long restless hours of tossing and turning, with sleep tantalizing him by its closeness and frustrating him by remaining just out of reach.

"I can give you a pill," the doctor offered.

"For what I have, there are no pills," Heller told him.

He grew stronger and ate more, and drank more, and learned to dread the nights. The few times he managed to doze off, he became trapped in his recurring dream—hauling a huge sack of pebbles along a beach, systematically studying the pebbles under his feet to find one that matched a pebble in his sack. Once he picked a small flat pebble, about the size of a fifty-cent piece, out of the wet sand, then found its twin in his sack and turned to throw them both into the sea—only to discover he was standing at the edge of a high cliff looking out over a moonscape canyon that was filled with seething lava pits.

His days accounted for now that he was back at work, Heller took to staying out late at night. He ate in small restaurants that smelled of cooking fat and cigarette butts, and usually lingered over his coffee until all the other customers had left and the waiters started putting on their overcoats. He took the habit of going to late night movies, the plots of which he never remembered the next day. Once he actually sat through half an hour of a film before he realized he had seen it several days before.

Carrying a sardine sandwich and a wedge of chocolate cake and threading his way through the crowded Company cafeteria one day, he bumped into the secretary he had spent the night with. He arranged his face into what he thought was a smile and asked her what she was doing after work. "Whatever I'm doing," she answered with exaggerated sweetness, "I'm not doing it with you."

Over lunch with Slater, Heller laughed too loudly at some-

83

thing that wasn't funny. People glanced their way; the Shadow, Mudd, eating by himself at a corner table, took out a pen and paper and jotted a note.

Slater put it on the line to Heller: "You don't ask for cigarettes anymore. You don't smile your Mona Lisa smile. If I ask you to guess what was in those wooden barrels we spotted going into Ethiopia, the only thing you come up with is pickles. *Pickles!*" He waved his hand in disgust. "In short, you're not the stimulating companion you once were." He leaned closer to Heller. "She's dead, Charlie, dead and buried. Life has to go on." He looked sharply at Heller, who hadn't touched his sardine sandwich. "What's really bugging you, Charlie?"

"What's really bugging me," Heller said—he found he was carefully listening to see what words would come out of his mouth —"is the idea of those people living it up in Czechoslovakia. Sarah's father was right—the only thing that will save my life is their deaths. The guy who wrote 'an eye for an eye' knew something important. It's a reasonable formula for survival. An eye for an eye!"

"There's nothing you can do about them," Slater said flatly.

"That's the heart of the problem," admitted Heller.

Heller ate dinner that night in a Chinese restaurant that sprinkled too much monosodium glutamate on the dish from column B. He lingered as long as he decently could, then at a downtown theater took in a film that the critics had made quite a fuss over. Heller was hard put to follow the story line; at several points he wasn't even sure there was one. Near the end of the film, one of the characters challenged another to a game of Russian roulette. Barely breathing, Heller stiffened in his seat as the first character slowly placed a pistol to his skull and squeezed the trigger. Heller clamped his hands over his ears and stumbled from the theater. Outside, gasping for breath, grateful for the cold air that filled his lungs, he leaned for a long moment against a poster on the wall with the words COMING NEXT WEEK printed in bright red diagonally across it.

The gray-haired woman counting the night's receipts in the fortresslike ticket booth looked over in alarm. "Are you all right?" she called out, and suspended chewing gum to catch his reply.

Heller nodded and thanked her profusely and started walking in the general direction of his apartment, his head angled into a wind that wasn't blowing. The store windows were all brightly lit and covered with metal grills and plastered with notices proclaiming that the premises were protected by a variety of infallible burglar alarm systems. The crossing lights for as far as Heller could see (the few times he looked up) were stuck on red; the occasional car that passed at that hour simply ignored them completely.

Heller turned to look at his reflection in one store window, and then looked through his reflection to the objects *in* the window. It was a small stamp store, and there was a collection of several dozen red stamps displayed on black pages. *Red stamps!* Heller never knew she collected red stamps until—

Suddenly Heller had the sensation that he was not alone. The skin on the back of his neck crawled (with fear? with anticipation? with *hope?*). He lifted his eyes from the stamps and made out two dim reflections in the store window, standing on either side of him.

Fighting the sudden heaviness of his limbs, Heller dragged himself around to face them.

He found himself before two husky teenagers in crisp black leather jackets with too many zippers. They were both white; one chewed gum; both had blank-looking faces, as if they were bored to tears, as if they had never experienced thoughts or emotions.

"You don't make no trouble, we don't make no trouble," warned the first boy sullenly.

"Jus' hand over your wallet, is all," ordered the second boy. He took a step in Heller's direction and started to reach a hand inside his sheepskin jacket. Heller instinctively pushed his hand away. The boy, furious, grabbed Heller by his lapels and flung him backward into the metal grill that covered the store window. Both boys began to close in on him.

Suddenly the violence they offered seemed to Heller like a rite of communion, a ritual appropriate to the situation in which he found himself. It dawned on him that it didn't matter whether he was on the giving or the receiving end of the violence; it all amounted to the same thing. He dropped into a half crouch and beckoned the two muggers with his finger tips, which had lost all

85

feeling. "Come on," he whispered hoarsely through clenched teeth, inviting the violence; longing for it. "Come on."

The two muggers stared at Heller with something very close to embarrassment, all the while stamping their feet on the cold pavement, blowing out clouds of frosted breath, casting sly sideways looks at each other. After a moment they burst out laughing, as if the whole thing were a misunderstanding, a simple case of minds that didn't meet. Slowly they backed away from their reflections in the store window. Then they pivoted, like two dancers in a chorus line, and sauntered off.

Straightening stiffly, Heller watched them go with what can only be described as *disappointment*. They had promised violence and not delivered. Then another look came into his eyes. Gradually his features relaxed, his breathing became more regular—and a trace of the Mona Lisa–like smile clung to his lips.

That night he turned out all the lights in his apartment and slept like a baby. He dreamed his recurring dream and found a pebble on the beach that matched one in his sack. When he turned to fling them both away, the sea was just where it was supposed to be, spread out before him, rippling with soft waves against the curve of the beach as if it had always been part of the landscape of his dream.

Slater noticed the change immediately. "Whatever you had for breakfast," he quipped as Heller came charging up to the lunch table, "hasn't done you any harm."

"How you fixed for cigarettes?" Heller demanded.

Slater beamed. "You gave up smoking almost a year ago." The smile evaporated. "Sarah made you stop," he added heavily.

"She said she'd never live with someone who smoked," Heller explained calmly. He actually managed a smile. "After that it was easy."

Slater sat back in his seat and regarded Heller soberly. "You *have* changed," he said quietly.

Heller nodded. "I figured out how to save my life," he said mysteriously. He attacked his grilled cheese sandwich with an appetite. "What are you up to in crateology these days?"

But Slater only shook his head in wonder. "Welcome back,"

he said with a certain amount of emotion, "to the land of the living."

Heller solved five "unbreakable" ciphers that day, and even had time to help the man who shared his office copy off a list of high waters and low waters in Vladivostok for the coming year. In the later afternoon he wandered over to Rutledge's office and stuck his head in the door. "Sorry to bother you," he said, smiling brightly.

Rutledge, who was in the middle of having the mechanics of an all-plastic "bug" explained to him, looked up. "What can I do for you, Heller?"

"If it's all right with you, I'd like to work on my Shakespeare ciphers," Heller said.

Rutledge took a long hard look at Heller. "No problem," he agreed finally.

"I'll need your authorization to use my old computer evenings," Heller explained. "It has a lot of combinations I've already tried stored in its memory bank."

Rutledge said, "As long as the new man there isn't using it, go ahead. Do you good to keep your hand in."

Heller smiled warmly. "Thanks. I'll ask your secretary to type up an authorization for the housekeepers."

Rutledge stopped by on his way out that night to see what Heller was up to.

Heller had written out on his blackboard Ben Jonson's dedicatory poem entitled "To the Reader" that appeared next to Shakespeare's picture in the First Folio.

> *This Figure, that thou here seest put,*
> *It was for gentle Shakespeare cut;*
> *Wherein the Grauer had a strife*
> *With Nature, to out-doo the life:*
> *O, could he but haue dravvne his wit*
> *As well in brasse, as he hath hit*
> *His face; the Print would then surpasse*

All, that vvas euer vvrit in brasse.
But, since he cannot, Reader, looke
Not on his Picture, but his Booke.

                                             B.I.

"First," Heller explained enthusiastically, "I'm going to run this through the computer to see if it contains a simple acrostic, acroteleutic, numerologic or something of the sort. Then I'll get into more complicated things"—Heller squinted professionally at the writing on the blackboard—"Bacon's biliteral cipher, various transposition or substitution systems that were used in Elizabethan days . . ."

Rutledge made for the door. "All that's a bit over my head," he said. He was obviously quite pleased with the way Heller had pulled himself together. "If you do manage to find something, it will be quite a feather in the Company's cap."

As soon as the door closed behind Rutledge, a Mona Lisa smile crept over Heller's face—and stayed there. He pulled a chair over to the computer's keyboard, rolled up his sleeves and started hunting and pecking away. All the one-time pad messages that Heller had broken in the past seven years were stored in the computer's memory bank, so that Heller, in devising new ciphers, would have access to the systems he had already used. The messages were filed not according to their contents or origins but rather their enciphering characteristics.

Heller keyed the computer and punched in a particular enciphering system:

INTERROGATORY ONE-TIME PAD MESSAGE USING DOUBLE
LATERAL SUBSTITUTION OF VOWELS.

With his forefinger, he hit the retrieve key. The magnetic tapes whirred. Then the computer's printout system started up, and out spilled the response:

FROM STATION CHIEF MEXICO CITY FOR DIRECTOR'S EYES
ONLY STOP COMMUNIST PARTY SECRETARY'S DEATH RULED
ACCIDENTAL STOP FORENSIC STUDY FAILED DISCOVER

EITHER PELLET OR TRACE OF POISON STOP REQUEST YOU
DEPOSIT HUNDRED THOUSAND SWISS FRANCS IN ZURICH
ACCOUNT OF LOCAL MEDICAL EXAMINER ANOTHER
HUNDRED THOUSAND TO ATTORNEY GENERAL WHO AC-
CEPTED ACCIDENTAL DEATH RULING AND CLOSED CASE.

Heller tore off the message, punched in a new "interrogatory" and hit the retrieve key again. Once more the printout
system started up.

FROM STATION CHIEF ROME FOR DIRECTOR'S EYES ONLY
STOP MONEY DEPOSITED IN GENEVA STOP UNION OFFICIAL
ALREADY ISSUED STATEMENT DENOUNCING COMMUNISTS
FOR SUPPORTING BIRTH CONTROL STOP HAVE LEFT WING
SENATOR WHO WILLING PLAY BALL WITH US FOR SIMILAR
FEE STOP AS WE ALREADY OVER BUDGET REQUEST ADDI-
TIONAL UNTRACEABLE FUNDS FOR FISCAL YEAR.

And again:

FROM STATION CHIEF DJAKARTA FOR DIRECTOR'S EYES ONLY
STOP GENERAL REPLIES HE WILL DO ANYTHING GUARANTEE
SAFETY OF HIS DAUGHTER STOP REQUESTS IMMEDIATE
PROOF SHE STILL ALIVE STOP CAN YOU SUPPLY SOONEST
TAPE OF HER VOICE AND PHOTOGRAPH OF HER HOLDING
LATEST ISSUE OF WASHINGTON POST.

And still again:

FROM STATION CHIEF MANILA FOR DIRECTOR'S EYES ONLY
STOP URGENTLY REQUEST YOU RECONSIDER ORDER TO
TERMINATE LEFTIST SENATOR STOP FEEL POLITICAL CLI-
MATE WOULD MAKE HIS TERMINATION COUNTERPRODUC-
TIVE STOP SUGGEST PUTTING PROJECT ON BACK BURNER
UNTIL AFTER ELECTIONS WHEN ACCIDENT MORE LIKELY GO
UNNOTICED.

Working late every night that week and the next, Heller retrieved almost a thousand messages. Of these he selected three

dozen that he considered the most compromising; the others, which dealt with more routine matters, he shredded, stuffed in his burn bag and deposited in the basement burn room on his way out at night. The messages he decided to keep he folded into thin strips and smuggled out wedged between his sock and his boot.

Back at his apartment, Heller set up his photographic equipment and went to work. Each message was flattened and taped to the kitchen wall, illuminated with a desk lamp and photographed with his tripod-mounted Pentax. The original computer printout was then pasted up in an ordinary scrapbook, two messages to a page. The photographs Heller developed in his bathroom, which he had rigged up as a darkroom. He hadn't done any developing since high school, and it took him a while to get it right. The first roll came out too dark, the second too light. He went through the whole process again, photographing the messages for a third time. This time the contrast seemed just right. He didn't make prints; he only required the developed negative. He dried it on a clothesline stretched between the medicine chest and the window, which had been sealed with black paper. Then he rolled the film strip as tightly as possible, and taped it closed.

On the following Sunday, carrying the scrapbook in a brown shopping bag and the roll of developed film in his jacket pocket, Heller set out at the crack of dawn in his yellow Pinto. Heading north on the turnpike, he passed the service station where Diamond had had his windshield wipers changed. At midday Heller pulled up at the same roadside diner he and Diamond had eaten at. Clutching the brown shopping bag under his arm, he took a seat at the counter and ordered a number two club special and a beer.

Behind him, at the alcove entranceway, the manager gave the Astro-Flash computer a sharp kick. Heller, who had a healthy curiosity about computers, wandered over.

"What's the matter?" he asked.

"Damn thing's been printing gibberish again," complained the manager, a young man with apple-red cheeks and flattened down hair that looked like a toupee. "It'll take me a month to get a repairman down here. You don't know anything about these contraptions, do you?"

"As a matter of fact, I do," Heller admitted. "I'm a computer programmer for the government." He set his beer down on the computer, and his brown shopping bag on the floor. "Here, let me take a look. It's probably something in the storage differential."

"I really appreciate this," said the manager. "The lunch's on the house. If you need any tools, just yell." And he retreated to the relative security of something he understood—the cash register.

Alone in the alcove, Heller opened the lid of the memory bank and began tinkering with the printout system, punching in instructions, then trying to retrieve what he had punched in. A waitress brought over his sandwich, put it next to his beer, watched curiously for a moment and then left him to his work.

Forty or so minutes later, Heller had the Astro-Flash running smoothly again. "It was the storage differential, just as I thought," he told the grateful manager. "They have to be cleaned every so often or they act up. After that it's just a matter of tripping the memory bank key into automatic, and off she goes."

"I don't understand a word you're saying"—the manager laughed—"but I'm mighty grateful. Did you at least treat yourself to a printout?"

Heller said he hadn't. "Give me your birth date and hour," demanded the manager. "I'll do it for you. They're really a lot of fun."

"I'll stop by for it another time," Heller promised.

He returned to the turnpike, a bit behind schedule but with a feeling of having accomplished something. The New York skyline loomed out of a thick haze and then slipped by on his right. Near Hartford, he turned off the highway and began driving along two-lane back roads that had no white line down the middle and no shoulders. When the road narrowed to one lane, Heller stopped at a roadside store with MORNINGSIDE FLOWERS hand-lettered over the door and bought a bouquet of long-stemmed red roses. He pulled in for a quarter of an hour at the Jewish cemetery, a half mile down the road from Morningside Flowers, left his car under the wrought-iron Star of David over the entrance and made his way on foot to Sarah's grave.

It was marked by a small granite tombstone with a simple inscription: SARAH DIAMOND / Jan 24 1945–Dec 12 1972.

Heller cleared away some dried roses tied into a bouquet with a metal band and laid his bouquet in its place. He contemplated the grave for a long moment, then nodded as if he had reaffirmed something important and turned briskly back toward his car. He took the dried roses with him. He intended to press the petals between the pages of a thick book and keep them on his desk.

In town he parked around the corner from Diamond's house, walked over and rang the bell. He could hear the old man grumbling before he reached the door.

"So it's you," Diamond said, studying Heller carefully. "It don't surprise me you're back."

Inside, Heller came right to the point and explained why he had come all this way, and why he would return before anybody had a chance to miss him. Standing in the foyer amid raincoats and umbrellas, the old man listened intently. An ember (of admiration? of recognition?) began to glow deep in his eyes. When Heller finished, he agreed instantly.

"You came to the right place," he said, panting little excited stale breaths into Heller's face.

"I appreciate your not asking questions," said Heller.

"I wasn't born yesterday, sonny boy," the old man assured him. "Any idiot can see it's better I don't know the answers to the questions I'm not asking."

Heller explained the situation carefully. "If anything happens to me . . . if I disappear . . . if you hear I'm dead, for instance . . . anything . . . you'll know what to do."

Diamond fingered the roll of film that Heller had given him. "I take the film from the hiding place. I print up copies. I send them to this newspaperman named Frank Molton."

At the door, Diamond offered Heller his hand for the first time. "I wish you good luck, Charlie," he said very formally. He added, "You don't mind I call you Charlie, do you?"

Heller accepted his hand. "If things work out," he said, "I may save my life."

Heller was dog-tired but walking on air when he got back to Washington. He had the car washed at an all-night service station on the way into the city to get rid of the traces of the long drive. And he removed the tag on the motor that showed the date and mileage the last time he had the oil changed. The next morning he showered and shaved and turned up for work bright and early.

He was waiting at her desk when the Director's icy appointments secretary arrived at the stroke of nine.

"You again," she said without trying to mask her lack of enthusiasm. She took her sweet time about hanging her coat in the closet. Then she planted her body in front of the office safe so that Heller couldn't see the combination when she retrieved the Director's appointment book. "The situation with respect to the Director's time," she informed Heller loftily, sliding into her seat, arranging her skirt, "hasn't improved since you were last here."

Heller flashed his Mona Lisa smile. "Yes it has," he said softly. He removed his scrapbook from the shopping bag, tore out a page at random and flipped it onto the secretary's blotter. "Give that to the Director," he instructed her. "Tell him that I can squeeze him in between ten and ten-five this morning. Tell him not to be late."

In the event, he arrived seven minutes early, storming through the door with Rutledge and the Shadow close on his heels looking for all the world like fawning bishops attending an upwardly mobile cardinal. "Out," the Director barked at the poor man slaving away on tide tables. He scurried from the room in panic.

The Director was a Midwesterner who had come up through the ranks and only recently acquired an Eastern Establishment veneer: a second wife, thinner and brighter than the first; an ear-to-ear smile that he wore like a badge; a way of talking that hinted he knew where all the bodies were buried. Which in fact he did. For in the course of a long and successful career he had left a great many people stranded on a great many limbs—Cubans, Khambas, Sumatran colonels, Ukrainian partisans, Meos, Montagnards, Kurds, to name a handful. The only visible result was a vague sense of regret, not so much for the people involved—they had been consenting adults!—but for the opportunities lost: to change a government, to change the course of history. If someone had reproached him, he would have conceded that great powers warring for long periods do come to resemble each other, but he would have argued with boyish enthusiasm the notion that despite the occasional assassination plot or the odd Operation Phoenix, the resemblance was only skin deep.

Brandishing the loose-leaf page, he turned on Heller and asked coldly, "What in Christ's name is this all about?"

Heller swallowed—and plunged. "That," he explained, "is one page out of a nine-page scrapbook. Here are the other eight."

Heller handed the Director the loose-leaf book. He flipped through it, his eyes narrowing as he scanned the messages, some of which he must have recognized. He passed the book to Rutledge, who paled visibly as he leafed through it.

The Director sank back onto the edge of a desk. Heller caught a glimpse of hairless white skin where his sock ended and his trousers began. "If I have you right," the Director said carefully, his forefinger twitching nervously, "you're asking for something, but you're not asking very gracefully."

"I'm asking for something," Heller acknowledged, "in a way you can't say no."

"That is generally referred to as blackmail," the Director noted. "And you are making the supreme error of doing it before witnesses. You could be put away for twenty years."

Heller stood his ground. His voice was fairly steady, but his hands gave him away—they shook uncontrollably. "I photographed these pages," he said, "and hid the roll of film. If anything happens to me—anything at all—copies of these messages will turn up in every newspaper in the country."

For a long moment no one said a word; Rutledge looked as if he had stopped breathing. Then the Director said, "I see."

It was the Shadow who put two and two together. "He wants those terrorists killed. That's what this is all about."

"Of course!" Rutledge exclaimed. His face darkened as he began to consider various aspects of the situation. "It's the terrorists he's after."

The Director looked at Rutledge. "What terrorists are we talking about?"

"I don't want them killed," Heller informed Rutledge in a barely audible voice. "I want to kill them myself!"

The Director's fist came smashing down on his desk. Various objects on it, including a small printed sign that read CONTRARY TO PUBLISHED REPORTS, THE BUCK NEVER STOPS! jumped into the air. "God damn it," snapped the Director. "I thought 'eyes only' meant *my* eyes only. How the hell did he get his hands on this material?"

Rutledge, trying to disappear into the soft depths of the Director's couch, and Mudd, standing next to the window in the spacious corner office and wishing he could *jump* the seven floors to the ground, looked at each other. Rutledge shrugged. "The messages were programmed into Heller's computer so he could keep track of the cipher systems . . ." His voice trailed off uncertainly.

The Shadow put in lamely, "He was cleared for top secret, eyes only, atomic—the works."

"Nobody dreamed he'd make use of the *contents* of the messages," fumbled Rutledge.

The Director shook his head in frustration. "Nobody dreamed! You're not paid to dream. You're paid to know." He slid open a desk drawer and found a pill and popped it into his mouth from his palm and took a gulp of Perrier to swallow it. "All right," he started in more calmly. "First, I want the barn door closed. I want computer access restructured so that nobody—and I mean nobody—gets to see my eyes-only messages except the warm bodies in this room."

Mudd asked. "What are we going to do about Heller?"

"My God," groaned Rutledge, "do you know what'll happen if the Senate Intelligence Oversight Committee gets its hands on those messages? We've denied under oath . . ."

The Director pressed his finger tips to his temples; he felt a migraine lurking behind his closed eyes and was trying to discourage it. "I have one client," he said softly—Rutledge and Mudd had to strain to hear him—"the President of the United

States. I am his obedient servant. I do what *I know* he would want done, but I leave him in a position where he can plausibly deny he ever heard of any of this." He opened his eyes to find both Rutledge and Mudd nodding in sympathy. "If just one of these messages finds its way into print . . ." The Director fixed his gaze on the sign that read CONTRARY TO PUBLISHED REPORTS, THE BUCK NEVER STOPS! "Nobody blackmails me," he declared carefully. "Nobody." He toyed with a solid gold paper clip, a gift from Henry Kissinger. Finally, peering past Rutledge with clouded eyes, he said, "We'll buy time. We'll go through the motions. Give him anything he asks for. Give him things he doesn't ask for. Pack him off to the Farm. Let them work him up for a penetration. Teach him to shoot. Teach him codes—"

Mudd made the mistake of saying, "He already knows codes."

The Director wheeled on him coldly. "Teach him codes he doesn't know. I don't give a damn what you do, as long as it takes time." He swiveled to stare out the window; he was on the opposite side of the building from the parking lot, and there was a view worth looking at. "Meanwhile," he continued, almost to himself, "we'll concentrate on the film. He's an amateur at things like this. He's bound to have stashed it with a friend or in a safe deposit box. And when we get our hands on it, we'll break your Mr. Heller in two and we'll throw away the pieces."

CHAPTER
SEVEN

AT midday the small delivery truck passed through the single entrance in the twelve-foot-high cyclone fence and pulled up in front of an unpretentious farmhouse. A guard cradling a shotgun in his arms opened the front door and called back over his shoulder, "He's here."

An athletic-looking Englishman, fortyish, with wavy red hair and a flamboyant reddish mustache that he waxed every morning, sauntered out onto the porch. He was in his shirt sleeves, but the cold didn't seem to have any impact on him. He adjusted a pair of silver-rimmed National Health spectacles, tilted his head quizzically and watched Heller jump down from the back of the delivery truck.

"Hello," called the Englishman, a mocking belligerence to his tone. He regarded Heller as if he were an insect that could be stepped on at will. There was no question of shaking hands. "I'm Colonel Henderson. Henderson isn't my real name. Colonel isn't my real rank. No matter. My friends call me Hank. You will call me Colonel Henderson. Understood?"

Heller squinted up at the tall Englishman. As far as he could make out, there was absolutely no trace of humor in the colonel's ice-blue eyes, which stared out at the world with total, unblinking lack of interest; he looked as if he would be bored by the man who killed him. "Understood," replied Heller.

Henderson nodded distantly. "In the unlikely event you haven't already guessed it, I am to be your case officer. Next to God, if you believe in God, a case officer is the most important person in the world for an agent about to penetrate an enemy country. Do precisely as I tell you and there is a slight chance you may come out of this alive."

"Only a slight chance?" Heller asked sarcastically.

Henderson permitted a faint smile onto the rigorously controlled contours of his face. "I am overestimating your chances to build up your confidence."

Behind Henderson, the guard with the shotgun barely restrained a laugh.

"Right," snapped the Englishman. "Follow me. Let's see what you don't know."

Heller had arrived at the Farm, a sprawling wooded facility near Williamsburg, Virginia, that was officially carried on the books as a Pentagon research and testing center. In fact, it was strictly a Company show, 480 acres of weapons ranges, jump towers, lecture centers, classrooms, barracks, officers' clubs and the like; there was even a country mile of "Communist border"— complete with guard towers, dogs, minefields, electronic sensors and all the paraphernalia designed to make the crossing what the professionals called a "wet" affair. The Farm was used mainly as a basic training center for Company recruits; Heller himself had been through it when he signed on. But the facility had a number of heavily guarded off-limits sites tucked away in isolated corners for its more secret projects—debriefing defectors or training important agents. The isolation was so complete that the people in charge of the Farm were able to boast of training foreign agents who never suspected that they were in the United States.

It was in one of these secluded "isolators" that Heller had landed. The farmhouse itself served for sleeping, eating and classroom courses on "tradecraft." A nearby barn had been converted into an indoor shooting range. And a "pit" in the woods behind the barn was used for a course with the academic title "Introduction to Explosives."

Immediately after lunch, Heller was outfitted in Army fatigues and taken off to the barn for his first session with firearms. An Army master sergeant with the name Smith printed on the nametag clipped to his pressed uniform was waiting for him inside the barn, which had a thick wall of hay at the far end and a bank of bright neon lights overhead.

"Don't tell me," Heller teased the master sergeant. "Smith isn't your real name, master sergeant isn't your real rank."

Henderson, leaning against a wall, commented dryly, "Very humorous indeed."

The master sergeant didn't crack a smile. He was the total professional, a veteran of years in the field; a cold-blooded killer from the look of him. He treated Heller with the disdain reserved by total professionals for total amateurs. Holding up an extremely large handgun, he asked Heller if he knew anything about firearms.

Heller admitted he didn't.

"If you had to guess," the master sergeant inquired, his head tilted back at an angle which emphasized his nostrils, "which end would you say the bullet came out of?"

Heller glanced uneasily at Henderson. "Writing lines for you guys must be a full-time job."

As if it explained their bad humor, Henderson said, "We are only used to dealing with professionals."

"What is a professional?" asked Heller.

It took a long time for Henderson to answer, so long it seemed that he had forgotten the question. Finally he said, "A professional is someone who thinks that if something is worth doing, it's worth doing well." He nodded crisply to the master sergeant. "Carry on."

The master sergeant hefted the pistol, then gripped it in both hands, spread his feet wide, crouched, thrust the pistol forward and sighted on a tin can propped up on a post at the far end of the barn. "We teach all our people to shoot this way," he explained, repeating the gesture several times as he spoke. "It's classical Company. If you see someone take up this stance, nine chances out of ten he's one of our alumni. You grip the handgun firmly with both hands. You plant your feet wide apart. You take a normal breath and expel half of it. You thrust the firearm forward. You sight above the target and let the pistol drift down onto it from its own weight. As the firearm bears, you squeeze, don't jerk, never jerk, the small movable piece of metal technically referred to as the trigger. You do it right, he's dead as a doornail."

Heller muttered, "Sexist."

The master sergeant reacted as if he had been accused of being a homosexual. He slowly straightened from the firing position and looked at Henderson. "He called me a sexist."

"Not to worry," Henderson reassured him. "He's making what he thinks is a witty comment. He's suggesting, in the peculiar way that intellectuals have of saying things, that the target may be a *she* rather than a *he*."

Master Sergeant Smith shook his head as if to say, "What will they send me next?" and in one smooth, flowing motion sank back into the firing position. He barely seemed to aim before he pulled the trigger. At the far end of the barn, the tin can flew from its perch and clattered around the cement floor.

"Your turn," Smith said, offering Heller the pistol, butt first.

Heller gripped the pistol as if it would bite him. He spread his feet wide, sank into an awkward crouch, thrust his hands forward, sighted on another tin can. Standing behind him, the master sergeant recited chapter and verse on the pistol. "This," he said, "is the famous P-thirty-eight, a nine-millimeter Parabellum used by the German Army during the Second World War. You've heard about the Second World War? The manufacturing firm of Walther resumed production of the weapon after the war, and it was adopted as the Bundeswehr's official sidearm. It is eight point three eight inches long. Unloaded, it weighs two pounds and two ounces. The barrel has six grooves, which send the bullet on its merry way with a right-hand twist. The magazine contains eight rounds. A signal pin protrudes from the slide to indicate that the pistol is loaded. The weapon has a nasty recoil because of its muzzle velocity, something in the neighborhood of eleven hundred feet per second. But at short ranges it will penetrate almost anything. The theoretical drawback of the weapon,

of which you probably are blissfully unaware, is the leak of pro-
pelling gas between the front face of the cylinder and the rear
face of the barrel, which reduces the efficiency of the weapon. In
well-machined pistols, such as the one you hold in your shaking
hands, the tolerances are such that this drawback is negligible
until the weapon becomes worn. The weapon you are about to
fire is brand-new."

"You don't say," Heller commented. He squeezed the trigger.
The pistol seemed to explode in his hands. The "nasty recoil" sent
him sprawling on the cement. Grinning sheepishly, he climbed to
his feet.

Smith watched him without expression. "Colonel Henderson
here tells me you are going to try and kill someone," he remarked.
"I wonder if you could tell me who?"

Heller asked him why he wanted to know. The master sergeant grinned a particularly ugly grin. "Because I'd like to bet on
her." Laughing wickedly, he added, "Sexist my ass!"

Heller looked from the master sergeant to Henderson and
back again. "Whose side are you guys on?" he groaned.

"We're the good guys," snickered Henderson. "Wait till you
see the bad!"

First one lock snapped open. Then the second. Then the
door swung back on its hinges and a small army of agents, wearing white coveralls and carrying tool kits of various sizes and
shapes, poured into Heller's apartment on Cherry Hill Lane.
"Don't rush," the Shadow instructed everyone as they filed past.
"We've got all the time in the world. The owner's not expected
back for quite a while. If there's a cockroach under the sink, I
want to know whether it's male or female."

The agents fanned out, four to a room, and set to work.
They pried molding from the wall and picked the carpeting off
the floor. They went through every open box of food in the
kitchen and defrosted the ice trays in the refrigerator. They unscrewed joints on radiators and toilets and sinks. They searched
every page of every book on every shelf. They inspected the record jackets. They studied every inch of pillow and mattress and
quilt for the faintest sign of a newly stitched seam. They felt

through every single item of clothing, and took apart the television and radio and hi-fi and clock and hair dryer and electric percolator and toaster and gas range and refrigerator motor and dishwashing machine. They emptied the fire extinguisher and the garbage can under the sink. They took photographs out of their frames. They even dug up the potted plants, dying from lack of water, and sifted the dirt.

The Shadow, experienced in such matters, wandered from room to room, spurring everyone on with caustic comments on what would happen to them if they didn't find what they were looking for. According to him, raises, pensions, summer vacations, a shot at plush overseas assignments would all go down the drain. "Which reminds me," he called to the team in the kitchen, "don't forget to search the drain while you're at it."

Four hours later they had come up with nothing. Or next to nothing. "A big fat zero," Mudd told Rutledge over the phone. "Except for a key to a bank vault." He looked at the key that he held in the palm of his hand. "Might be something worth taking a peek at."

Rutledge cursed under his breath. "We've got to find the film," he said. "You're sure you didn't overlook something?"

Mudd surveyed the wreckage of Heller's apartment; it was an extraordinary sight, something that could only be achieved by sixteen professionals working like bees for the best part of an afternoon. "He couldn't have hidden a paper clip here," he said flatly. "I'd stake my career on it."

Rutledge laughed viciously on the other end of the phone; to Mudd's ear it sounded almost like the static he used to hear so often on the radiotelephones in Vietnam. "You're staking more than your career," Rutledge said, and the line went dead.

Heller's days were filled with activity—mental as well as physical—from the moment Henderson woke him at six-thirty until he stumbled tiredly off to his room, usually about ten. Mornings were generally spent in the barn with Master Sergeant Smith. Heller gradually got to the point where he could squeeze the trigger of the P-38 without flinching beforehand, and actually hit one of the tin cans now and then, an occurrence that brought no visible reaction from Smith or Henderson. Once, after he had missed eight consecutive times, the master sergeant retrieved the P-38, rammed in a new clip, then returned the pistol to Heller. "Before you can hit something," he said, studying him through narrowed eyes, "you have to *want* to hit it."

"That's very Zen," noted Heller.

"Who's Zen"—the master sergeant sneered—"another one of your sexist friends?"

"He's a foreign national," Heller said sweetly, "who developed a technique for accurate shooting."

Wanting to hit the target, oddly enough, seemed to make a difference. Pushing his eyeglasses back up along his nose, crouching with his feet spread, his two hands gripping the pistol in front of him, Heller imagined that it was Horst Schiller he was shooting at. Crack went the P-38—and the tin can leaped off its perch.

Henderson, observing from his usual place along the wall, clapped his hands together insolently. "Congratulations," he said, "you finally managed to hit something you aimed at."

"I did it for you, coach," Heller retorted. But he immediately regretted it; he was determined not to play Henderson's game.

Before the lunch break, Heller put in an hour with a Polish judo instructor whom everyone called "Ski" for short. At first Heller had balked at the idea of hand-to-hand combat. "I don't intend to maim anyone," he complained when the Polish instructor started to hold forth, in barely understandable English punctuated with an occasional demonstration, on "crippling blows."

"It isn't a question of maiming anyone," Henderson explained with his usual air of total superiority, "it's a question of putting you in the right frame of mind—in the mood, if you like. We're training your *head* to accept violence as something not at all out of the ordinary."

"I'm ready to accept violence," Heller said tightly, turning back to face the Polish instructor.

When Heller was thrown for the dozenth time, he picked himself off the mat and eyed his adversary; he was no bigger or heavier than Heller, but he moved with incredible speed and catlike grace, lunging or dropping back out of range of Heller's awkward "attacks." It became an obsession with Heller—he had to land at least one blow. "He's got to have a weakness," he said somewhat breathlessly to Henderson.

"It's not physical, old boy," Henderson replied mirthlessly. "It's intellectual. Right up your alley. If anybody can find it, you should be able to."

Heller gamely tried. But he never did find the weakness.

A conservatively dressed man, more or less similar in appearance to Heller, leaned over the attendant's desk and scratched his name on the card. The attendant, a smartly turned out woman in her fifties, pulled a card from her files and compared the two signatures. They were precisely alike.

She looked up and smiled. "If you'll come with me, Mr. Heller. You haven't forgotten your key, I hope?"

The man returned the smile. "I never go anywhere without it."

The attendant led the way down rows of strongboxes, found the right one and inserted her master key. The man who called himself Heller inserted his key and turned it. The door opened. The man withdrew the strongbox and carried it to a booth. He emptied the contents of the box on the table and started to go through them item by item.

There were various papers, a birth certificate, insurance policies, a government bond, a collection of first day covers, an old pocket watch, a much thumbed book of chess openings, a copy of the Company retirement plan with Heller's name printed in by a secretary and the words "Byzantium's benefits" scrawled across in Heller's hand.

The man went through everything a second time, then replaced the items in the strongbox and rang the buzzer for the attendant. Minutes later he was telephoning from a public phone in the lobby of the bank.

"A blank," he said. "No film. No leads. Just some chess openings if you're interested."

Afternoons at the Farm were devoted to what the profession-als called "tradecraft"—mostly a rehashing of things Heller had studied in the Company's basic training program eight years be-fore. There were sessions on flaps and seals (opening and closing letters without leaving a calling card), how to make homemade Molotov cocktails, how to select meeting sites, how to change your silhouette, how to follow someone on foot or by car, how to make sure nobody was following you.

"What do you remember about secret writing?" Henderson asked one afternoon.

Heller racked his brain. "I remember in a pinch you can always use urine—the writing is brought out by gently heating the paper. I remember you can write with Pyramidonia powder, which you can get in pharmacies in Europe—it's a headache pow-der. The developer is iodine vapor."

For once, Henderson seemed mildly impressed. He handed Heller a white linen handkerchief. "You'll carry this with you when you go in. All you have to do is dip it in water and it creates an invisible ink that's heat developed. Remember to use good paper, and rub it in all four directions with a soft cloth before and after to conceal the writing within the texture of the paper. Use a Q-tip sharpened with a razor or knife for a pen."

"Why will I need to use invisible ink?" Heller asked in frus-tration. "I'm going to kill some people, and then I'm coming out."

"You'll need the secret ink"—Henderson reverted to type—"to give us the details of your failure."

One afternoon in the middle of a tradecraft session—they were going over the theory of crossing borders illegally before actually going through some dry runs on the Farm's mile of sim-ulated Communist frontier—Henderson abruptly looked up at Heller. "I've been meaning to ask you," he said, "what you have on them?"

Startled, Heller said, "What makes you think I have some-thing on someone?"

Henderson peered at Heller through his National Health spectacles. "It must be rather hot for them to put up with you. If I can offer you a word of unfriendly advice: Whatever you've got on them, don't lose it."

Heller felt a chill shoot up his spine. "Who's side *are* you guys on?" he whispered.

Henderson didn't answer.

Two dozen men and women, all wearing white lab coats and rubber surgical gloves, were seated at high tables systematically steaming open letters. Once opened, each letter was put into a plastic tray, along with the envelope, and passed in a sort of assembly line operation to someone who flattened it under glass and photographed it and the envelope. The tray then went to another technician who folded the letter along its original creases and sealed it back into its envelope with a special spray-on glue.

The Director, on an inspection tour of the lab, chatted with the head technician. "How many can you process on a given day?"

"Right now," reported the head of the lab, "I'm two under staff—I had to send one man to Hong Kong and another's on loan to the Egyptians—but we still manage to keep up, oh, roughly a thousand or twelve hundred a day. I could speed things up, but it's important to do the steaming slowly if you don't want to leave a trace." The head technician laughed uncomfortably. "Haste makes waste."

"Indeed it does," agreed the Director. "Indeed it does."

The Shadow came into the lab on the trot and whispered something to Rutledge. Rutledge nodded and pulled the Director aside near a window. He talked to him in a low voice for nearly a minute.

"Damn it," exploded the Director. Several of the technicians looked up from their work, then immediately went back to their steaming.

"They have to be out there somewhere," the Director said more quietly. "Start with the relatives. What does he have?"

"There's a brother, there's a father," said Rutledge.

"Try them," ordered the Director. "When you talk, talk national security. Then work back through his friends. I want to know who he played handball with in high school." He shook his head stubbornly. "They're out there somewhere. He doesn't have nerve enough to bluff us."

Rutledge hesitated. "What if we let Heller loose? The worst

that can happen is he'll kill Schiller. With any luck, Schiller will kill him first."

The Director dismissed the idea with a quick jerk of his head. "It's too risky. There's too much at stake. I want Heller stopped in his tracks. I want those films."

"Those," said the master sergeant, indicating the wooden ducks that had been installed at the far end of the indoor range, "are known in the trade as moving targets. Presumably the he, or *she,* you will be shooting at will not do you the favor of standing still."

Henderson came up with a rifle wrapped in a blanket and handed it to Smith. The master sergeant removed the blanket and held up the rifle. "Say hello to the Fusil, Model F-one," he lectured. "This is a bolt-action magazine-loaded sniper's rifle of considerable precision. It was used by the French Army team that won the 1966 Prix Leclerc NATO shootout." Surprisingly, Smith's French pronunciation wasn't as bad as it might have been. "The rifle is no great shakes designwise, but it is carefully machined. The weapon is basically a competition rifle which has been militarized for a sniping role, which is a more intelligent approach than trying to improve the accuracy of a standard military rifle, which was never meant to shoot accurately to begin with. The butt length is adjustable. The folding bipod"—Smith flicked it down with his hand—"makes for steadier aiming. The trigger pull can be adjusted by a micrometer screw. The weapon is forty-four inches long. It weighs eight pounds and two ounces unloaded. The magazine holds ten rounds. The muzzle velocity is 2,800 feet per second."

Henderson said in a bored voice, "If you have use for something along these lines, it will be supplied to you by your cut-out in Prague."

Master Sergeant Smith brought the rifle to his eye and adjusted the sniperscope mounted on it. "The rifle has been fitted with a laserscope device," he went on with his explanation, "that normally makes it difficult to miss whatever it is you're shooting at. You depress this button and you project a small red dot, which you then see through the sniperscope. Where the dot is, that's where the bullet will be when you squeeze—don't jerk, never jerk —the trigger."

Smith handed the rifle to Heller. "Of course, moving targets," he pointed out, "present more of a problem than still ones. You have to"—he turned to Henderson—"dare I employ a technical term?"—then back to Heller—"you have to *lead* the target so that the target and the bullet meet at what amounts to an intersection."

Heller sighted through the sniperscope. Sure enough, there was a small red dot dancing on one of the wooden ducks. "This shouldn't be too difficult," he muttered. He lowered the rifle and judged the distance to the target. "What did you say the muzzle velocity was?"

Smith and Henderson exchanged glances. "Two thousand eight hundred feet per second," said Smith.

Heller calculated the time it would take the bullet to reach the target line, then the distance the target would travel in that time. He worked backwards, geometrically, until he had figured out the lead angle. "Hmmmmmm."

Smith and Henderson exchanged a second look.

Heller steadied the rifle on its bipod, projected the red dot onto a target, then offset it—and fired. The wooden duck flipped over on its side.

A trace of a Mona Lisa smile flitted across Heller's features. "It's just a question of calculating the lead angle," he explained sheepishly. "I'm fairly good with numbers."

Rule one: Put the subject at ease. "I can tell you," Mudd assured him, "that there is absolutely nothing to be concerned about. Your son performs valuable services for his government and his country."

Heller's father, a short gray-haired man in his mid-seventies who peered out at the world through thick lenses, nodded and smiled. "I never thought otherwise," he said. "I don't know exactly what it is Charlie does for you people, but I always had the feeling it was important work."

Rule two: Mask the real purpose of your visit. "Let me put

you in the picture, Mr. Heller. We have reason to believe that members of the Soviet mission here in New York, posing as representatives of a European travel organization, have been approaching the close relatives of some of our more important employees and offering them what amounts to a free trip to the Budapest trade fair."

Mr. Heller, listening intently, said, "Budapest is behind the Iron Curtain, isn't it?"

Mudd nodded knowingly. "That's the entire point."

"Ah," said Mr. Heller. "So this kind of thing really does go on."

Mudd lowered his voice. "I can only tell you so much," he apologized.

"Of course, I understand that."

"Once they get a close relative on their home ground, there's no telling what they can pull. They'll try to find your weakness— wine, women, whatever—and set you up for a fall. And when you've fallen, they play you back on the member of your family who has access to secret material."

"I can assure you," Mr. Heller said eagerly, "that no such people have contacted me. Between us, I would have suspected something the moment I heard the word Budapest."

"Vigilance," said Mudd, "is the name of the game. If you are contacted—"

"I'll get in touch immediately," promised Mr. Heller.

"Don't refuse them outright," Mudd instructed him. "Play them along. Say you want to think about it."

"Count on me."

Rule three: Put the question you came to ask as if it were an afterthought. "By the way"—Mudd turned to Mr. Heller at the door—"did you get the pictures Charlie sent you?"

"Pictures? Charlie never sent me pictures."

"I thought he said he sent them to you." Mudd seemed puzzled. "We took them"—he appeared to search his memory—"oh, ten days ago, two weeks on the outside, on a drive along the Potomac." He watched the father's eyes, and especially his lids, for the telltale rapid movement that would indicate he was lying.

There was no mistaking the father's honesty. "Must have

been lost in the mail," he said. "Damn system is getting out of hand. Just the other week, I had to get them to put a tracer on one of my retirement checks."

After dinner one night they got down to the business that really interested Heller. "To find Schiller and Juan Antonio," Henderson said, reading from briefing notes in a worn file folder with a red ribbon around it and the words "Top Secret" stamped in a dozen places, "you have to find the German girl Gretchen. And the key to Gretchen is a Russian named Rodzenko."

"Who is Rodzenko?" asked Heller.

Henderson took a sip of cognac; he helped himself to a snifterful every night, but it never occurred to him to offer one to Heller. "Rodzenko," he said, studying Heller carefully, "is carried on the books as a cultural attaché at the Soviet embassy in Prague. He's an odd bird actually—he holds a degree from Moscow University in Elizabethan literature." The very idea of a Russian being interested in Elizabethan literature left Henderson with a bad taste in his mouth, and he made no effort to hide it. "His thesis, which was published in an obscure English quarterly that prints anything submitted as long as it's typed, made the case that Edward de Vere was the real author of certain plays written by an Englishman named William Shakespeare."

Henderson set down his cognac and noisily blew his nose in a tissue, which he then threw onto the burning logs in the fireplace. "Actually," he continued, "Rodzenko is a lieutenant colonel in the KGB. He was also Schiller's roommate at Patrice Lumumba University. He is also Gretchen's case officer. He is also her lover."

Heller said, "I think, for propriety's sake, we should draw the line at you being my case officer."

Henderson glanced sharply at Heller, but Heller only adjusted his eyeglasses with a forefinger and buried himself in the photographs that Henderson had tossed onto the low table between them. One, taken by a telephoto lens from a great distance, showed Rodzenko in civilian clothes buying a newspaper at a kiosk. The Russian was a heavy-set man, with a high brow and an alert look to his eyes. His hair was thick and brushed straight back without a part. Another shot showed him ducking into the back of a car. The door was being held for him by a burly chauffeur. A third photograph, also taken from a great distance, showed Gretchen and Rodzenko walking through the countryside with their arms around one another, deep in conversation.

Heller absently asked, "Can I bum a cigarette from you?"

"Why are you always asking for cigarettes?" Henderson demanded. "You never smoke the ones we give you."

Heller looked up from the photographs. "I'm testing," he explained.

"Testing what?" asked Henderson. "Testing whom?"

"I'm testing to see if I'm the same man today that I was yesterday."

Henderson shrugged mentally and pulled another sheet from the briefing dossier. "Once in Prague," he went on in a bored voice, "you will be under the wing of the chief of station, a man named Yaneff."

"How will I recognize him?"

"You won't be able to miss him," said Henderson. "He's a fat man—almost twenty stone, I should think."

"What's a stone?" asked Heller.

"A stone," Henderson informed him, "is fourteen pounds."

"Two hundred eighty!" Heller whistled. "He's certainly not your ordinary unobtrusive spy."

Henderson told Heller where he would contact Yaneff on his arrival in Prague, and what the recognition signal would be. "Yaneff will set you up with a place to stay. He'll probably use one of his safe houses, but that's up to him to decide. He will also provide whatever logistical support you need—explosives, a rifle with a laserscope, whatever. When you're ready for exfiltration, he'll turn you over to the people who will take you out." Henderson extracted a sealed envelope from the dossier, tore it open with a finger tip and scanned the note inside. "One more item: If you are caught in the act, as they say, we shall write you off completely. As far as we're concerned, you are a private person who took it upon himself, for understandable personal reasons, to seek revenge. Period. You would do well to stick to the same story. Understood?"

"Understood."

Heller went over the details until he had them committed to

memory. Henderson was downing the last of his cognac when Heller turned on him and said, "I think it's time for school to let out."

Henderson seemed amused at the idea. "Agents usually go through this training program in three months. You've been here a week and a half."

"I'm not going to get better," Heller insisted stubbornly. "I'm just going to get staler."

"It's not up to me," said Henderson.

"Whoever it's up to, tell him"—Heller smiled sweetly—"or *her* that I'm chafing at the bit. I want to begin the operation, or I'll—"

The crackling of the burning logs filled the still room. "Or you'll what?" Henderson inquired curiously.

"Or I'll become very annoyed," retorted Heller. "And the last thing anyone wants is for me to become annoyed."

CHAPTER EIGHT

THE thick black drapes had been drawn in the Director's seventh-floor office. He, the Deputy Director and several aides were watching slides of Soviet missile bases taken by orbiting satellites.

"How long between the time they gave the alert and the missiles were in firing configuration?" asked the Director.

"Fourteen minutes," replied the Deputy Director.

An aide pointed out, "That's almost eighty seconds less than we've seen before."

The Director said, "They didn't trim eighty seconds by training the crews. There's a technical improvement somewhere in there."

"That's my opinion too," agreed the Deputy Director.

Rutledge slipped into the darkened office and handed the Director a typed memo. He held it up to catch some of the light from the projector and read it.

"There must be something you haven't thought of," he

snapped, twisting in his chair to return the memo to Rutledge. "Have you briefed him on escape routes?"

Rutledge nodded in the darkness.

"How about local political conditions? How about clothes?"

"We never figured it would get as far as clothes," said Rutledge.

"Well, it obviously has," said the Director. "Outfit him. And make sure the tailor takes his sweet time about it." The Director turned back to the screen and waved irritably at the projectionist. "Let's have the next series of slides."

The man from Clothing and Accessories stepped back and squinted professionally at the shoulders, then made several marks with his chalk. "We don't want it fitting too well, do we?" he asked rhetorically. Heller, wearing pleated trousers with wide cuffs and a double-breasted suit jacket, studied his image in the mirror.

Henderson, sitting on the windowsill, said, "He'll need an overcoat, a good hat—give him one of those Russian models with fur—gloves, thick-soled shoes that resist water."

The man from Clothing and Accessories, who had a dozen pins handy in his own lapel, removed the suit jacket and attacked the trousers, which were far too big around the crotch.

Henderson went on with what they had been discussing when the tailor arrived. "Where was I? Ah, yes. You can put drops of tetraethyl lead—the additive in high octane gasoline—on the skin. Death comes quickly. No lesions. No evidence of what the detective writers refer to as foul play. You can freeze someone to death. You can smother them with a pillow, being careful not to leave any bodily marks that indicate violence. You can always strangle them with a wide piece of cloth—a bath towel will do nicely, thank you. Done with a bit of attention to detail, none of these methods will leave pathological evidence of murder."

"Ouch," cried Heller. The tailor had jabbed him with a pin.

"Sorry," he said, looking up from the floor.

"What have I left out?" Henderson's brow furrowed. He toyed absently with the tip of his mustache. "X rays. I've left out X rays. You can expose someone to lethal doses of X rays. Death isn't immediate, but if you handle it right you might actually scare someone to death by letting him—or *her*—know what you're doing. Bring on a rather splendid cardiac arrest, I should think."

Heller said over his shoulder, "Personally, I prefer your German pistol."

Henderson snickered. "If you ever actually shoot anyone, I would advise you to get quite close."

"How close?" Heller asked.

"Oh, I should say that at point-blank range, you stand a fifty-fifty chance of hitting something."

Heller started to remove the trousers, careful not to scratch himself with the pins the tailor had stuck in them. "When these are ready," he announced, "I want to put our little sideshow on the road."

"I'll pass that valuable piece of information on," Henderson said without visible enthusiasm.

The Director took the call in the hallway just off the living room. Behind him he could hear the sound he had come to know so well—the distinctive hum of the Georgetown cocktail party.

"What's up?" he asked into the phone. On the other end, Rutledge talked intently for the better part of a minute; he had a way of delivering bad news in long bursts and coming up for air only when the worst had been said.

The Director took a deep breath through his nostrils. Grimly he issued his instructions. "Tell Henderson to take as much time as he can getting there."

As he hung up, the hostess appeared from the living room carrying two glasses of champagne, one for the Director, one for herself. "Enough of your daggers and your cloaks." She laughed gaily. "Don't you people ever *play?* "

The Director, his old charming self once again, accepted the champagne. "All the time," he assured her. "All the time."

Henderson had flattened the map of western Czechoslovakia on the table in the crews' briefing room, and weighted down the corners with whatever came to hand—a saltshaker, two coffee cups, a model of the Russian Backfire bomber. A flight crew—

their crew, as things turned out—lounged around the television set at the other end of the room, out of earshot. Heller, wearing a Czech overcoat one size too large for him and a Russian style fur hat, peered over Henderson's shoulder.

"We'll fly in an Air Force plane to Munich," Henderson said quietly. "Then we'll rent a car and drive to Linz in Austria. From there, we'll make our way to the frontier."

Heller eased his eyeglasses back up along his nose. "What happens when I get to the frontier?"

"You'll pick up your guide and cross just south of Ceske Budejovice."

"What about patrols? What about minefields?"

"There are both," Henderson said calmly; he watched Heller closely to see if the first shoots of panic would blossom. "It's a question of knowing where they are. The guide who will take you over has done it half a hundred times—twice with me in tow."

"You've been into Czechoslovakia?"

"My dear fellow, there are very few frontiers in Eastern Europe that I haven't crossed—at night, on my stomach, with the dogs barking away just over the rise. It's good fun, actually. I quite came to enjoy the whole thing." He tapped the map with a fingernail. "Here, at Ceske Budejovice, you will be handed on to a woman who will run you up to Pisek. From there, you will follow the Vltava to its widest point."

"What's at the widest point?"

"Prague. Do you remember the address?"

"Number forty-five Vinohrady, behind the museum. Fourth floor, first door on the right. I say to whoever answers the door, 'There is no history.' Your man in Prague'll reply, 'There is only biography.' " Heller laughed under his breath. "That's a very classy recognition signal. Someone at the Company must be reading books!"

Henderson glanced sharply at Heller. "There's an old saying which you may have heard: 'He who laughs last laughs best!' "

"I was making a joke," protested Heller.

"So," Henderson announced, "was I."

The Company's Inspector General was adamant. "My brief is in black and white," he argued. "The rumor is enough for me. I want to see all the relevant paper. I want to interview the warm bodies. I want to flutter anyone I suspect of lying. I want to fire anyone I find covering up. I want to bring charges if the rumor turns out to be true."

"Frank, Frank," the Director tried to soothe him, "there are a thousand rumors a day here—"

"There aren't a thousand rumors a day like this one," the IG fired back, and he rolled his eyes in their sockets and muttered, "Thank the good lord."

The Director tried another tack. "Suppose, for argument's sake, that it were true. Suppose one of our cipher people *was* trying to blackmail us. Isn't that exactly the kind of thing that's best dealt with internally, and quietly?"

The IG shook his head stubbornly. "You know where I stand. Something like this is bound to come out eventually. It's better for the Company if it comes from us. It's better if we clean our own house rather than have some Senate committee come in here and do it for us." The IG raised his right hand as if he were taking an oath. "Save the big secrets, give away the little ones, that's my motto. If one of our people is trying to blackmail us, he ought to be called on it."

The Director smiled blandly. "I was taught to keep *all* the secrets, Frank, not give them away at the drop of a rumor." He looked the IG in the eye. "Nobody's trying to blackmail us. I give you my word on it."

The IG actually sighed. "I'm sorry," he said. "That's not enough."

The Director took a deep breath. The IG thought for a tense moment that the Director would simply explode. Instead he slowly let out the breath.

The IG spread his hands, palms up. "Look, if someone is trying to blackmail the Company, he must think he has his little fingers on some hot material. I want to see the material just in case it's as hot as he thinks it is. Also, I want to make sure the Company doesn't give in to blackmail. What is it the guy wants the Company to do that the Company is not willing to do? There's a pretty good chance it's something the Company shouldn't be doing." He sat back in his chair. "I want to see the paper. I want to interview the warm bodies."

The Director stood up very suddenly. "All right."

The IG, taken by surprise, rose too. For a long moment neither man said anything. Then the IG nodded and turned on his heel and left the office.

The Director was on the phone to Rutledge as soon as the door closed behind the IG. "How the hell do I know where he picked it up?" fumed the Director. "The important thing is that he's onto it." He lowered his voice. "The IG's a tenacious son of a bitch. If he finds a loose thread and pulls, the whole thing will unravel. I don't need to remind you, there's a lot more at stake here than Heller. Or even those messages he pasted up in that ridiculous scrapbook of his."

Later, in the Director's office, Rutledge mused gloomily, "We're trapped between Scylla and Charybdis."

Mudd said, "On the one hand we can't let those messages see the light of day. On the other hand—"

The Director supplied the rest. "On the other hand, we can't let him loose in Czechoslovakia with a pistol, even if he barely knows how to use it. The wrong people are bound to ask the right questions."

The Director studied his fingernails. The last few weeks had taken their toll. To his own eye, his skin looked yellowish, wrinkled; the face that stared back at him from the mirror appeared older. "I always assumed the job would kill me," he muttered to himself. He smiled tightly. "I don't know why I'm surprised by all this." Through sheer will power, he shook off the depression. "First things first," he told Rutledge and Mudd. "The IG shouldn't be hard to sidetrack. This will be just another rumor he'll never get a handle on. He'll be down to see you both. You take the position that you wouldn't put up with blackmail if you knew about it, but you don't know about it. He'll talk to the cipher people in Section D, but they really don't know anything. If he wants to talk to Heller, you tell him what happened to his lady friend, and say he's been given a leave of absence. What's left?"

"Mudd's crew that went through his apartment," remarked Rutledge, "but he won't get the time of day out of any of them. They're all professionals."

"What are your people doing now?" the Director wanted to know.

"They've run out of places to look," Mudd admitted.

"We've interviewed his relatives, his friends, male and female, his college roommates, male and female," recounted Rutledge. "There weren't many; he was always something of a loner. We even fluttered his closest friend here at the Company, someone who works in crateology—"

"If anything happens to Heller, the person he stashed the films with will publish," said the Director. He seemed to be reviewing the options open to him.

"Perish and publish," wisecracked Rutledge. He was instantly sorry.

"If there's something humorous in this"—the Director scowled—"I'd appreciate being let in on it." He swiveled toward the window and stared out into the countryside. "They're out there . . . someplace . . . someplace. You checked his apartment. You checked his bank vault. You checked his car . . ."

Rutledge and Mudd looked at each other quickly. Mudd said, "I didn't know he owned a car."

Eight minutes later Mudd was on the phone rounding up his people. In the early hours of the morning, one of the agents walked into the public garage where Heller had left his Pinto, and a few moments later drove down the ramp, paid the parking bill and disappeared into the night. He took the car to a special garage across the Virginia line that the Company had a "relationship" with. There the agents went to work. Using compression equipment, they unscrewed everything that could be unscrewed. Two agents ducked into the well under the car and began unbolting various parts of the motor. The wheels were taken off, tires deflated and searched. The interior rugs were lifted out. All the lights on the car—interior and exterior—were dismantled and examined.

Off to one side, Mudd supervised the operation. He glanced down at the various parts of the car spread out on the cement near his feet. His eyes fell on a bouquet of dried roses that had been found on the floor on the passenger's side, searched and thrown away. A piece of metal—a thin band holding the stems together—caught the light and glinted. Mudd bent down and looked more closely. He touched it with his finger tips, the way a blind man reads braille, then he carefully undid the metal band and held it up to the light to make out the words.

It said "Morningside Flowers."

The band, flattened on the Director's blotter, became the subject of intense study. The Company computer that had digested every telephone directory in the country racked its memory (a chore that took thirty-five seconds) and spewed out thirty-three shops from coast to shining coast with the name "Morningside." A further check eliminated seven (which were no longer in business), three (which sold only plastic flowers), eighteen (for geographic reasons; they were out of one-day driving range of Washington), and two (that hadn't handled red roses in months).

Which left three.

Mudd himself telephoned each in turn from the Director's office, with the Director and Rutledge looking on. He mumbled something about a lovely bouquet of red roses, asked if he could get more. "I got your name," he explained, "from the metal band around the stems."

"What band?" the owner of the first flower shop replied.

"We use ribbons," the saleslady at the second shop said.

At the third call, Mudd hit pay dirt. "I always believed in advertising." The woman who responded to Mudd's call laughed. He asked her where her shop was located. He listened, thanked her profusely and hung up. "I've got it," he told Rutledge and the Director. "Morningside is where the girl is buried!"

"Of course," murmured Rutledge and the Director in one breath. Rutledge added, "The girl!"

Mudd and four agents went by helicopter to Hartford, where they rented a car at the airport and drove the last leg to the cemetery. Flashing an exhumation order so quickly that the cemetery manager didn't have time to really read it, Mudd ordered the coffin dug up and opened. The manager hemmed and hawed until Mudd understood what the problem was: Who would pay the workmen who did the digging? He quickly solved this by distributing twenty-dollar bills (several to the manager himself) and the work began.

In short order, the coffin was hauled up to ground level and the workmen who had done the digging dispatched to the nearest bar with instructions to return in half an hour. Mudd and his men pried off the lid with tools they had brought along with them and went about the grisly business of searching the interior, and what was left of the decaying corpse, for the roll of film.

The cemetery manager, meanwhile, had gotten around to thinking about the credentials that had been flashed across his field of vision. He toyed with the idea of calling the police, but decided he might look like a fool if the men were, as it appeared, agents. But agents of what? The question nagged at him. And why were they digging up the grave of the poor girl who had been killed by terrorists in Germany? The manager had a nodding acquaintance with Diamond; their paths crossed every now and then when they played pinochle together.

Looking out from his office window over the tombstones, the manager made up his mind. He picked up the phone and telephoned Diamond.

"But who are they?" Diamond demanded when the manager explained what was happening. The old man was very worked up. "And what right do they have to dig out Sarah's coffin?"

"To tell the truth," the manager admitted, "I saw the exhumation order but somehow I didn't get to actually read it."

"I'm coming right over," Diamond announced.

He gunned the old Ford until the motor vibrated and arrived just as the agents, under Mudd's watchful eye, finished searching through the clothes of the corpse. The sight of the decaying body *stark naked* drove the old man almost crazy. "What in God's name?" He grabbed the first agent he came to and pulled him away from the coffin, and turned back and stared at the body and covered his eyes with his hands and sank to his knees and began rocking back and forth, moaning incoherently.

When Diamond had calmed down enough to speak, Mudd asked him, "Who are you?"

Mudd's team (bolstered by the addition of four other agents who arrived late in the day) went about the business of ransacking Diamond's tiny house. The old man, drinking tea in the kitchen, got up every now and then and wandered around, watching expressionlessly. "I have had dealings before with people like you," Diamond commented to one of the younger agents who was searching through Sarah's collection of red stamps.

"Where was that, old man?" the agent inquired politely.

"My flat in Cracow was searched by the Gestapo," Diamond explained tonelessly. "They were nice young men, clean-shaven, good complexions, short hair, sure of themselves the way you are sure of yourself. They were looking for copies of an underground newspaper." When the agent didn't react, Diamond added, "I had crumpled up the newspapers in the stove and put kindling on top, but they found them anyway. We were packed off in cattle cars to a place you maybe heard of. It was called Auschwitz. A wife. Two little girlies. I was the only one to survive."

If the agent was embarrassed by the story, he didn't show it. "This is not the same," he insisted.

"How not the same?"

"This is a matter of national security," the agent explained.

"Ah," remarked the old man, "I didn't realize." But the irony went right over the head of the agent, who, having finished with the stamp collection, turned his attention to the ugly Chinese doll propped up on the pillows of Sarah's bed. The sight of the agent *feeling* the doll's boneless limbs struck Diamond as grotesque and he cackled obscenely. "In my day," he snorted, "men your age were interested in flesh-and-blood girls."

Mudd came by and asked the young man how he was doing. "There's just the bed left," he reported, "and this room is clean."

In the corner, the muscles in the old man's face tightened— and Mudd, like a sailor alert to the faintest breeze, noticed it. "I'll give you a hand," he told the agent, and together the two of them started to search it. Mudd removed the old high school yearbook that was under one leg and went through it page by page and flipped it aside with the other books piled in a heap. He eyed the old tarnished brass bed, then felt around to see where one part screwed into another. He found the joints, unscrewed the top of the post, trained a flashlight down into the hollow and then glanced at the old man who was sinking slowly, silently to the floor, his right hand weakly massaging his heart. Gurgling sounds seeped from between his compressed lips, as if he were under water and trying desperately to say something.

They laid the old man on the bed. Mudd, alarmed at the sound of Diamond gasping (for air? for life? for memories?), unbuttoned his shirt and began feeling for his pulse.

Suddenly Diamond opened wide his eyes and grabbed Mudd's lapel and muttered something and then sank back dead.

Neither Mudd nor the young agent could figure out what the old man's last words had been. He had spoken in Polish, a language neither of them understood.

The Director listened to Mudd's report on the phone. "All right," he said, "put the place back together, get your people out of there and then square the cardiac with the local police. You were questioning him on a matter of national security, he keeled over, you massaged his heart, et cetera, et cetera."

The Director hung up and turned to Rutledge. "They found it. In the bedpost."

Rutledge smiled in relief. "With people like that, it's always in the bedpost."

The Director's eyes burned with hatred. "Where is Heller now?"

Rutledge's smile faded. He looked at his watch and made a quick calculation. "He's crossing over tonight. He may already be out of our hands."

The Director didn't mince words. "If he's not across, I don't want him crossing. If he's already across, I don't want him coming out."

Rutledge, who knew an order when he heard one, made tracks.

CHAPTER NINE

UPSTAIRS a toilet flushed and the water spilled noisily through the pipes in the walls. In the storage room behind the kitchen at the rear of the hotel-bar, a long stone's throw from the Austrian-Czech frontier, Heller slept fitfully on an old mattress that had been laid on the floor. He was once again caught up in his recurrent dream—trying to find a pebble on the beach that matched one in the huge sack he carried on his back. At one point he spotted a coal-black pebble with a white line encircling it. He found the duplicate in his sack and threw them both into the sea —and unaccountably started in after them. He could feel the coldness and wetness of the water washing around his ankles, the sponginess of the sand underfoot. He wondered if he would go through with it, then found himself being sucked into the sea by an undertow, sucked farther and farther from the beach—

"Wake up!" Henderson was shaking him by the shoulder. "It's almost two—time to go."

Heller sat up. The Czech guide, a young man about the same height and build as Heller, was sitting on the floor near the back door drinking beer from a can. An odd-shaped hunter's cap with a long peak was pulled low over his forehead, so that all Heller could see was a deep shadow where the guide's eyes should have been.

Henderson, wearing hunter's clothes and a sheepskin jacket, peered out the single window in the storeroom at the flat fields barely visible in the light of a quarter moon. "God, how I love borders," he said to no one in particular, and he breathed deeply through his nostrils as if he expected to *smell* the frontier. He turned to Heller, all business. "It'll be light out in five hours. Whatever happens, you have to be well across by then. All right, let's go over it for the last time. You cross those fields"—he gestured with a toss of his head toward the window—"to a small stream. You cross the stream and cut diagonally across a woods until you come to more fields and a small village. The village is just on their side of the frontier. You skirt the village until you come to a wide, shallow river. You go upriver until you come to a railroad bridge—"

"Normally it's not guarded." Heller picked up the thread. "If it's not, we cross on the bridge. If it is, we wade across the river and make for the railroad tracks farther along."

Henderson nodded. "You follow the track, being careful to walk on the ties—the area is mined—until you spot the farm with the windmill. Fifty yards away is a small shed. Be sure to go to ground in the shed, not the windmill. You stay in the shed during the day. Tomorrow night, a car will fetch you and take you to Ceske Budejovice."

Heller got to his feet, adjusted his eyeglasses, climbed into his Czech overcoat, which he had been using as a pillow, and set the Russian fur hat squarely on his head with the earflaps tied up so he could hear better. Then he took out the heavy P-38, removed the clip and punched it back in again and checked to make sure he had the three spare clips in his pocket. He put the pistol in his overcoat pocket. Across the room the Czech guide rose lazily to his feet; moving with effortless grace, he stretched his shoulder muscles and grinned at Heller and tapped the crystal on his wristwatch with his forefinger.

Heller said dryly, "I suppose this is the moment we've all been waiting for."

Henderson, still gazing at the world with an unblinking lack of interest, didn't offer to shake hands. "Have fun" was all he said.

Heller said, "Fuck you too," opened the door and stepped out into the field. The guide came out, flared his nostrils at the wind, took in the clouds racing across the quarter moon, then said something in Czech, pointed with his fist and set off across the field at a fast pace. Heller followed close on his heels.

Behind them, Henderson watched the two figures disappear in the darkness. Henderson was a good soldier, someone who did what he was told without asking questions, without judging the orders or the person who gave them. But in all his years of working for the Company, he had never come across a case quite like Heller's—and it made him wonder. The fact that the Company wanted to "terminate with prejudice" (as the in-house phrase makers put it) three terrorists struck Henderson as perfectly reasonable. But that Heller should have been chosen for the job—or, more accurately, that he should have chosen himself for the job and obliged the Company to send him in—struck Henderson as another example of the insanity that had seeped into the veins of the Company in recent years. If there was a logic to the madness, he, Henderson, couldn't put his finger on it. Still, orders were—

The wall telephone behind Henderson sounded shrilly. He stared at it, narrowing his eyes in thought, then decided to answer it. He lifted the receiver off the hook and listened for a moment. His eyes opened alertly. "You're too late. He's already on his merry way." He listened again. "You're not serious?" The voice on the other end cursed. "You are serious!" said Henderson. And he added with a touch of grim humor, "This is a hell of a way to run a cold war. I'll see what I can do."

Henderson hurried out the back door and circled the hotel-bar until he came to the parking lot in front. He went to the rented Opel, opened the trunk and took out a long object wrapped in a blanket. Back in the storage room, he removed the blanket and checked the sniper rifle with the laser projector to make sure it was loaded. Fairly scowling at the ridiculousness of the situation—what a story this would make on *his* Georgetown cocktail circuit!—he slung the rifle over his shoulder and started across the field after Heller.

The wind had died away. Nothing moved in the open field —not a blade of grass, not an insect—nothing. Very gradually a figure (the guide, judging from the silhouette of the distinctive peaked cap) rose up on his knees. A second figure (Heller, judging from the silhouette of the Russian fur hat) rose up next to him. They waited motionless, listening. Then the guide touched Heller on the shoulder and they set off toward the small stream.

Heller had never in his life been as aware of each footfall as he was now. He felt the change in the texture of the earth under the soles of his heavy shoes. He heard the stream before they got to within earshot. He picked up the first faint touch of the breeze against his cheek before the grass swayed to it. He imagined the trees looming on the other side of the stream before the wood came into view in the silver moonlight. He realized that the night *smelled* different than the day. It wasn't a matter of his imagination working overtime; it was more a question of his senses working for the first time.

They crossed the stream on a fallen tree trunk and cut diagonally through the wood. At the tree line the guide dropped to one knee and listened for a long moment before tugging gently on Heller's arm and setting out across the next stretch of open field. A few minutes later they came to a small rise. Heller, out of breath, sank to the ground. The young guide settled down next to him. Heller could see that he was looking at him strangely. Then the guide grinned and said something softly in Czech.

"I don't understand Czech," Heller whispered.

Still grinning, the guide took off his peaked cap and offered it to Heller. He indicated with gestures that he expected Heller to give him his Russian fur hat in exchange.

Heller shook his head. "This one goes with my overcoat," he whispered.

The grin on the guide's face evaporated. He repeated the gesture. He obviously had his heart set on trading hats.

Heller shrugged. "From your point of view," he muttered, "I can see that this is an ideal time to ask."

They exchanged hats. The guide's hunting cap was a bit tight, but Heller figured it was better than nothing. The guide, grinning happily again, set the Russian hat on his head at a jaunty angle, then turned and crawled the few yards to the top of the rise. He carefully raised his head above the skyline to get a look at the village just on the other side.

Somewhere in the village, a cat in heat screeched in a deep voice that sounded almost human.

Heller, watching the guide's back, suddenly tensed. Something was very wrong, but it took him a second or two before his brain assigned words to the thing that his eyes saw. *A small red dot of light was dancing on the guide's back!*

The laser projector from the sniper rifle! Heller opened his mouth to whisper a warning, but the sharp crack of a rifle echoed through the fields first. In the underbrush nearby a dozen birds scurried into the sky in panic. The guide pitched forward on his face. A soft sound came from his body—bubbles rising to the surface of a still lake. From the open field behind him, Heller heard someone running toward him. Henderson came into view; he had the rifle slung over his shoulder. Heller rose off the ground. He planted his feet wide apart, thrust the German pistol out in front with both hands and sighted on the advancing target.

Henderson's mouth sank in horror as he spotted the distinctive crouching position. It was Heller and not the guide who was waiting for him! He tried to stop running, but his momentum carried him almost up to Heller. He sank to his knees, panting for breath, frozen in fear. The rifle slipped from his shoulder to the ground. Breathing in short gasps, terrified that each breath would be his last, he brought an arm up in front of his face. "Please," Henderson begged in a voice that neither he nor Heller had ever heard before. "Don't."

Heller's pistol was only inches from Henderson's head. His finger began to squeeze, not jerk, the trigger.

"For God's sake," sobbed Henderson, "give me a chance." A warm stain spread along the inside of his thick trousers.

"You already have a fifty-fifty chance," taunted Heller. "I'm going to shoot you at point-blank range!"

He tried to do it; he concentrated on the muscle in his index finger and willed it to contract; he willed it so hard that his hand began to shake. To hit something, the master sergeant had said, you have to want to hit it.

With infinite slowness, the tension in Heller's finger relaxed and the pistol fell off until it was pointing at the ground.

Henderson's arms slipped limply away, exposing a face that no longer looked human. Stripped of his own image of himself, accumulated over a lifetime of posing, he was beyond humiliation, beyond terror. What was left was a whimpering infant, incapable of coherent thought or speech or motion. Simple gestures —getting to his feet, putting one foot in front of the other— would have to be relearned.

Heller picked up Henderson's rifle by the barrel and flung it into the night. Then he backed away from the figure that appeared to *melt* grotesquely like candle wax, awed at what had happened. When he was far enough from Henderson so that he could no longer see his eyes staring after him, he turned and raced away from the rise, away from the village; away from his first brush with violence.

Dogs barked wildly and strained against the chains that held them to the fenceposts. Lights came on in several houses. A door was flung open. A man called in Czech to his dogs.

Running heavily, making no effort to hide his presence, Heller skirted the village, plunged feverishly into some underbrush, flung his arms up to protect his face from snapping branches (a gesture that brought back the image of Henderson with *his* arm in front of *his* face). He burst through the underbrush and tramped across a small field planted with winter cabbages. He heard the river before he came to it, running in cold currents over smooth shallow boulders. Heller slid down the embankment to the river's edge. He paused to splash icy water over his face. It was so cold it stung his skin; for a while his fingers felt numb. Walking on the pebbly surface at the river's edge, kneading his fingers to get feeling back into them, feeling oddly as if he were in the middle of one of his recurring dreams, he started upstream.

He followed the curve of the river for ten or fifteen minutes, losing track of time, climbing over dead branches, rock formations that glistened like fool's gold in the moonlight, even an old car, rusted and falling to pieces, that had been pushed down the embankment and abandoned. Rounding a bend, he spotted the one-track railroad bridge.

Heller sank into the shadow of some shrubbery and studied the bridge. As far as he could make out, there was no movement on it. He decided to count to fifty and then take his chances. At thirty-eight, a match flared at the far end of the bridge. A sentry was lighting a cigarette.

A cigarette! What he would have given to ask for one, and then not smoke it!

Heller settled back into the shrubbery, then carefully inched back the way he had come. Once around the bend from the bridge, he removed his shoes, socks, trousers and overcoat. Testing the depth of the water with a stick he found on the bank, he practically danced across the shallow river. On the far bank he roughly rubbed his legs and feet with his overcoat until he felt life seeping back into them, then quickly dressed, tucked his frozen hands under his armpits and stumbled across fields that had been plowed but not planted, in the general direction of the railroad track.

He found it—or more accurately, it found him; he tripped over it before he saw it—about twenty minutes later. He crouched and listened for a full minute, but the only sounds that came to his ears seemed like normal night sounds. Stepping on the wooden ties, Heller turned away from the river and the bridge and started up the tracks.

For a long while he counted the ties, but then he gave up and concentrated on putting one foot in front of the other. He tried not to think about anything else, but a corner of his brain worked at fitting the pieces of the puzzle together. Henderson had tried to kill him while he was crossing the border, no doubt with the idea that his body, stripped of papers (and perhaps even fingers!), would never be identified—another victim of the cold war, a Czech from the look of him, killed trying to cross illegally into, or out of, Czechoslovakia. Which meant—Heller felt as if he were resisting the inevitable—which meant that the Company had recovered the film. *Whatever you have on them, Henderson had said, don't lose it.* Well, he had obviously lost it. A new thought sent an impulse of panic through his nervous system. He was getting deeper and deeper into a country where his safety depended on Company contacts, and the Company had already tried to terminate him. He would have to think about this aspect more carefully . . . more carefully . . . but now he was becoming exhausted, physically, mentally . . . exhausted to the point where the act of stepping from tie to tie seemed almost beyond his ability.

Heller had been on the ties for three-quarters of an hour when he looked up and spotted the strange silhouette. "The windmill!" he muttered to himself; the word confirmed the vision, gave to it a reality that it seemed to lack. Forgetting his exhaustion, he abandoned the ties and cut across the fields toward the windmill.

The message came in on one of the embassy's high speed printers. The night code officer ripped it off and took it up to the "floating" windowless room-within-a-room on the top floor where the keys were stored. There, working under a desk lamp with the appropriate one-time system, he deciphered the message, typed up a single copy, marked it "Original, No Copies," folded it into a metal clipboard and hand-delivered it to the night duty officer sleeping on the Ambassador's couch.

The duty officer went into the Ambassador's private bathroom, splashed some cold water on his face, then came back and read the message. The text made it crystal clear that it was to be acted on immediately. The duty officer signed the code officer's book acknowledging possession of message number 812, of which only one copy existed. As soon as he was alone, he dialed a number and let the phone ring until somebody on the other end finally answered.

"Yeah?" a sleepy voice inquired.

The duty officer said, "If I were you, I'd climb into some clothes and come on in."

The fat man on the other end of the line was instantly awake. "Be there in fifteen minutes."

He was as good as his word. A quarter of an hour later the duty officer met him in the lobby and handed him the metal folder with a single piece of paper in it. The fat man, breathing hard, settled into one of the seats that the Marines guarding the door used and studied the message. Without a word he handed it back to the duty officer and left.

The fat man was a professional. He spent twenty minutes doing some elementary street work to make sure he wasn't being followed. Then he parked under a streetlamp and printed out a set of precise instructions in minuscule letters (One: contact . . . two: offer to sell . . . three: don't appear to be eager) and deposited the folded piece of paper in a dead letter drop (behind a metal container for used bus tickets). Finally he ducked into a public phone booth near the bus stop and called his contact.

The man obviously slept with the phone near his bed, because he answered after one ring. "It's me," said the fat man. "I'm leaving a bag of fruit for you. It will rot if you don't pick it up within an hour."

The man on the other end of the line spoke English with a thick Polish accent. He was an older man, well educated and very formal. "Might I inquire what sort of fruit you have left for me?"

"Peaches," said the fat man. "Peaches, as in peaches and cream."

The Pole recovered the "peaches" half an hour later, memorized the message in a public toilet and flushed it down a drain. Then he phoned up the man at the Bulgarian embassy who ran him. They bargained in Russian for several minutes, settled on a price, and the Pole passed on the piece of information.

The Bulgarian woke his superior at home and described the information he had acquired. His superior passed it on immediately to his contact at Czech counterintelligence. He in turn woke up the Professor, who lived with his wife in a small apartment in an old building under Hradcany Castle.

The Professor, who had been up very late the night before working on the monograph he would deliver in a few days to the university seminar, took the call in the kitchen and whispered so as not to wake his wife, who was still asleep in the double bed that almost filled their tiny bedroom. "Where did the information come from?" asked the Professor. He cradled the phone between his chin and shoulder and used his hands to fill a kettle with water for tea.

"I got it from the Bulgarians," the caller explained.

"Where did they get it?"

"I don't know."

"Find out," instructed the Professor. "The single most important thing about any piece of information is where it came from. If you know where it came from, you may begin to know why you have it."

"Yes, sir."

The Professor, who was the chief of the counterintelligence directorate of the Czech Intelligence Service, cleared his throat; it always embarrassed him to give orders. "I'll want a car to pick me up in twenty minutes," he said.

"I've already dispatched it," said the underling, a bright young man named Karol.

"You should alert our people in Ceske Budejovice," the Professor added.

"Excuse me, Professor," said Karol, "but I've taken it on myself to send an alert to Ceske Budejovice."

The Professor was getting impatient with Karol's efficiency. "You have a way of making me feel replaceable," he noted dryly. "I will want a helicopter standing by," he said, "to take me down there." He grimaced inwardly; he detested helicopters—the way they had of hanging motionless in the air and then suddenly arcing off at some ungodly angle, as if gravity had never existed, as if "up" and "down" were mere technical terms and not a matter of essential orientation.

On the other end of the phone, Karol hesitated in embarrassment. "The helicopter has already been arranged," he finally informed him.

There was a moment of silence. Then the Professor said, "Karol, it is my considered opinion that you will go far in this business. You are intelligent enough to know how to. And ignorant enough to want to." And he put the receiver softly down on its cradle.

Somewhere in the distance a cock crowed. Faint ribbons of light streaked the bleak horizon. An icy wind swept across the flatland, chilling to the bone the Czech soldiers who had crept up in the darkness to surround the windmill. The Professor pulled his astrakhan over his ears and took the battery-powered bullhorn from the officer in nominal charge of the operation. Crouching behind a trough in which the water had turned to ice, he switched on the bullhorn and brought it up to his chapped lips. On every side of the windmill, the soldiers, wearing heavy winter overcoats and fur hats, threw the bolts on their rifles. The four dogs held on leashes by their handler perked up their ears for the kill.

"You there, inside the windmill," the Professor called through the bullhorn. He spoke meticulous English with only the vaguest hint of an accent. "Come out with your hands on your head. It is your only chance. You are completely surrounded."

The Professor lowered the bullhorn and watched the old wooden door of the windmill. There was no sound, no sign of life.

He raised the bullhorn again. "This is your last warning. You are instructed to come out with your hands on your head. We know you are in there. I give you three minutes."

The Professor fished an eighty-year-old Patek Philippe from his vest pocket and clicked it open. At two and a half minutes, he nodded to the officer in charge; he in turn raised his left hand. Around the windmill, the soldiers brought up their rifles and sighted on the only door and the windows. The Professor's watch indicated the three-minute limit had expired. He shook his head unhappily, replaced his pocket watch, placed his gloved hands over his ears and nodded again at the officer, who brought his left hand sharply down, as if he were administering a karate chop to an invisible victim. A ragged volley of rifle fire broke the morning stillness.

Fifty yards away, in the abandoned tool shed, Heller—sleeping on the floor wrapped in his overcoat—sat bolt upright. There was no mistaking the sound of rifle fire. He groped for his eyeglasses, fitted them on and peered through a crack in the door. He could make out splinters flying off the side of the windmill as the soldiers fired away. Heller grabbed his overcoat, climbed out a back window covered with tarpaper instead of glass and, keeping the tool shed between him and the soldiers, raced for the nearby wood.

Behind him, the soldiers—in reality, a well-trained border unit—increased their fire as several men dashed for the windows and the door. On cue, they flung grenades into the windmill. As soon as they exploded, the soldiers at the door kicked it in and, firing submachine guns in short bursts from the hip, disappeared inside.

Instantly the firing ceased; a professional calm settled over the scene. A moment later one of the soldiers emerged from the windmill, the metal butt of his submachine gun resting casually on his hip and angled up. "There's nobody inside," he called to his officer.

The officer looked at the Professor. "I thought you said . . ."

The Professor's brow furrowed. "The information was precise—an American infiltrator in the windmill."

The officer stood up and looked around. "Search the area," he called to the soldiers.

The soldiers spread out and began to inspect the interior of a collapsed barn, an abandoned chicken coop. Two troopers kicked in the door of the tool shed and entered. Almost immediately, one of them emerged, shouting excitedly. He raised his rifle over his head. An odd-shaped hunting cap with a long peak hung from the barrel.

"Dogs," cried the officer in charge. The handler let them smell the cap and the floor of the tool shed where Heller had slept. The dogs followed the scent to the rear window covered with tarpaper, then picked up the trace outside and started for the wood, straining at their leashes, their noses sniffing frantically along the ground. The border troops, their rifles at the ready, spread out in a line behind them. They had hunted people before and knew the drill.

Heller had a good head start, but he suspected it wouldn't be long before they picked up his trail. Wading through a field of winter wheat, he stopped for a moment to catch his breath. He could see a faint wisp of black smoke spiraling into the sky behind him—the explosions he heard must have set the windmill on fire —and then he caught the ominous yelp of the dogs. He broke out of the winter wheat and raced through an open field. Three-quarters of the way across he stopped next to an old broken bent tree that thrust its leafless branches into the air like so many arthritic fingers. At the far edge of the field a teenage boy with a peasant's cape draped over his shoulders was trying to force a mule to move. When the mule refused, the boy hauled back and kicked the mule in the testicles. The mule screamed in pain—and moved.

Heller could hear the dogs behind him. He had the impression they were in the wheatfield, closer if anything than before. Suddenly he remembered Rutledge telling the secretaries at the cocktail party how he had urinated to throw the dogs off the scent. Laughing viciously, his lips stretched tightly over his teeth, Heller urinated against the tree, then sprinted off toward a forest of new white pines.

He had barely disappeared into the pines when the dogs burst through the wheat onto the open field. The soldiers were right behind them, and the Professor, surprisingly agile for his age despite the heavy galoshes on his feet, not far behind the soldiers. The dogs bounded up to the bent tree and began milling around in confusion. The soldiers and the Professor caught up and stood around breathing heavily. The dog handler pulled the dogs from the tree. "Must be a professional," he called. "He pissed to throw the dogs off." The handler went out twenty paces and began to lead the dogs in a large arc looking for the scent. One of the dogs found it, barked twice and bounded off toward the pine trees.

Heller heard the dogs pick up the scent, and he quickened his pace. He stumbled down a steep slope, going from tree to tree, and emerged on a two-lane highway with a white line down the middle, and shoulders. From the woods behind him Heller caught the hollow sound of the dogs barking. They were drawing nearer and nearer. Across the road, flat treeless fields stretched off to the horizon.

In the woods, the officer in charge shouted over his shoulder to the Professor, "We have him now. There's a road just ahead, and beyond that nothing but flat land."

The dogs crashed through the woods, leaping excitedly down the slope toward the road. The soldiers flitted through the trees right behind them. In a rush, they burst through the tree line onto the road. The dogs, their noses to the asphalt, whimpered as they sniffed around.

136

The Professor lowered himself onto the road and looked across at the flat fields. There was nothing in sight. Then he looked up and down the road, but it too was empty. His eyes narrowed in what he hoped would look like annoyance. The officer in charge braced himself for the inevitable rebuke, but all the Professor said was, "Just so."

CHAPTER
TEN

THE sudden change in temperature had fogged Heller's eyeglasses, and he found himself peering out at the world through frosted lenses that blurred the edges of objects, and dissolved them into geometric shapes. The driver, for instance, talking out of the side of his mouth while keeping his eyes glued to the highway, looked vaguely like an octagon. "But they've already checked our bloody passports at the frontier," he complained.

The double-decker English tourist bus, with cots, toilets and a small kitchen down below, and seats topside, had hauled into view around a bend in the nick of time. Heller never hesitated; waving his arms over his head, he had stepped into the middle of the road. The driver had pulled up—Heller had left him no choice—and opened the door.

"Passports," Heller had called in an English that he hoped smacked of a handful of East European languages. He swung aboard and signaled with the back of his hand for the driver to continue on down the road.

The English tourists, eighteen days out of London and looking the worse for it, took in Heller's enormous overcoat and formless trousers. Heller wiped his eyeglasses on his handkerchief and fitted them on again; the world, such as it was, came into focus. He filled his mouth with saliva and repeated the word "passport" several times.

"I warned you it was a police state," sneered a man in suspenders to his bulky wife. "Well, 'ere's the bloody police."

A rail-thin schoolteacher with ruddy cheeks and a hairpiece raised a finger to attract Heller's attention. "Eh, excuse me, old boy. Do you happen to know how far it is to Prague?"

Heller stared back blankly.

The schoolteacher handed Heller his passport, which he fetched from the breast pocket of his double-breasted suit jacket. "Good God," he said loudly, "look at his clothes, will you! That overcoat must have been in its prime in the forties. He doesn't look all that fresh either, what?"

There were subdued giggles from several corners of the bus. The schoolteacher looked around, extremely pleased with himself.

Heller checked the passport of every passenger, studiously comparing the photograph to the original before handing it back. When he had finished, he settled into a vacant seat in the last row of the bus, next to the emergency exit. For a while, the English tourists kept looking over their shoulders at him and whispering among themselves. As the morning wore on, they seemed to forget all about him.

The bus passed through the wide, clean streets of Ceske Budejovice, lined with small buildings that looked as if they had been recently laundered and set out in the sun to dry. By the time the bus turned onto the four-lane highway that ran parallel to the river the West knows as the Moldau and the Czechs call the Vltava, Heller had been all but absorbed into the small community of tourists; when the hostess passed around sandwiches she had prepared in the tiny kitchen, she smilingly offered one to Heller. And he smilingly (and hungrily) accepted.

Heller actually dozed, albeit fitfully, on the eighty-mile run up to Prague. He was awakened when the rail-thin schoolteacher plugged in the hand microphone and began lecturing his compatriots on the history of Prague. "The city of Huss, of Kepler, of Rilke, of Kafka, of Smetana and Dvorak," he intoned, glancing at an eight-by-ten file card he had prepared the night before (the English took their touring seriously!). "Founded by Germans, invaded in the course of eight centuries by Swedes, French, Prussians, Germans and most recently . . . eh"—he glanced at Heller in the back of the bus and saw that he was staring out the window —"eh, most recently, our friends from the East."

The schoolteacher droned on ("Bohemian barons . . . baroque . . . rococo . . . thirteen bridges of which the Charles is universally considered the most . . . the city that Auguste Rodin called 'the Rome of the north' "). Outside, the gently rolling landscape of the Vltava gradually flattened, almost as if it had been pressed like a pair of pants, and the first of the hundreds of factories that ring the capital came into view—massive sprawling scars with functional lines. There were trolley cars now and cobblestones instead of asphalt and policemen with white gloves and batons which they twirled as they directed traffic from small circular platforms set dead center at important crossroads.

And a police roadblock. Heller, spotting it up ahead through the front window of the bus, thought at first there had been an accident. But as the bus drew closer, he saw the soldiers manning machine guns in the backs of jeeps, and teams of three men dressed in fatigues and red berets and carrying submachine pistols with folding stocks making their way from car to car in the queue, examining papers passed through the window, eying the cars to see how muddy they were—a likely indication of how far they had come.

Three members of the militia—a military auxiliary attached to the Ministry of the Interior—came up to the English tourist bus and one of them rapped his wedding ring against the glass door. The driver pulled the lever that opened it. One of the militiamen stationed himself on the first step of the door. The other two started down the aisle asking firmly but politely for passports.

"Not again," moaned the rail-thin schoolteacher. "This is becoming bloody boring, if you ask me." Still, when his turn came he handed his over without comment.

The militiamen, both serious young men, were obviously

professionals. It wasn't only the photographs that interested them, though they paid a fair amount of attention to the faces; it was also the date of birth and age and place of issue and the visa with the time and day of crossing the frontier stamped inside.

The militiamen took their sweet time as they checked the passengers. Finally they came to the last row of seats, saw the emergency exit door ajar, glanced at each other with a look that some of the passengers took for sheer satisfaction, and hurried from the bus.

Heller remembered looking it up in his office dictionary the first time he came across the name:

in•qui•line ′in-kwə-līn **** *n.* an animal living in the nest or burrow of another animal

There were other details Heller knew about the Company's asset in Prague: he lived under the approach pattern of an airport (which accounted for the earplugs he ordered); on the edge of a river, the Vltava probably, that had overflowed its banks recently (hence the size-seven waterproof boots); and he raised and exported guinea fowl, a turkey-sized bird with a bony casque on its head and dark gray spotted plumage, bought in Europe by people who wanted something more decorative than chickens running around their yards.

The idea had come to Heller during the bus ride to Prague: It would be suicide for him to contact his Company case officer after what Henderson had tried to do. Yet Heller had to find a place to operate from if he had any hope of locating—and eventually killing—the three terrorists.

Which is what made him think of Inquiline. If he could find him, he could supply enough details—his shoe size (seven), his culinary preferences (Indian), what services he rendered to the Company (sending Russian letters to the West hidden under newspaper at the bottom of his birdcages) to convince Inquiline that he, Heller, had been sent by the Company to . . . to what? Of course, to teach him how to encipher one-time pads correctly! There was always the danger that Inquiline might be in touch with the same case officer Heller was trying to avoid; that he would check out Heller's story with the case officer and bring the Company hatchet men down around his ears. But that would take time. And in any case it was a risk Heller would have to run; he didn't have that many options left open to him. He would hole up with Inquiline for a week or so, give him a refresher course on one-time ciphers an hour each morning and, pleading other business in Prague, disappear for the rest of the day. If he played his cards well, he might even get Inquiline to supply money, if he needed money, and wheels, if he needed transportation.

All this depended on finding Inquiline. Making his way through side streets, Heller headed in the general direction of Hradcany Castle, which hovered over the Czech capital like a falcon waiting to pounce on its prey. As he got closer, the streets narrowed and began twisting and turning the way streets that were laid out before the Great Plague usually did. Upper floors jutted over the gutters, and windowpanes were full of imperfections. The square in front of the castle, jammed with tourist buses, had a carnival atmosphere. The bus drivers warmed their hands over a fire burning in a trash can, glancing impatiently every minute or so at their watches to see how long they had to go before their charges returned from the various museums in the castle. People with cameras over their shoulders crowded around the sidewalk stands fingering cheap trinkets with "Prague" written on them, or examining picture postcards. An old lady wrapped in layers of clothing hawked hot wine from a large metal thermos. Kneeling over a cardboard valise, a young Czech with a badly pockmarked face moved three playing cards around in a version of the old shell game. Several Russian soldiers who had been visiting the museum put their money where they thought the ace of spades was. No matter how slowly the Czech moved the cards around, the Russians always seemed to lose.

Working his way downhill toward the Vltava, Heller emerged from the old section around Hradcany into streets arranged in a perfect grid (a sure indication that they were planned after the Great Plague). The buildings were grayer and more businesslike, and the windowpanes thicker and without imperfections. The street teemed with children hurrying home in the twilight; the younger ones carried their heavy books in backpacks, the older ones in imitation leather briefcases. Heller paused on the Charles Bridge, between the statues of St. Gaetanus and St. Augustinus, tb stare down at the Vlatava running silently underneath, its whale-gray surface splashed with faint traces of pink, reflections from a cold winter sunset.

Across the river, the shadows were thickening, and the silhouettes of church spires and tall government buildings etched themselves into the sky. Prague, Heller thought, wears its culture like an old winter coat, its frayed collar turned up against the icy winds that existed as often as not in the imagination. Many people considered Prague a beautiful city, but the chances were good they also liked wedding cakes.

Heller found what he was looking for on Pruchodni, a narrow cobblestoned street across from an old cathedral. A small bell attached to the inside of the door jingled as he entered the pet store. The woman behind the counter looked up from her newspaper.

"Do you speak English?" asked Heller.

"A little, yes," The birds had started chirping at the intruder, and she had to talk up to be heard.

Heller explained that he was interested in guinea fowl.

The woman shook her head. "Parrots. Tropical birds. Doves even. No guinea fowl."

"I don't want one bird," Heller said. "I want many. I want to import them to England. I heard there was someone in Prague who raised them for export."

The woman nodded carefully. "There was someone, yes. A poet, I think. In the suburbs. Along the river. That was maybe years ago. I am not knowing if he is still being in business." She forced her face into a tired smile. "You are sure to be not interested in parrots? I have one called Engels, he repeats the word 'alienation' all the time."

Heller shook his head. "I have my heart set on guinea fowl," he said. The bell on the door jingled behind him; a man and a child entered the shop. Heller hurriedly thanked the woman and left.

He walked back to the river and hesitated. Should he go upstream or down? He was still trying to decide when he heard the faint but unmistakable sound of a jet plane off to his right.

The airport! Feeling as if he had been *pointed* in the right direction, he hurried off toward the north.

Following the river was easier said than done. For a long while the road ran parallel to it. There were several swimming barges, closed for the winter, tied to rusting bollards by thick hawsers with plastic rat guards. There was also a brightly lit barge that had been turned into a restaurant; Heller could see the waiters in white jackets lighting candles on each table. But soon after, the river widened; and the road simply ended in a high fence that surrounded a warehouse.

Heller turned inland and found a narrow street with a trolley track that ran parallel to the river. Every few minutes a trolley jammed with bodies (the central city disgorging its suburban migrants!) rolled quietly by on rubberized wheels.

After half an hour the trolley tracks turned inland, and a few minutes later the street too turned inland and then twisted back until it was once again parallel to the river, only it was no longer paved. There was a long series of three-story blocklike apartment houses, relatively new judging from the lack of pavement and the wooden boards stretched between what passed for the street and the front doors. There weren't many private cars, but the few that existed were covered with black tarpaulins tied down with ropes.

Heller passed a small park with a high fence. Inside, a teenage boy in a warmup suit scurried around, a ghostlike figure in the gathering darkness, slamming a soccer ball into the fence with so much force that the sound reverberated from apartment house to apartment house. Oddly, the sight and the sound seemed to Heller not at all inappropriate.

Further along, the apartment houses thinned out. There was construction equipment—a Russian bulldozer, the pieces of a crane laid out neatly on the ground like a giant erector set—where new buildings would rise.

And then came the first fields, frozen mud flats, with garbage strewn at the edges. An old man carrying a leash and plaintively calling a name hurried up to Heller and asked him something in Czech, looking anxiously all the while for a glimpse of his lost dog. Heller never actually heard the old man's voice. It was drowned out by the roar of the jet plane passing just overhead on

144

the final leg of its approach to the airport out of sight over a rise on the other bank of the Vltava.

Heller watched the plane, its powerful wing lights stabbing out like an insect's antennae, disappear across the river, barely visible in the west. And then he saw it, sitting on the near bank of the Vltava, looking for all the world like a giant nest. "Inquiline," he breathed.

Behind him he could hear the old man wandering off, still calling for his lost dog. Heller turned and trudged across the fields toward the nest.

The house—for that was what it was—had been built in that modern age of innocence (the period before Anschluss) by a whimsical Czech architect for a rich Prague businessman who spent his weekends bird watching on the banks of the Vltava. The idea had been to construct a giant bird's nest in poured concrete and wood; philosophically (if so heavy a word can be used for so light an undertaking) the building represented art deco carried to its logical (some critics at the time preferred "laughable") extreme. It was bowl-shaped and laced with stripped tree trunks placed almost haphazardly to represent twigs. For windows there were slits in the wall between the tree trunks. Off to the right were two long low wooden buildings from which emerged the high-pitched chatter of birds. Even the guinea fowl were accounted for!

The house was pitch dark and without any visible sign of life. Heller gripped the butt of his German pistol in his overcoat pocket—what if the Company had anticipated he would turn up at Inquiline's?—and he approached the nest cautiously, stopping every few paces to listen. All he heard was his own heart thumping away (with excitement? with fright?). He made his way along the side of the building, feeling the roughness of the poured concrete with his finger tips, peering in windows as he came to them, seeing nothing, no movement, no light, until he found himself at what he took to be the back door. He tried the handle, but it was locked. He took out his German pistol, wrapped the hem of his overcoat around the butt and tapped on the pane over the lock. There was the tinkle of falling glass. Heller held his breath. Still no sound came from inside. He reached in with his left hand, flipped the lock and quickly let himself into the nest.

It came to him, standing there with his back pressed to a wall, with the force of a religious revelation: there was something psychologically satisfying about breaking and entering! Locks, after all, were in the deepest sense anti-human; an obscene contraption for barring people from doing what they would normally have a standing invitation to do—come in, take shelter from the elements, share whatever there was to be shared. In the old days, before locks (designed to keep people out) but after doors (designed to keep the cold out), the peasants used to set food on the table before going off to the fields in case a visitor should happen by. But that instinct died when people began accumulating *things;* the second thing they always accumulated was a lock.

Feeling extremely pleased with himself, Heller took a look around. He helped himself to a handful of raisins drying on a board, and a crust of bread he found on the kitchen table. If he needed further assurance that he had come to the right place, he found it on the small shelf over the sink—a brand-new copy of Madhur Jaffrey's *An Invitation to Indian Cooking.* It lay open to a recipe for *khitcherie unda* (scrambled eggs, Indian style). And set out on a newspaper near the door was a pair of rubberized boots. Heller held them up to the moonlight filtering through the window. He could just make out the number seven printed on the size ticket.

Suddenly the dishes and glasses stacked on various shelves around the kitchen began to rattle, gently at first, then fiercely, almost as if they had taken on a life of their own. And then the house itself seemed to quiver as it was engulfed in the roar of a low-flying jet.

When the sound faded, Heller made his way into the main part of the nest—a large area, two stories high, with slits for windows through which shafts of moonlight angled down onto the bare polished marble floor. There was mildew in the corners. Paint peeled from the walls. The cryptlike room was bare of furniture or objects; the slightest sound tended to resonate. On the side of the house facing the Vltava, there was an enormous picture window covered with a curtain of plants hanging at different levels, their vines full of leaves of rusts and reds and greens tumbling away from the macramé that held the pots.

Heller explored the upstairs too. There was a bathroom with

an enormous art deco tub and a gold-inlaid mermaid spout through which the water arrived. Next to the bathroom was the bedroom, a small low-ceilinged space filled with piles of cushions covered in wildly clashing fabrics. There was a wicker double bed, and above it on the whitewashed wall an old ikon with a wafer-thin candle on either side of it. Next to the bed, in an ornate antique frame, was a formal wedding photograph of a belliger-ent-looking middle-aged man (obviously Inquiline) and a younger unsmiling woman with uneven teeth, dressed in white. It struck Heller that she was very plain-looking—not at all what you would imagine the wife of a spy would be like.

Heller had picked up the photograph for a closer look when he heard the car heading down the unpaved track that led to the nest. He hurried out to the top of the stairs winding down to the main room. Another low-flying jet hurtled by overhead, filling the crypt for a terrifying moment with a noise so intense that Heller thought it would drive out all the air and he would suffo-cate. When the noise subsided, the headlights from the car pull-ing up before the nest flashed through one of the slits that served for windows. A car door slammed shut. Heller drew his pistol, felt for the protruding signal pin to make sure it was loaded, spread his feet and sank into a firing crouch, the P-38 thrust out in front in both hands pointing directly at the front door.

There was a scraping of a large key in a large lock. Then the door opened. A figure came in. The door closed behind it. There was the soft click of a light switch being thrown. High overhead at the top of the nest, a crystal chandelier in the form of a swan with its wings spread wide came on. The sudden spray of light seemed to affect the crystals, and they tinkled like a distant aeo-lian harp in a soft current of air.

At the door a woman was slipping out of her shoes and into felt-soled slippers that polished the marble floor as you walked. Absently she glanced up at the chandelier, and caught sight of Heller on the top step with his pistol pointing at her. Her features and her limbs froze, as if the absence of motion would save her life. There was no visible panic, but an infinitely profound fear. She appeared to accept his presence as *inevitable*. It dawned on Heller with a shock: she expected him to *shoot!* Her body was braced to receive a bullet, and it came as a surprise (or a disappointment; Heller wasn't sure which) to her when one wasn't forthcoming. After a moment she began to draw breath again, and she swayed until her back was against the wall.

She said something softly in Czech.

Heller's pistol wavered and fell away until it pointed at the marble floor. He straightened. Embarrassed, he said, "I don't speak Czech."

The woman advanced to the bottom step and peered up at him. Heller could make out the curve of her lashes, the fright in her eyes. "You speak English?" she asked in Czech. She repeated the question in English.

"American English, yes," Heller said.

"What is it you want of me?"

Heller laughed nervously. "A cigarette."

The woman's eyes were fixed on his pistol. She seemed confused. "I don't smoke." She hesitated, as if she were working up the nerve to ask a delicate question. "Could you . . . could you put that thing away. Please."

Heller shoved the P-38 into his overcoat pocket. "I'm looking for . . . Inquiline," he said.

The expression on the woman's face changed. Her lips parted. Heller spotted the uneven teeth, and realized that she was the woman in white in the photograph.

"What do you know about Inquiline?" she demanded.

Another jet passed overhead. Heller anxiously followed the roar with his eyes. The woman kept her gaze glued to Heller. When she could make herself heard again, she repeated the question. "What do you know about Inquiline?"

Heller told her what he knew—the Indian cookbook, the size-seven boots, the Italian earplugs, the letters hidden in the birdcages.

The woman said, "It's me, Inquiline."

Now it was Heller's turn to be surprised. "You're . . . I'm the person in Washington who deciphered all your messages," he explained. "You made an error almost every time you sent one. One of the reasons I'm here is to give you a course on enciphering."

It wasn't something the woman could easily check. Her only

contact with her case officer in Prague, a fat man who worked out of the American embassy, usually came at his initiative. She would receive a postcard in the mail from a fictitious aunt vacationing on the Black Sea, a signal that a package awaited her in a dead-letter drop, an abandoned garbage bin at the edge of the Vltava halfway to the center of Prague. If she wanted to contact him, she wrote out her message in invisible ink on a picture postcard, then filled it with tourist chatter from an imaginary visitor to Prague to her sister in Paris, and dropped it in a mailbox.

There was also a certain logic that encouraged her to believe Heller; if he were not who he said he was, she would have long since been carted off to prison by agents of the Czech MV.

"You must be hungry," she said matter-of-factly, and she smiled up at Heller for the first time—a smile so tentative it looked as if the muscles were resisting. "Take off your shoes, please. Here they are not permitted."

Padding after her in felt slippers to the kitchen, watching her go about the business of preparing something to eat, Heller got his first good look at her. She had rust-colored hair, and enormous eyes that looked like a summer sky before a sudden storm —the color of ash and permanently angry. She unbuttoned her overcoat and flung it over the back of a chair. Underneath she was wearing a man's suit that was at least one size too large for her. The effect was just short of being Chaplinesque.

"How come you wear clothes that are too large for you?" Heller asked. "Did you used to be bigger?"

She looked at him with her angry eyes. "I used to be poorer," she shot back.

Heller said, "I don't know your real name."

"My given name is Elizabeth. My married name . . ." She seemed to lose the trend of thought, then abruptly got it back again. "My married name you would not be able to pronounce, or remember."

Heller, bone-tired, sank gratefully into a kitchen chair. Elizabeth announced, "I have no refrigerator. I also have no meat."

"I don't eat meat," Heller informed her. "I'm a vegetarian."

"I'll make you an omelet of guinea fowl eggs," Elizabeth offered.

She swept up the broken glass on the floor, stuffed the hole in the door with newspaper, then took five eggs from a bowlful of eggs and began cracking them open. "The radio speaks of an incident at the frontier," she said. She hunted in a drawer for a fork and began beating the eggs. "They speak of a dead body. They speak of someone who escaped into the countryside . . . of a manhunt."

Heller sensed the last reserves of energy draining out of him. "Why do you wear two wristwatches?" he asked, glancing at her thin arms. She had rolled up her sleeves to beat the eggs.

Elizabeth pulled an old frying pan from a shelf covered with a scrap of linoleum. "One tells the hour it is now," she explained. "The other is set to the hour I'd like it to be."

Heller was intrigued. "What time would you like it to be?"

She looked directly at him. "Any time but now," she said moodily. "How did you come into Czechoslovakia?"

Heller ignored the question. "What's a nice girl like you doing working for the Company?"

"What Company are you talking about?" she wanted to know.

"*The* Company," Heller said. "The CIA."

"You *were* involved in the affair at the frontier," she decided.

Heller watched her as he spoke. "I don't know what happened. Someone shot the guide." His gaze drifted. "I almost shot the someone who shot the guide. I should have. That would have left one less of *them* in the world."

Elizabeth heated the frying pan on the one plate of her three-plate electric stove that worked and poured the eggs into it. There was a sizzling sound. She glanced out of the corner of her eyes at Heller. An ironic smile distorted her lips. "We have become *them,*" she observed quietly.

Another plane roared overhead. Dishes and glasses jumped on their shelves. Heller asked, "Does that go on all the time?"

She nodded. "It's not something you get used to."

"I didn't expect to. What effect does it have on your guinea fowl?"

"They sleep less, and lay more."

Elizabeth divided the omelet in half and served the eggs on cheap china plates that were chipped at the edges.

Heller regarded the guinea fowl omelet suspiciously. "You don't happen to have a cigarette?"

"I still don't smoke," said Elizabeth.

"Oh."

After dinner she stacked the dirty dishes in the sink and led Heller to the upstairs bedroom, the only one in the house, as it turned out. She switched on an electric heater—its coils grew red quickly—and arranged the cushions into a bed for Heller. Then she went into the bathroom and started to run a bath. When she came back to the door, Heller thanked her for the omelet.

"It wasn't very much," she protested.

"It was enough," Heller said.

The restrained smile flickered across her face. "The peasants have a saying." She said it in Czech, and repeated it in English. "Enough is as good as a feast."

She turned off the tap and came back to collect a towel from the bottom drawer of a dresser. "You said that teaching me ciphers was *one* of the reasons you came to Prague. What are the others?"

Heller could see no harm in telling her part of the truth; she might even be able to help him. "I'm looking for a Russian," he said.

"In Prague? That's like looking for a thread in a haystack!"

Heller said, "You mean, *needle* in a haystack."

"Thread. Needle." She shook her head in annoyance. "It's the same thing. They're both hard to find in a haystack. What does he look like, your Russian?"

Heller produced a photograph from his breast pocket. Elizabeth dropped to her knees and took it to examine more closely. "His mouth is too big for his features," she said. "I don't particularly like the eyes either. They're too"—she fished for the right word—"*alert* to suit me." She handed back the photo. "If you have a choice, look for another Russian."

Heller said, "I don't have a choice."

Elizabeth shrugged. "This one gives me the Williams."

The clichés that were almost, but not quite, right stirred Heller's memory. For a moment he couldn't put his finger on it. Then it came to him—the cliché in one of her enciphered messages had been slightly wrong too. "You mean willies," Heller corrected her. She didn't react, and he added weakly, "You said Williams." When she still didn't react, he muttered, "Forget it."

"Not to be annoyed," Elizabeth said. "I am an Americanophile. I adore everything American."

"You don't know anything about America," Heller protested. "How can you adore it?"

"I collect clippings," she said. "I see old films occasionally. I listen to your Voice of America. Yesterday they had a special program on the American Society for the Advancement of Cruelty to Animals."

Heller leaned against the wall, all patience. "What *is* a nice girl like you doing working for the CIA?"

Elizabeth sank back on her haunches. "Someone showed up at my door one day and offered me a job."

"Just like that? Out of the blue?"

Elizabeth looked uncomfortable. "Not quite . . . out of the blue, as you say." She fingered her wedding ring, turning it around and around on her finger. "My . . . husband . . . had been jailed by the Communists."

Heller nodded. "What did he do? Or what didn't he do?"

The story poured out in a torrent. "He was a poet. Not yet a great poet. But a very good poet. The young people adored him. He committed the crime of writing a poem about the Russian occupation of Czechoslovakia in 1968, and then reciting it at a poetry reading. You must understand, this"—she bit her lip—"this is very difficult for me. My husband went off to jail with a pair of spare socks in one pocket and a copy of *Leaves of Grass* in another. Do you know the American poet Walter Whitman? The man who turned up at my door brought me a page from my husband's book. In the margin he had written a short message to me. The man told me that my husband had died in prison. He asked me if I wanted revenge."

Heller was suddenly very interested. "And you jumped at the chance?"

"Not immediately," said Elizabeth. "I got cold teeth—"

"Cold feet. You got cold feet."

"I was frightened. Then I stopped being frightened and

started being angry. I decided I did want revenge after all. It seemed like a fine idea at the time."

Heller said quietly, "At the time?"

Elizabeth shrugged off the implication of the question. But Heller persisted. "And has it made a difference?" he asked.

"It didn't bring him back to me, if that's what you mean." She stood up, a distant look in her eyes. "But it offers certain . . . advantages."

Heller looked up at her sharply. "Name one?"

Her ash eyes brimmed with tears and she turned away to hide them. "It fills my days," she said vaguely.

"With what?"

She wheeled on him. "With fear," she said coldly, in total control now. "It fills my days with fear."

She disappeared into the bathroom, and Heller could hear her climbing into the tub and later getting out. He switched off the overhead light and undressed in the dark and pulled the blankets she had given him up to his chin. He heard her emerge from the bathroom and turned his head toward her. She was wearing only a T-shirt. She switched off the bathroom light behind her. Heller could hear her hesitate next to her bed. Then, speaking quickly, as if it were a formality to be gotten out of the way, she announced, "If it is important to you, we may make love."

Heller was tempted; he could imagine her body, angular and lean, in his arms. In the silvery moonlight that streamed through the slit in the wall of the next, he could make her out. She was looking off to one side. He followed her gaze and saw that she was staring at the wedding photograph next to her bed.

"It's not important," Heller said huskily—he had ghosts of his own to deal with—and he turned his face to the wall and tried to empty his mind and sleep.

CHAPTER
ELEVEN

HER childhood was not something Elizabeth remembered much about. It had slipped through her fingers almost without her being aware of it. The few memories she did have were whimsical ones. Her mother died when she was very young; Elizabeth could summon up a vague image of an almost bald woman wasting away in an enormous four-poster. In her innocence, the little girl thought that the bed was growing larger. It never occurred to her that the woman in it was growing smaller. And then one day the servants were whispering in corners and her father appeared with a black band on his sleeve and the bed was empty. From the look of the sheets, it had not been slept in.

Elizabeth was swept by a sense of relief, and then guilt at having felt relief. Her father, a cultivated man with a warm, inventive glint to his eyes, took the guilt for grief and cast about for ways to distract her. Which is when the trips began—to Persia, to Afghanistan, to Egypt, to France, to Spain and, once, to England. They always started out early Sunday morning, and wound up with the little girl tucked safely back in her own bed in Prague that same night. Her father, carrying a wicker hamper packed with a picnic lunch, would cart her off bright and early to the train station. An hour or so later, they would arrive at some nearby town. Her father would walk up to the station master or a porter or a ticket taker and speak to him in a language he made up on the spot. The little girl trailing shyly behind him would giggle with delight at the idea that she was visiting Paris or Madrid or whatever city her father's imagination had conjured up.

On one such trip—Elizabeth thought it was to Alma-Ata in Central Asia—her father (speaking fluent "Central Asian") arranged for them to ride in a plane that had no engine. They were towed into the clear Asian sky by a small plane that did have an engine and then set adrift. For what seemed to the little girl like an eternity they soared high over the flat grass field of the glider club, dipping and climbing on currents that the pilot, a serious young man with thick glasses, felt through his finger tips resting on the controls. To this day, Elizabeth remembered the sensation of soundless, effortless flight—the feeling of being cast loose from the earth, of teasing it; of not really needing it.

She didn't remember landing. But she remembered the heaviness of having her feet once again on the ground. For days afterward she walked around as if her shoes had lead soles.

Elizabeth developed into an intense young woman with a complex about the ugliness of her feet and (as one of her first lovers put it) a non-Euclidean mentality. For her, the shortest distance between two points was a meandering line. Her attention span was relatively short and her thoughts had a tendency to wander; people she spoke to often had a hard time following her drift. Her "hobby" at the time was eavesdropping—collecting disjointed phrases against the day when she would hear the one thing that would cause everything to fall into place.

Several years after her father succumbed at a relatively young age to a heart attack, she heard *it*. She was squeezed around a table at the university canteen with a dozen or so students. Directly across from her sat an older man; Elizabeth guessed he was roughly the age her father would have been if he had lived. The young people around the table treated him with a deference they were unable to obscure even with all their casual chatter and quick laughter. It developed that he was a poet. He kept glancing at Elizabeth throughout the meal. When she finished her salad, he asked her, "You don't mind if I drink your juice?" and without waiting for permission reached for her plate and tipped it up to his thick, sensual lips.

Elizabeth had been in love and had made love before, but it was the poet who relieved her of her innocence. It was an exhilarating experience, like soaring in a motorless plane. Though they never talked about it, they both understood the father-daughter quality of their relationship, and relished it. It added an incestuous dimension to the attraction that they felt for one another; it made the act of sex seem almost a religious rite, and the bed its altar.

The poet was never an easy man to live with. Even after they found the nest on the Vltava, even after they scraped together enough money to buy it and move in, even after the simple marriage ceremony in the cavelike main room (read between landing jets), she found that he kept part of himself back (a strategic reserve hoarded until he could be sure which way the battle was going?). He had a way of slipping in and out of the familiar "thou" form of speech, depending on his mood, or the time of day, or the weather, or the state of his bowels. When she complained, he muttered only that relationships were not poured in concrete. "To tell the truth, there are times when I love you, and times when I don't," he wrote her (important things he tended to set down on paper) three months after their marriage. "On the other hand, the times when I love you seem to be occurring more often, and growing longer."

They argued about his love affairs, and hers, and drifted apart for several months and then came back together again with more intensity than before. Those were exuberant days: poetry readings in the nest or in some out-of-the-way classroom at the university; knots of people talking politics late into the night; friends huddled around a radio listening to Alexander Dubcek's latest speech; articles in the newspaper openly criticizing some of the "excesses" of the past. Everyone was convinced that they were about to stand socialism on its head, to democratize it, to give the world a third way.

And then, on August 20, 1968, the house of cards in which

they all lived caved in. Soviet troops poured across the frontier. The students jeered at the Russians who poked their heads through the tank hatches, and they scrawled anti-Soviet graffiti on walls pockmarked with bullet holes. But everyone understood the futility of it all. The experiment in "socialism with a human face" was over.

The poet was arrested early on a Wednesday morning. He had read some of his poems at the university the previous night, then returned home and calmly stuffed a pair of warm socks and his well-thumbed copy of *Leaves of Grass* into his overcoat pockets, along with some pads and pencils and several tins of Baltic herrings that he was particularly fond of. They undressed and went to bed and made love, and then slept, and then made love again. At three-thirty, a black four-door Skoda pulled up in front of the nest. The people in it waited until the plane roaring overhead had passed, and then honked once. The poet dressed carefully and stepped out to speak to them. When he came back, he seemed relieved. "They only want me," he told her.

"Let them at least come out of the car for you," Elizabeth cried, but he only shrugged and muttered something about useless gestures and turned away without kissing her goodbye and disappeared into the back seat of the car.

For the better part of a year Elizabeth had no idea what his fate had been. Along with hundreds of other wives, she took to making the rounds, which involved waiting on endless queues for a hurried word with someone who might know someone who might have access to dossiers of convicted criminals. She wrote letters to her husband and sent them in care of every prison she had ever heard of, but she had no way of knowing if any of them reached their destination. Once, an assistant to the Deputy State Prosecutor, a tired man with stale breath, hinted he might be able to help her if she could see her way clear to returning the favor. Elizabeth never hesitated. She was ready to do anything to end the uncertainty, to know simply if he was alive or dead.

She became the eager mistress to the assistant to the Deputy State Prosecutor. There was nothing she wouldn't do to please him—literally nothing. Twice a week he drove out to the nest in a chauffeured limousine. He was a demanding lover with a vivid, if somewhat warped, imagination. Three months went by. Then one day as he was pulling on his trousers he announced that it was his last visit and handed her as a payment for services duly rendered a slip of paper bearing the name of a prison and the duration of her husband's sentence—ten years.

Elizabeth dispatched packages every month, a process that involved more queues in snow-filled streets before a special window at the central prison. She also wrote long rambling letters in which the most important things were said between the lines. She quit the university and, acting on the suggestion of a friend, started raising guinea fowl in the long low empty buildings on the property in order to make a living.

And she waited.

Three years later she learned that her husband had died in camp of pneumonia, or so they said. Once again she was swept by a feeling of relief—for him, for herself—and then a feeling of guilt at having felt relief. That night, standing at the edge of the Vltava, the *sense* of his death struck against her, washed over her, drowned her in agony, in grief. She stumbled back to the nest and banged her head against it until her hair was matted with blood, and then she wept until dawn. And then took a deep breath and considered the proposition that the fat man had made to her. It would either save her life or put an end to it.

Either alternative seemed acceptable.

When Heller woke up the next morning, Elizabeth was nowhere in sight. He eventually found her in one of the low buildings collecting guinea fowl eggs in her straw basket. She made him poached eggs for breakfast and settled into the lotus position on the marble floor in the cryptlike main room for an hour-long lecture on enciphering one-time pad messages, which was interrupted once every ten or twelve minutes by the roar of a jet passing low overhead on its way to the runway.

"Does it ever let up?" Heller complained at one point.

Elizabeth seemed to enjoy his discomfort. "Heavy rain, thick fog, blinding snowstorms and easterly winds bring peace and quiet," she said.

"Why easterly winds?"

"Something to do with using another runway," she said.

"Oh."

Heller looked at her strangely.

"What is it?" she asked.

He shook his head. "Nothing."

She said, "I thought perhaps you wanted a cigarette."

"I don't smoke," he said.

They both smiled; it was the first conspiracy between them.

Later she offered to drive him into Prague, and he found himself accepting, not only because of the prospect of having transportation laid on, but also . . . also, for the second time in his life, he had no desire to go around in ones.

At rush hour they were sitting in Elizabeth's tiny Fiat parked down the block from the Soviet embassy on Pod Kastany. "That's him," Heller said, excitedly tapping Elizabeth on the elbow, "coming out now."

Through the front window they could see Rodzenko. He was crew cut, fortyish and wearing civilian clothes; but his bearing was distinctly military. He carried a long thin cardboard box tucked under one arm. He had stopped to light a cigarette just outside the embassy entrance, an everyday gesture that permitted him to glance up and down the street before ducking into the back seat of a Czech Skoda parked at the curb. Rodzenko leaned forward to give instructions to the driver, another military man in civilian clothes. The driver nodded, started the motor and nosed the car into the late afternoon traffic.

Elizabeth turned the ignition key on the Fiat and pulled out several cars behind Rodzenko's. Heller said, "His full name is Viktor Vladimirovich Rodzenko. He's listed as the embassy's cultural attaché, but he's really the KGB station chief."

Elizabeth, concentrating on her driving, asked, "Why are we following him?"

"We are following him," Heller explained, "in the hope that he will lead me to a very unpleasant German girl named Gretchen. Rodzenko is her case officer in Prague." He watched the ripple of Elizabeth's thigh muscles under her skirt as she braked and changed gears and regretted not accepting her offer of the night before. At the very least he should have taken a rain check. "Next to God," he continued, "if you believe in God, a case officer is the most important person in the world for an agent."

Elizabeth lost sight of the Skoda for a moment, swerved around a truck and spotted Rodzenko's car rounding a corner. "I have a case officer," she observed. "His name is Yaneff. He's very fat."

Heller said, "Rodzenko's wife is very fat. She's in Moscow. The German girl Gretchen is not as fat. She's in Prague."

Elizabeth got the message. "Rodzenko is her lover! Why didn't you say so in the first place. When the mouse is away, the dog will play!"

"When the cat is away," Heller corrected her, "the mouse will play."

"Cat?" Elizabeth seemed confused. "Mouse?"

"Cat. Mouse." Heller noticed the distance between the two cars closing as the Skoda slowed down. "Careful," he warned Elizabeth, "don't get too close."

"Have you done this kind of thing often?" Elizabeth asked.

"Every day," he told her. "I'm a persuader."

Elizabeth jumped a light that was changing to red. At the next light she asked, "What are you going to do with the German girl when you find her?"

Heller glanced sideways at Elizabeth, and then back at the Skoda four cars ahead of them. "I'm going to persuade her to tell me where two other people are."

Elizabeth sensed she was on sensitive ground. "And afterward," she said softly. "After she tells you? What will you do then?"

Heller stared straight ahead without answering, and she didn't press the question.

They were north of the city now, in a section of high-rise apartments with a ratio of glass to concrete that smacked of Western influences. Ahead, the Skoda pulled up in front of one of the buildings. The driver, his right hand fingering something in his overcoat pocket, ducked into the lobby of the building for a look around. He appeared at the front door a moment later and waved to the passenger in the back seat. Rodzenko emerged from the Skoda and walked briskly into the building. The driver, who had been holding the door for him, followed him inside.

Elizabeth, watching from the Fiat, reached for her sack and came up with two apples. She handed one to Heller and bit into the second. Talking as she chewed, she said, "Your Russian is very prudent." She indicated Rodzenko's building with a toss of her head. "What do we do now?"

"Now we wait," Heller said.

"Wait for what?"

"Wait for the German girl to come in or out."

Elizabeth finished the apple, opened the window a crack and dropped the core into the gutter. Then she sank down into her seat. "Patience," she mused, "is next to godliness."

Heller rolled his eyes in their sockets and settled back to watch the building with the Skoda parked in front of it. On the fourth floor, a light came on in an apartment, and Heller could make out the figure of Rodzenko flitting past a window. The chauffeur appeared squarely in one of the windows. He looked out, then reached up and closed the curtains. After a while the chauffeur came out of the building, got into the Skoda and drove off.

Heller kept his eyes glued to the fourth-floor apartment. Elizabeth took a blanket folded on the back seat, wrapped herself in it and appeared to doze. With her eyes still closed, she sighed. "I am not very worldly," she said. She might have been talking to herself. "Until my husband introduced me to Walter Whitman, I thought Brooklyn was a bridge." She laughed quietly at the memory, but Heller understood it was a laughter on the edge of tears.

Heller studied her face, which was almost lost in the shadows. Outside, herds of people, their heads lowered, charged soundlessly toward the relative warmth and quiet of their apartments. Soon the streetcars that rumbled past the corner were less crowded, and then almost empty. Children bundled up in scarves and knitted hats pulled low over their ears played in the street until dinnertime, and then they too vanished. On the fourth floor of the apartment building, a figure parted the curtain and stared off into the night for a long moment, and then disappeared from view.

Elizabeth reached out and touched Heller's arm with her finger tips. "Say it," she ordered. "You find me"—she racked her brain for the right word—"melancholy. I am not offended. It is more or less true. When I walk in the countryside, I see a clearing and think of the trees that were cut down to create it. What is melancholia except the capacity, which only humans have, to compare the ways things are with the way they might have been." Her voice quivered, and Heller realized that she was crying. "I am nostalgic for things I never experienced. I miss people I never met. I weep over poems that were never written."

Heller thought of Sarah turning up her face toward a sun that wasn't shining. "History," he observed, "has a way of playing with people—"

There was a snort of derision from Elizabeth's side of the car. "History," she sneered, "has been licked clean like a bone and hidden in the garden." And with a sudden viciousness that originated somewhere deep in her body, she muttered, "Let sleeping pigs lie."

Heller didn't have the heart to correct her.

At ten minutes to midnight, the light in the fourth-floor apartment went out. Elizabeth turned on the car motor and ran the heater for a while, and then turned it off again and fell asleep in her corner with her head against the window. Heller wiggled his toes inside his shoes and his fingers inside his gloves and concentrated on staying awake. Several times he caught himself starting to doze off. Once he actually did fall asleep, and woke with a start to find Elizabeth's head on his shoulder. She sat up with a jerk too.

"What time is it?" she wanted to know.

Heller glanced at his watch. "After two," he said. "Let's call it a night."

Elizabeth looked at Heller in the darkness. "What does this mean, call it a night? What else can you call it?"

"Let's get out of here," Heller said. He felt very discouraged.

She started up the car with stiff fingers and headed toward the Vltava and home. At the corner she passed a black Mercedes parked at the curb. As soon as the tail lights of Elizabeth's Fiat could no longer be seen, the Mercedes pulled out and drove back toward the center of the city. It double-parked next to the first phone booth it came to. A fat man emerged from the Mercedes and squeezed into the phone booth with an effort. He dialed a number, let it ring, then inserted a coin. "Guess who?" he said into the phone. Then: "Just where you thought he'd turn up, right behind our Russian friend." He listened for a moment. "He wasn't alone. He was with Inquiline." He listened again. "How the hell do I know how he found her. The important thing is he did. Listen, I can't touch him while he's with the girl. It'd only put her in hot water with the locals." The fat man snorted. "Don't rush me, Colonel. Everything in due time."

Elizabeth opened the front door and closed it after Heller. "Where's the light switch?" he asked. He ran his hand along the wall until he found it. Overhead, the chandelier in the form of a swan burst into life. Elizabeth slipped out of her shoes. Heller followed suit. Shuffling along in felt slippers, polishing the marble floor with every step, they made their way to the upstairs bedroom, which was ice cold.

"You should have left the heater on," Heller said, shivering despite his overcoat.

Elizabeth bent down and switched it on. "There's always hot water," she said.

"What can you do with hot water?" Heller asked innocently.

Elizabeth looked at him with her enormous ash-angry eyes. "We can submerge ourselves in it," she explained as if it were the most obvious thing in the world.

She spilled some thyme oil in the art deco tub and then filled it with steaming water. With a kind of European disdain for prudishness, she peeled off her clothes, pinned up her long hair and stepped into the tub. Heller, a product of American reticence, undressed in the bedroom, wrapped himself in a bath towel and slid into the other end of the tub as discreetly and as quickly as he could. The water burned his limbs until he grew used to it and began to relax, his head back on the rim. Steam and incense filled his nostrils and fogged his glasses. He pushed them up on his forehead and regarded Elizabeth. She looked mythological, with only her long neck and head above the still water. Under the surface, he could make out her breasts and limbs. Partly to make conversation, partly out of curiosity, he asked, "What was your husband like?"

A faint smiled played on Elizabeth's lips. "He was a saint of sorts. He was incapable of swatting a—" She couldn't think of the word in English and made a soft buzzing sound to indicate what she meant. A low-flying plane drowned her out.

When it passed, Heller supplied the word. "Mosquito?"

"Mosquito, yes. He couldn't support violence in others, or in himself. And he was stubborn. He didn't know when to give in. He would drive me crazy mad at times, the way he refused to even consider a compromise."

"For instance?"

"For instance." She searched for an example. "For instance, he was a poet, but his ambition in life was to write a novel. He had a theory that everything in the world was either poetry or prose. He didn't mean how it looked on the page; he called that the geography of the written word. No. He meant how it *feels*. How it affects the silences that surround each word like parentheses. So he sat down and took the"—her eyes sparkled as she came up with the correct cliché—"bull by the horns—it was a torture for him—and wrote a novel."

Elizabeth sank into the tub until her mouth was under water. She stayed there as long as she could and then surfaced with a splash for air. "But the bastards who control the cultural production as if it came from an assembly line demanded changes."

"And he refused?"

"He borrowed an electric typewriter and X'd out the entire novel and sent it to them and went back to poetry, where you can say anything you want as long as it's between the lines."

She fell silent for a while, brooding. Heller asked, "Have you had many . . . visitors like me before?"

Elizabeth perked up. "You are my first genuine spy. Up to now the only thing I've done is smuggle out letters in my birdcages and, occasionally, supply a written report to my case officer at the embassy."

Heller asked what kind of report.

"Things I hear," Elizabeth said vaguely. "Things people tell me." She rearranged her legs under the water. "I heard a story about a man in prison for some unspecified crime. He went on a hunger strike to win some unspecified concession. They put food in his cell, but he left it untouched. Finally, when he was faint from hunger, someone came to his cell and told him he had won.

The prisoner smiled weakly. His mind wandered; he had trouble concentrating. He couldn't remember what his demands were. He refused to eat until he could remember. They reminded him, but he didn't believe them. They tried to force-feed him. He died several weeks later."

"The system is rotten," Heller burst out. "The regime is rotten. What else do you expect?"

Elizabeth sat up in the tub; her round shoulders and her breasts broke water. "America the beautiful has a lot to answer for too," she said with sudden vehemence.

"I thought you were an Americanophile," retorted Heller.

"I am," she declared. "I'm the best kind. I know the faults and still love it." She yanked out the plug in annoyance, jumped from the tub, wrapped herself in a huge bath towel and stomped out of the bathroom.

Heller dried himself, turned out the light and followed her. The only light in the bedroom came from the glowing red coils of the electric heater. Elizabeth was under the covers. Her bath towel lay where it had fallen on the floor. Heller hesitated next to her bed. Barely daring to breathe, he announced with mock formality, "If it is important to you, we may make love."

Elizabeth considered the offer. After a moment's hesitation she replied, "It is not important either way." And she reached out and lifted the covers so that he could slide in next to her.

Another jet on the final leg of its approach to the runway hurtled overhead, but the roar of the engines was drowned out by the storm of passion that burst over them—the sudden joining performed with all the violence and disdain for niceties of someone who, dying of thirst, stumbles on a stream of fresh water. Somewhere along the way Heller, his limbs twined around hers so that he no longer knew where he stopped and she began, pressed his mouth to her ear and demanded, "What is it you want from lovemaking?"

At first Elizabeth couldn't find a voice with which to answer. Then she found a voice which didn't sound anything like her own and said, "To pass time." And a moment later she blurted out, "Painlessly."

Still later she screamed (Heller couldn't tell whether it was in pain or pleasure) and cried out in Czech (he couldn't tell whether it was in poetry or prose) and, gasping for air, muttered breathlessly in English, "Enough!"

Heller, lost in the vast silences around the word, whispered, "Enough is as good as a feast," and finding himself hard, thrust back inside her.

The second joining was an exploration of latent possibilities. They made love slowly, barely moving, lingering over surfaces and textures, savoring the short gasps that passed for breathing, holding back until it was no longer possible and the fault opened and, clinging to each other, they fell in.

After a while Heller rolled over and felt around the floor for the towel and dried himself and then passed it to Elizabeth, who lay on her side staring at the glowing coil of the electric heater. Very gently Heller said, "A pfennig for your thoughts—or whatever the money is here."

Elizabeth's voice came from the far end of a long tunnel. "I have no thoughts," she said. "I've emptied my memory. Nothing rings a bell. Someone once asked me to free-associate. He said 'hot.' I couldn't think of anything." She breathed deeply. "He didn't believe me."

Heller said, "I believe you."

Elizabeth rolled over and stretched. "The lovemaking was extremely well done. You were very good. In the end, Mozart is the only thing I like as much as sex." She looked at him seriously. "It is not possible to love a second time the way one loved the first time. Nothing can ever be the same. Neither the giving. Nor the taking. You must understand this."

Heller nodded in the darkness. "I understand," he told her. And he did. He understood that enough fell short of being a feast.

CHAPTER
TWELVE

IT was socked in the next morning with a thick pea-soup fog that rolled across the Vltava smelling of wet grass and the river. The planes were not landing, and the silence woke Elizabeth. She poked Heller, who sat up with a startled look on his face which evaporated when he saw her naked back disappearing into the bathroom. Over breakfast (guinea fowl *oeufs à la coque*), Heller tried to teach her everything she always wanted to know about nulls, but she seemed to have a mental block on the subject.

"It's simple," he explained for the dozenth time.

"It's simple for you," she complained, "because you already understand it. For me, it's still complicated. And it doesn't do any good to yell."

Heller took a deep breath. "About nulls." He tried again. "If you don't use them, someone trying to crack the cipher starts off with a very crucial advantage: He knows how many letters are in the plain text of the message."

"What I don't understand," Elizabeth conceded, "is how

someone else can break a cipher if you and I are the only ones with the key."

Heller had an idea. "Encipher a message without nulls," he ordered her.

She picked up a pencil. "What do you want me to say?"

"Say anything you want," Heller instructed her. He turned his back to her. "When you're finished, I'll break it."

"Right now?"

"Right now."

Elizabeth wrote out a sentence, signed "Inquiline" and enciphered the whole thing using one of the keys printed on the inside cover of a book of matches. She handed the enciphered message to Heller.

"Can I borrow your pencil," he asked. Then he started in. In short order he had recovered the three "i"s in "Inquiline," and a few minutes later he had the whole name. "It sticks out like a sore thumb," he lectured her.

Her eyes widened in delight. " 'Sticks out like a sore thumb.' That's very picturesque." She repeated the phrase several times to memorize it.

Heller, meanwhile, worked his way through her cipher. Twenty-five minutes later he looked up triumphantly. " 'The twin sisters Death and Night incessantly softly wash' "—his voice softened as he realized what he was reading—" 'again and ever again this soiled world.' "

"That's a line from Walter Whitman," Elizabeth said quietly.

Heller spotted a film of tears in her eyes. "We'll go over nulls again tomorrow," he said.

Elizabeth tended to her guinea fowl for the rest of the morning. Heller, browsing through the library alcove a few steps up from the bedroom, could hear the birds chattering away; they sounded vaguely like old women gossiping in a strange tongue. His eye roamed over the shelves, sagging in the middle from the weight of the books. Most of them were in Czech and he couldn't make out the titles, though he did notice that there were two copies of a great many of them. He did find a much-thumbed copy, in English, of Shakespeare's *Tempest,* which he took with him when Elizabeth summoned him to the kitchen.

Over lunch, guinea fowl eggs scrambled Indian style (Elizabeth kept glancing at her Indian cookbook as she made them), she explained why there were two copies of some books in the library. It seemed that her husband had a mania about books he particularly loved; he was afraid they would "wear out" with use. "Some people hoard food, some hoard books," she said. "I remember him hurrying off to a reading with two copies of Akhmatova's poems under his arm. He was a curious man who nourished himself with words; he was like a drug addict getting his daily fix. At the same time, he was aware of the dangers of words. He often said that speech organized behavior, and not the other way around. He thought clichés were wilted, tired poems. He complained that the world had been overdescribed; that often what we saw was the description, not the reality." Her facial muscles strained to hold back a sad smile. Her tongue played nervously over the edges of her uneven teeth. She breathed deeply and stared out a window, unable for a moment to focus. "On top of everything," she said, "he was a good lover!"

It was an awkward moment. Heller attacked his scrambled eggs with as much enthusiasm as he could muster. Between mouthfuls he explained about his search for a cipher in Shakespeare's plays. "I never paid much attention to *The Tempest*," he said. Behind his narrowed eyes an idea was taking shape. "It was the last play he wrote. The epilogue contains what amounts to his last words—what a logical place for the real author to sign his name in cipher. Hmmmmmmm."

Elizabeth asked, "Would it change anything?"

Heller didn't understand the question. "Would what change anything?"

"Would it change anything if it turned out that Shakespeare didn't write Shakespeare?"

Heller answered with a question of his own. "Have you ever read Shakespeare?"

Elizabeth shook her head. "I have trouble reading English. And I never read poetry in translation. The poetry is what's lost in translation."

Heller said, "Your husband read poetry in translation."

Elizabeth didn't see anything illogical in this. "He was a poet," she reminded Heller. "He was able to supply the poetry when it was missing."

They picked up Rodzenko as he left the Soviet embassy at the end of the workday. He wore a raincoat with the collar turned up and carried a long thin cardboard box tucked under his arm again. Following discreetly behind in her Fiat, Elizabeth threaded her way through rush-hour traffic, past the radio station with its bullet-chipped walls, a grim reminder of the Soviet occupation in 1968. A few minutes later she turned into Wenceslas Square and started downhill toward the Vltava, past the museum, past the fountain just below it where Jan Palach immolated himself to protest against the Soviet presence. The morning fog had thinned considerably, a light rain was falling and the wet cobblestones and trolley tracks, slick and glistening, threw back reflections of the streetlights, which had been switched on earlier than usual. Near the Old Town Square, the Skoda pulled up at a kiosk. Rodzenko darted out to buy a newspaper, then turned into a narrow cobble-stoned street. Heller started to follow Rodzenko.

Elizabeth said, "Not to worry. I'll carry the fort."

Heller had one foot out of the car. "Hold. Not carry. You'll hold the fort."

"That's what I said," snapped Elizabeth.

Heller shook his head and shrugged and hurried off after Rodzenko, who was just disappearing around a corner into the Old Town Square.

As Heller rounded the corner, the great clock in the town hall tower was striking the hour. Figures of Christ and the disciples wheeled out of a door alongside the clock into view. Despite the rain, several dozen tourists pressed in and craned their necks at the sight. Rodzenko stopped to check his wristwatch.

Across the square, a fat man wearing a green loden coat heavy with moisture drifted in Heller's direction. People flowed around him. An old man sharpening knives on a pedal-operated grindstone sent off a shower of sparks in his path, but he walked through them without taking his eyes off Heller. A child tried to trap some of the sparks in her mittens, and almost got run over by the fat man, so intent was he on his prey across the square.

When he was several paces from Heller, he casually opened the coat with his left hand—a gesture that had all the obscenity of a man exposing himself. His right hand, which had gone through a slit in the loden pocket, was holding a pistol fitted with a silencer.

Heller never did figure out what attracted his attention—the curious obscenity of the open coat, the metallic glint of the pistol, the intensity with which the fat man concentrated on him. Something made him turn his head, and he saw the fat man sinking into a crouch, the pistol held with both hands in front and coming up to point at him.

Heller dove off to one side just as he heard the distinctive *pfffft* of the silenced pistol. Behind him, a woman was slammed back by the impact of the bullet and fell to the sidewalk clutching her stomach. Above the crowd's heads, Christ and the disciples retreated in orderly fashion to the interior of the clock. People milled excitedly around the fallen woman. A dog strained on its leash, its jaw opening and closing in soundless barks. A teenage girl spotted blood seeping from under the fallen woman's hands and screamed.

The fat man tried to draw a bead on Heller, sprawled on the sidewalk, but milling people kept getting in his way. Then, for an instant, there was no one between the fallen man and the pistol arcing up to bear on him. The fat man had actually begun to squeeze the trigger when he was jarred by a frightened woman running down the street. Frustrated, he closed his overcoat over his pistol, backed away and disappeared down a side street.

Heller, white and shaken, made his way back to the Fiat and climbed in. "You look as if you've seen a ghost," said Elizabeth. "What happened? What's happening?"

In the distance there was the first faint wail of sirens. On the sidewalk people were running in every direction. Heller wiped the moisture from his face. "What's a nice guy like me," he said grimly, "doing working for the CIA?"

After the fifth or sixth pot of tea it had become ridiculous, and the Professor had summoned Karol and announced, in the tones and rhythms that senior bureaucrats reserved for their ambitious juniors that he was going home for the day. Karol had anticipated an early getaway; he had noticed that the Professor had not bothered to remove the galoshes that his wife obliged him to wear, come sun or snow, every day of the winter. Also, the Professor's secretary had just delivered to him (with trembling hands; there were two corrected errors in the text) the typed monograph, handsomely bound in black with a red ribbon around it. The black had been the Professor's idea, the ribbon the secretary's.

Clutching the monograph, the Professor heaved himself into his overcoat, planted his astrakhan firmly on his head and fled from Karol's failure to ask questions that solicitous juniors were expected to ask in such situations ("Are you feeling all right?" or "Is there something I can do for you?").

His wife was waiting for him at the door of their apartment. "I have it," the Professor said nervously, brandishing the monograph.

"How long did it turn out?" she asked, plucking his hat from his head, helping him off with his coat. He practically pirouetted out of it in his eagerness to get at the typed pages.

"Sixty-six pages," he told her. "Thirty-four lines to a page, an average of ten words to a line—that makes twenty-two thousand four hundred and forty words."

They settled down in the kitchen. It was the warmest room in the apartment because the Professor's wife was baking an orange cake in the oven. She carefully poured out two cups of jasmine tea. The Professor untied the red ribbon and, using only the tips of his fingers so as not to smudge the white pages, started to read parts of the monograph to his wife.

"I begin with a general statement, you see: 'By reason of his birth, his breeding, his travels, his learning, his command of languages, his place at the court, his knowledge of law, Francis Bacon was the sole among all of his contemporaries capable'—you see where I'm heading? Here"—he flipped through several pages—"I go into his commonplace book in some detail, and draw parallels between entries and certain passages . . ."

The Professor's wife scraped her chair closer and looked over his shoulder, following his finger which underlined the text.

"Here I get to the heart of the matter—my discussion of

whether he was in fact guilty of taking bribes as lord high chancellor and, as I see it, why in the end his sentence was remitted and he was put out—here I managed quite a nice phrase, 'put out to painless pasture.' "

"This is bound to have a big impact," the Professor's wife predicted. "Your footnotes look very impressive too."

They were poring over the short bibliography an hour later when Karol rang up.

"What is it?" The Professor, cradling the phone between his chin and shoulder, made no effort to hide his irritation.

Karol apologized profusely for the intrusion and quickly told him why he considered it necessary to bother him at home.

"When did all this take place?" the Professor wanted to know.

Karol told him and added some other details. The woman who had been hit in the stomach was being operated on at this very moment; the doctors were hopeful; several vague reports had been received about a fat man in a green loden coat, though no one remembered hearing the sound of a pistol being fired.

The Professor asked Karol if the relevant microphones were still harvesting. Karol assured him they were, and made the mistake of adding, "If they succeed in killing him, we will never know whom he's after."

The Professor permitted himself a noncommittal "Just so," hung up and turned back to the relative incomplexities of his monograph.

Elizabeth pulled the blanket across her legs, fetched a jar of bee pollen from her handbag, spilled some of it into her palm and started to lap it up with the tip of her tongue. They sat for a long while in absolute silence, each absorbed in fleeting thoughts. Heller glanced at his watch—it was just midnight—and then back at Rodzenko's windows on the fourth floor. The lights had been out for an hour now. Several people had come and gone from the building, but none of them resembled Rodzenko or the German girl Gretchen. Out of the blue, Elizabeth slipped her fingers into Heller's hand and challenged him: "Describe your first sexual experience."

The question amused Heller. "It was in a bar in Piraeus, the port that Socrates used to walk to from Athens," he began. "I was hitchhiking around Europe after my junior year at college. A girl took me back to her room, inspected me to make sure I didn't have anything that she could catch, then turned out the lights. She was chewing peppermint gum and I couldn't stand the taste. She took it out and stuck it on the base of the night lamp, and when we finished the first thing she did was put it back in her mouth." Heller looked at Elizabeth. "How about you?"

"Mine was also in Greece," Elizabeth said. "I was seven, eight on the outside. I was visiting cousins who lived in Athens; that's what my father told me when we took the train to a nearby town. The cousins were obviously in on the game. I remember they served strange food for lunch which they claimed was Greek. And they spoke to each other in a funny language which sounded made up, but they swore on a book they said was a Bible that it was Greek. After lunch everyone disappeared for a nap. I wandered up to the attic, looking in drawers and closets for treasures. I heard steps. I hid behind a rack of winter clothes. Two of my cousins, a boy about twenty and a girl about sixteen, came up. The girl lay down on the rug. The boy kneeled between her legs, reached under her skirt and removed her pants. He must have noticed something move in the clothes rack because he glanced in my direction. I froze, but I always suspected he saw me. He smiled as if he knew a secret and bent his head to the girl's sex. I remember . . . I remember thinking the whole thing was very . . . religious . . . the way an Arab prays in a mosque."

Sometime later Heller looked up at Rodzenko's apartment. "It doesn't figure," he muttered to himself.

"What doesn't figure?" Elizabeth asked. She shivered from the cold, and started the motor to warm the car.

"It doesn't seem like your typical hot love affair."

"What is your typical hot love affair?"

Heller laughed under his breath. "I suppose it's different things to different people." He looked at her in the darkness; he had the impression she was studying him intently. "I suppose it's a question of experience," he said quietly.

Elizabeth jumped on the word, and they got into an argument about the nature of experience. "You're wrong," she insisted. "Dead wrong. You don't have to experience something to be nostalgic for it." She turned her head away to hide the rush of emotion. "Take for instance a wedding anniversary. I never had one. They took him before—"

"At least you had a wedding," Heller said bitterly.

Elizabeth turned back, intrigued. "You are not what I expected."

Heller shrugged. "Come on, let's—"

Elizabeth finished the cliché: "—call it a night."

Sunlight streamed through the slit in the wall of the nest the next morning, illuminating the specks of dust that drifted on gentle currents through the bedroom. Overhead, planes roared in every twelve or fifteen minutes, setting off little vibrations on the shelves and tabletops.

Downstairs, Heller put the finishing touches on the breakfast table, then bounded up the narrow stairs to wake Elizabeth. She sat up blinking in the cold sunlight.

"Welcome to the world." Heller laughed.

Elizabeth wound a blanket around her thin body and padded in bare feet to the bathroom. "The early bird catches—"

"—the worm!"

She stopped in her tracks. "That's what I was going to say."

"I'll bet you were," teased Heller.

When she entered the kitchen a while later, Elizabeth stared at the table, which looked like something out of *Alice in Wonderland*. Heller had set it whimsically. Instead of spoons and knives, he had used large wooden cooking utensils and whisks and a can opener. In place of plates he had put salad bowls and pot covers. He had substituted a measuring bowl for a teacup.

"Aren't I handy to have around?" Heller asked sheepishly.

But Elizabeth was not at all pleased. "Why did you do this?"

Somehow all the humor had disappeared. "I wanted to make you laugh," Heller explained seriously to her—to himself too.

They stared at each other over the table. Elizabeth warned with mounting anger, "Don't try to make me laugh. Don't become

175

part of my life. When you finish whatever you have to do, go back where you came from. I don't want happy endings. I only want endings."

Elizabeth was still sulking when Rodzenko came out of the Soviet embassy. He was earlier than usual and carried the long thin cardboard box tucked under his arm. The Skoda set off quickly, almost as if Rodzenko were late for an appointment.

Elizabeth kept behind a truck, peeking out every now and then to make sure Rodzenko was still up ahead. Heller had a scare when the Skoda suddenly turned left onto a narrow one-way street near the museum and Elizabeth got trapped behind a trolley discharging passengers. But she jumped a light and made the turn and they spotted the Skoda up ahead heading into the university grounds.

"This must be what we're looking for," Heller said excitedly, leaning forward, his hands flat against the dashboard. Elizabeth pulled into the parking lot and stopped. Through the front window they could see the Skoda parked at the curb next to the front entrance of the main building. The chauffeur stood with his back against the car door, taking the sun. Rodzenko was just disappearing into the university.

Heller started to get out of the Fiat, then remembered something he had meant to ask Elizabeth. "You said your case officer was a fat man. Describe him?"

"I only saw him once," she said. "That was when he recruited me. He wore a loden coat. I remember his skin was soft and his face almost beardless—like a teenager's. He seemed to be a very gentle man actually. Why do you ask?"

"Just curious," muttered Heller, and he started toward the university, careful to keep an eye peeled for the gentle beardless fat man who had tried to kill him once already, and was likely to try again.

Inside the university entrance, Rodzenko was shaking hands with two men in caps and gowns. Then all three marched off down a corridor and disappeared through a pair of swinging doors.

Heller pretended to read the notices on a bulletin board, and watched out of the corner of his eye to see how difficult it would be to get into the university proper. There was a uniformed guard at the inner door, and he appeared to be checking the student identification cards of everyone who entered.

Heller retreated to the street again and looked around in frustration. Rodzenko's chauffeur had apparently had enough sun for one day and had taken shelter in the back seat of his Skoda to read a newspaper. To his left, Heller spotted a delivery man carrying cases of soft drinks from his truck into the building through a service entrance. Heller meandered over, casually helped himself to a case of soft drinks, hefted it onto his shoulder and followed the delivery man down the ramp and through the door. The student assigned to guard it never raised his eyes from the textbook he was reading. Heller deposited the case outside the storage room, and hurried off through the narrow basement hallways. He spotted a staircase, climbed one flight and found himself in the main corridor full of students and teachers standing around in knots talking. Above Heller's head, a bell shrilled. The groups broke up and everyone hurried off toward a classroom.

Heller wandered down the corridor in what he took to be the general direction of the front entrance. Ahead, he caught sight of the entrance and the uniformed guard checking identity cards. And then he saw the swinging doors through which Rodzenko had disappeared.

He pushed through and found himself in the back of an enormous auditorium. The fifty or so students, along with a dozen professors who had come from London for the seminar, had been swallowed up by the vastness, and the auditorium looked empty. Up on the platform half a dozen panelists sat at a long table. There was a small microphone in front of each panelist and a nameplate. Rodzenko, the last panelist on the right, sat with his head tilted back, his eyes closed, listening intently to a man in the middle, whose nameplate identified him as Professor Emeritus Lako, read in meticulous English from a monograph bound in black with a red ribbon.

Off to one side of the platform, a hand-lettered sign on an easel read:

Professor Emeritus Lako seemed to be gathering confidence as he went along; he raised his eyes from the text more often and tapped the table with his right hand to emphasize a point. "There is absolutely no record of his having attended a university. The real author of the plays exhibited firsthand knowledge of Spain, France, Italy, Denmark, Navarre and Scotland; but there is no record that *he* ever set foot outside England. And then there is the matter of his handwriting. The known signatures are almost illegible, the scrawl of an illiterate. Yet we have the word of various editors that they received the manuscripts of the plays with 'scarce a blot.'" The Professor paused for a sip of water, then plunged on. "Francis Bacon, on the other hand . . ."

In the back row, Heller suddenly understood what they were talking about and moaned out loud.

Professor Emeritus Lako described how Bacon had risen from knight to attorney general to lord keeper and, finally, lord chancellor. And then had come the fall; the Professor's voice, normally even (he believed in letting the words carry the emotion, not the tone with which they were delivered; as a matter of principle, he preferred movies without music), waxed passionate. Bacon had been accused of accepting bribes. He had pleaded guilty and was fined forty thousand pounds, banished from the court and sentenced to the Tower of London. At which point Bacon was pardoned; the fine, the banishment and the jail sentence were remitted. Why? the Professor asked rhetorically, and he proceeded to offer his own theory, developed over a period of ten years of intensive reading and research, including three glorious months spent poring over old court records in London itself. It was the Professor's conclusion that Bacon in fact had taken the bribes—his fingers were as sticky as the next man's when it came to matters of the pocketbook; and there was his own admission of guilt to reckon with—but was pardoned because the King, James I, and a small circle at court knew Bacon to be the real author of the plays attributed, as was often done in those days, to the head of the troupe that performed them, an obscure actor by the name of William Shake-spear. Keeping his finger on the text so as not to lose his place when he looked up, the Professor cited chapter and verse; fragments of letters, court rumors that found their way into print, bits and pieces of official records, circumstances that meshed with other circumstances, obscure references in diaries that could only be explained if one accepted a certain view. By the time he had finished, his case seemed overwhelming —if circumstantial.

Rodzenko listened to all this almost as if he were in a trance. When the Professor had closed the black cover of his monograph, and the smattering of applause had died down, Rodzenko was introduced. "The respected cultural attaché from the Union of Soviet Socialist Republics, the author of numerous papers on the question of the authorship of the plays, a specialist in Elizabethan literature with a degree from Moscow University, Viktor Rodzenko."

Rodzenko, speaking English as well as the Professor, began with a graceful acknowledgment that he was a fish out of water. Here, in the midst of Baconians, he would argue that Edward de Vere rather than Francis Bacon was the real author of the plays. And spicing his speech with anecdotes and a healthy sense of Elizabethan humor, he made the case for de Vere: his coat of arms as Lord Bulbeck was a lion *shaking a spear;* his lifelong obsession with the theater; the fact that he personally owned two companies of actors; that it was one thing to *own* a company and another for a nobleman to participate as actor or author; that because of his position and standing he was obliged to work anonymously; that *Measure for Measure* recorded de Vere's own well-documented love affair with Anne de Vavasour.

Rodzenko read excerpts from an old copy of *Deutsche Baconiana,* published by the German branch of the Bacon Society in the early 1930s, translating the German into English as he went along, occasionally looking up to comment on what he had read. One of the other panelists put in a word and the students in the auditorium burst into laughter. Rodzenko smiled and nodded and continued reading.

Diagonally across the auditorium another swinging door

opened inward, and a fat man in a green loden coat appeared. He stood with his back to the wall listening to Rodzenko's lecture, never once glancing in Heller's direction.

His heart beating wildly, Heller slipped out of the auditorium and turned toward the main entrance of the university. He could see the uniformed guard at the door checking identity cards, but he was only concerned with people coming in, not those going out. Heller started forward—and then stopped in his tracks. The fat man had emerged from the auditorium between him and the uniformed guard. Heller backed away, then spun on his heel and hurried off in the other direction. He rounded one corner and another and glanced over his shoulder and was terrified to see the fat man thirty yards behind him. He moved the way fat people often do, with a light flowing gait, on the balls of his feet, darting in and out of groups of students with all the agility of a broken field runner.

Heller spotted a fire exit, dashed through the door and started down a flight of steps, taking them two at a time. He tried the door at the next landing, but it was locked. Above him he could hear the door slamming closed and the light balletlike steps of the fat man as he started to descend. Heller hurried down another flight, but that door was locked too. He raced down another flight and pulled desperately at the door. It opened, and he rushed through into a sub-basement that housed the university's heating system.

Heller went to ground behind a boiler, drew his German pistol, gripped it with both hands, spread his feet and crouched with the P-38 thrust forward and aimed directly at the door through which the fat man would appear. Then he concentrated on his breathing and waited.

Any instant he expected the door to open and to find the fat man squarely in his sights. Once again Heller had the curious sensation of being both the participant and the observer at the same time. He could see himself crouching behind the boiler aiming at the door, and he wondered vaguely if he would have the nerve to squeeze, not jerk, the little piece of metal known technically as the trigger.

Behind and off to the right, behind another boiler, the fat man thrust his pistol out in front of him, slipped into a comfortable firing crouch and sighted on the figure of Heller. The fat man had slipped into the sub-basement through another door and come up on his quarry. As his pistol sights sank down toward Heller's head, the fat man expelled half the air in his lungs and began to squeeze the trigger.

Heller, surprised that nobody had come through the door he was aiming at, suddenly leaned to his left for a better view—just as the soft *pffffft* sounded behind him. A neat puncture hole appeared in the boiler where his head had been an instant before. More startled than afraid, he turned and caught a glimpse of the fat man in his firing crouch, with the pistol sinking down toward him for a second shot, and he darted off through a maze of catwalks and steam pipes, twisting and running until his breath came in great gasps. He rounded a corner and stopped to listen. He could hear the fat man stalking him. As Heller disappeared behind a ventilator shaft, another *pffffft* came from behind him, and then a third, and there was a rattling sound in the ventilator, as if someone had tossed a piece of metal into it.

Heller sprang up a short ladder and raced along a catwalk that angled off through the sub-basement toward a heavy fire door. He paused for a moment and heard the distinctive tap-tap of the fat man's footsteps. Acting on instinct, he reached down and took off his shoes and backed toward the fire door.

Behind Heller, the fat man had stopped to listen. There was a sudden sound of a push bar as the fire door was flung open. The fat man sprinted along the catwalk. As he came up to the fire door, it was swinging closed. He thrust his pistol out and started to push the door open with his foot in case Heller was waiting on the other side.

Heller, who had been hiding behind a pillar, stepped up behind the fat man and jammed his large pistol into his spine. The fat man froze. "Do me a favor," Heller said. "Drop your pistol." When the fat man hesitated, Heller added, "If I were in your shoes, I'd do exactly what I tell you. I'm fairly new at this, and very nervous."

The fat man's pistol clanged to the catwalk.

Heller said, "You're doing very well. So am I. Let's both keep up the good work. Now I wonder if you could push it over the edge with your fat toe."

The fat man did as he was instructed. "They told me this was amateur hour," he said in a wooden voice. "You learn fast."

"Who told you?" Heller demanded. "And where'd you learn to shoot a pistol like that? At a farm in Virginia maybe?"

The fat man only sneered.

Heller jammed his pistol deeper into the fat man's back. "I suggest you come up with answers, or I'll shoot you without trying out my other questions."

"There's nothing I can tell you you can't figure out," said the fat man sullenly.

"You're a Company man," Heller said.

"You're very bright."

The pieces were all coming together for Heller. "You followed Rodzenko knowing I'd also be following Rodzenko. You want to stop me before I get to the German girl."

"You don't need me," said the fat man. "Why don't you carry on this conversation with yourself."

It suddenly dawned on Heller; he had nibbled at the edges of the idea, but he had never bitten into it. Now he did. "They don't want me to find the terrorists!" Heller was looking at the back of the fat man's head, but he was talking to himself. "But why?"

The fat man wheezed through his nose. "You're finished," he snarled. "If I don't do it, someone else will."

Heller's face contorted in disgust. "We have become them," he whispered.

The fat man tried to psych Heller. "You couldn't pull the trigger if your life depended on it," he said. His voice was soft, almost musical now; he seemed very sure of himself. "You *are* an amateur. You're in over your head." Then he barked an order: "Go on, run."

Heller was sorely tempted. But he knew he couldn't run far enough or fast enough. He would have to face the fat man eventually. Better do what had to be done now. He stepped back, still gripping the pistol in both hands, and brought it up so that it was pointing directly at the back of the fat man's head. And he wrestled with himself to shoot, to squeeze the trigger, to send the bullet speeding into his skull.

He almost succeeded. He came very close—as close as it's

possible to come and still not do it. Then, with infinite slowness, the pistol wavered. Furious at himself, Heller brought the pistol down until it was pointing at the back of the fat man's left knee. And then he angrily jerked the trigger.

The shot reverberated through the sub-basement like thunder; the sound was out of all proportion to the space it filled.

The fat man collapsed as if a prop had been knocked out from under him. He grasped his knee and peered up at Heller through a film of pain. "Just proves . . . you're . . . amateur. Now you won't . . . won't know who's trying . . . trying . . . kill you."

Heller made his way back to the Fiat. He found Elizabeth propped up against a fender, her eyes closed, her face turned toward the last rays of sun. Her shadow stretched across the pavement. Some sixth sense made her open her eyes, and she gazed at him without a word for a long moment. Finally she said, "What took you so long?"

"I was talking to a fat man," Heller explained.

"With soft skin? With a loden coat?" When Heller made no reply she said, "What about Rodzenko?"

"He was lecturing on Edward de Vere."

Elizabeth asked, "Who's Edward de Vere?" but she was obviously not interested in the answer.

Heller noticed that she was squirming uncomfortably. "Is something the matter?"

Elizabeth looked down at his feet. "You're standing on my shadow." Heller followed her eyes. Elizabeth said, "It brings bad luck, standing on someone's shadow."

Heller moved aside. "I beg your pardon," he said. "It won't happen again."

CHAPTER
THIRTEEN

THE Professor loved paper. There was nothing he liked more than to settle down in his straight-backed wooden chair, all incoming calls on hold, his favorite Mozart sonata playing quietly on the East German tape recorder that came with the office, and systematically attack an enormous pile of reports: on the comings and goings of American diplomats, the volume of incoming and outgoing cipher traffic from the American embassy, a vague rumor from the Czech military attaché in Washington about a scandal brewing in intelligence circles, Karol's analysis of where the tip-off about the American agent crossing the frontier originated, a rundown on the fat man's movements during the past twenty-four hours. The Professor was drawn into his reading the way others were sucked into a novel; after a while, he wouldn't have heard the phone if it had rung. Lunch hour could go by, the tea in the pot on his desk could grow cold and still he would plunge on without looking up from the stack of papers before him. The Mozart tape might run out, but even that didn't matter. Savoring a sentence here, relishing a paragraph there, he delved into one of the few subjects in the world that interested him as much as Francis Bacon.

It was the Professor's theory and profound belief that if you read enough, what he called "trails of inquiry" would emerge. It would start with a discrepancy, or the lack of it where there should have been one. Or an obscure detail that would suddenly take on a significance in the light of another obscure detail.

The Professor had been reading professionally for thirty years. He had started out as a junior detective on the Bohemian police force during the German occupation. The very first case he solved (with clues he picked up from routine reports on black market operations in Prague) was the murder of a young Czech actress by a German Army sergeant. When the Professor tried to press charges, the German authorities had the sergeant in question quietly transferred to the Russian front (where he froze to death in a stalled tank) and the Professor quietly fired.

Footloose, he drifted to Slovakia, got involved in printing an underground newspaper and became an important member of the body that planned and led the Communist uprising against the Germans in 1944. At the height of the uprising, the Professor was betrayed by a double agent, a half-German functionary whom the Czechs had taken for a sympathizer and the Professor had taken for a friend. The Professor was picked up by the Gestapo and tortured by a professional with an affinity for pliers. It was an experience the less said about the better. In the end, he revealed the names of the others in his underground cell (though he held out for the prescribed twenty-four hours, enough time for some of them to get away). What was left of him was shipped off to Auschwitz. When the Russians overran the concentration camp at the end of the war, the Professor was still alive—but only just. It was another experience the less said about the better. He convalesced for the best part of a year, then returned to police work in Prague. After the Communists took over in 1948 he was transferred to counterintelligence on the strength of his former membership in the Communist underground.

In the late 1950s, the Professor finally succeeded in tracing the double agent who had betrayed him into the hands of the Gestapo. He was a prosperous businessman living in West Germany. Through police channels, the Professor sent a dossier to the West German authorities with proof of the German's role as a double agent. The West German state prosecutor dutifully reviewed the evidence and ruled that the German had not committed a war crime but rather fulfilled a legitimate role assigned to him as agent provocateur, and he politely declined to prosecute.

Now there was a soft knock at the Professor's door. He ignored it and went on with his reading. He was in the middle of a report on the Central Intelligence Agency's *résident* in Prague. The fat man had apparently made preparations to receive a visitor at a safe house near the museum, but the visitor in question never showed up. The past several days, the fat man had been staking out the apartment house in which the KGB's *résident*, Rodzenko, lived. The Professor looked up, a thoughtful expression on his face. Rodzenko was the case officer controlling, through contacts with the German girl named Gretchen, the terrorist team that had pulled off the raid on the American consulate in Munich. He was also the lover of the German girl. The agent who had written the report surmised that the fat man was either trying to turn Rodzenko or trying to locate the three terrorists—for what reason he didn't care to guess.

The Professor took another sheet from his pile. It was a transcript of several conversations between an American, presumably the one who had slipped through his fingers at the frontier, and the Czech girl who exported guinea fowl to the West. His arrival had come as a complete surprise to the girl. They had made love, that much was clear. The American was apparently an expert on ciphers. He was teaching the girl how to correctly encipher one-time pad messages. He also spoke about Shakespeare, but that part of the conversation had been garbled by an intermittent microphone. The American also expressed a healthy interest in the Russian Rodzenko, and the German girl Gretchen. All this provided food for thought.

Whoever was at the door was rapping again. Insistently. The Professor's eyebrows came together in annoyance. He ran a finger between his collar and his neck, where a red welt was forming; he still wore starched collars, but his neck refused to get used to them. In the end, the twentieth was not the Professor's favorite century, and he felt distinctly uncomfortable with anyone who was at home in it—computer programmers, helicopter pilots, ladies in trousers, ambitious assistants like Karol who wore soft button-down collars, associates who smoked at the dinner table without first asking permission of the host, to name a few. Still, one was trapped in the century one was born into—or was one? Was there a way out? A trail of inquiry that could lead you back in time, out of the multiple frustrations of the twentieth-century labyrinth?

Early evening shadows were falling across his desk. He reached to switch on the old-fashioned lamp. There was another respectful knock on the door. The twentieth century, no doubt, wanted his attention. The Professor shrugged inwardly and called out with a certain fatalism, "Come."

Karol entered and closed the door. The Professor looked up. "You've changed the part in your hair, haven't you? Well, how is he?"

"Yaneff will live," said Karol, "but he won't walk on his left foot for a long time."

"What about the bullet?"

"It's from a German P-38," Karol reported. He shook his head in disgust. "Very unprofessional weapon, if you ask me. Penetrates anything, but the enormous recoil invariably spoils the second shot."

"How are the Americans taking it?" the Professor inquired solicitously, as if he were asking after the next of kin.

"They're making all the appropriate noises," Karol said. "They plan to fly him out to *their* Germany as soon as he regains consciousness. Our doctors are advising them to wait a few days, but they seem quite determined. They have someone from the embassy with him day and night, so there's not much chance of questioning him."

The Professor waved his hand in the general direction of Germany. "Let them go when they want to," he instructed Karol. He bent his head to his reading, but Karol was still lingering in the circle of light cast by the desk lamp.

"Do you think he came in to kill the fat man?" Karol asked in a puzzled voice.

"In what country," the Professor replied, "do they teach agents that a bullet in the back of the knee is lethal?"

Karol was furious with himself for having asked the question. He tried to regain the lost ground. "The fat man got in his way then." Karol inclined his head at an angle that indicated confusion. "The man who crossed the frontier is an American. He came in to assassinate someone. The fat man is an American. He was trying to stop him from assassinating that someone."

"You have a fairly good grasp of the basics," said the Professor.

Karol said, "I've never seen anything quite like this before."

"Just so," the Professor commented, and he escaped back to the mountain of paper and the trails of inquiry that would inevitably offer themselves up to his observant eyes.

Heller couldn't believe his eyes. It had come up at him the way a print developed in a tray—slowly, inexorably, the darker "skeleton" appearing first, then the details, until the whole thing was spread out in all its glory before him.

He had been intrigued by the epilogue to *The Tempest* from the moment he came across it in the alcove of the nest. When he wasn't following Rodzenko or giving Elizabeth a quick course on nulls or getting shot at by the fat man, he *thought* about the epilogue. Earlier that night he had taken a pencil and had drawn longitudinal lines on a piece of loose-leaf paper (turning it into graph paper) and had printed out the epilogue, starting with "Now my Charmes are all ore-throwne" and ending on "Let your Indulgence set me free."

He had been particularly struck by the ninth and tenth lines:

> *But release me from my bands*
> *With the helpe of your good hands.*

Was the author of those lines hinting that there *was* a cipher hidden in the text, only waiting to be "released" with the help of the decipherer's "good hands"? Assuming that there was a cipher to be found, "good hands" seemed to suggest some sort of manual system. And then Heller dredged up from a corner of his memory the little known "string cipher." It was the first described by the Duke of Braunschweig-Lüneburg in 1623 in a book entitled

Cryptomenytices et Cryptographiæ. The method involved the use of a flat rectangular piece of wood divided into longitudinal columns, with each column representing one letter of the alphabet. The edges of the wood were then notched and a string was wound between the notches, starting at the upper left and finishing at the lower right. Knots tied in the string then fell in various columns of the ruled surface, and the position of each knot represented a letter.

On a hunch, Heller counted the capital letters in the epilogue. There were thirty-four, with one, two or three to a line. It was only when he had been at it for several hours that it struck him: The spacing of the capitals could be translated into the distance between knots on a string. Thus if the supposition were correct, he would have a thirty-four-letter message that could only be deciphered with the use of *good hands!*

"Do you know what time it is?" Elizabeth called from down in the bedroom. Heller was sprawled on the floor of the library alcove, inches from the glowing coils of the electric heater. "Come for God's sake to bed."

Heller looked at his watch; it was almost 4 A.M. "You know what I like about you?" he called back.

"What?"

"You recognize the male nipple for what it is—an erogenous zone worthy of attention."

A slipper came flying up into the alcove, and then another. The bathroom door slammed. Heller, oblivious to everything but the cipher unraveling under his finger tips, went on with his work. He tried various alphabets, some twenty-six letters long, some twenty-four letters long (in which the "I" and the "J," and the "U" and the "V," were each represented by one letter). But the only thing he came up with when he laid out his knot-capitals was gibberish. And then, with the first silver streaks falling across the sill, the puzzle tumbled into place. Using a twenty-four-letter alphabet that began with the letter "F" and ended with the letter "E," the knots fell one by one into syllables, and then words, and then a sentence. *And what a sentence!* Almost feverish with excitement, Heller repeated the operation from scratch a second time and then a third to be certain. Each time it came out exactly the same. The thirty-four-letter sentence came off the page at him as

189

if it was *alive*. He stared at it, the Mona Lisa–like grin spreading across his features: FRANCISCO BACON WRIT SHAKE-SPEARS PLAYS

Above the nest, the first plane of the morning roared toward the tip of the airport runway. Heller slipped out of his clothes and crawled into bed. Elizabeth, sleeping on her stomach, stirred restlessly and muttered something in Czech and reached for him.

"I found it," Heller whispered triumphantly. "I can prove that Francis Bacon really wrote Shakespeare's plays!"

But Elizabeth had inserted her Italian earplugs and didn't hear a word he was saying.

That night, sitting in the parked Fiat, his eyes glued to the windows of Rodzenko's fourth-floor apartment, Heller shook his head impatiently as the lights were turned off. Elizabeth started to say something. Heller held up a hand to cut her off. "Don't tell me. I already know it. Patience is next to godliness." He went back to studying Rodzenko's dark window. An idea occurred to him. "He was carrying that cardboard box again tonight, wasn't he?" he asked carefully.

"He carries it every night," noted Elizabeth. "What of it?"

Heller smiled at the thought of what his crateologist friend, Slater, would say if he could hear him now. "It's long and thin," Heller mused. "He carries it tucked under his elbow, which means it isn't heavy! A long, thin, light white cardboard box, with heat-sealed seams probably, that the lover of the German girl takes home with him every night." Heller stared at Elizabeth. "Of course! Roses! Long-stemmed roses!" He slapped his palm against his forehead. "I need a phone."

Elizabeth drove back toward the center of town until they came to a booth. She watched Heller thumb excitedly through the directory, running his fingernail up and down columns until he found what he was looking for. He dialed a number and let the phone on the other end ring for several minutes before he slowly hung up the receiver. "What an idiot I am," he told Elizabeth when he returned to the Fiat.

"No one answered?"

"Of course no one answered! What's the best hours for a hot love affair?"

Elizabeth started to catch some of his excitement. "It's as plain as the mouth on your face."

Heller laughed happily. "Nose," he corrected her. And he planted a kiss on the tip of her nose. "It's as plain as the *nose* on your face." He kissed her on the lips for a long, luxurious moment. When he came up for air, he said huskily, "Not mouth."

The next night they didn't bother picking up Rodzenko when he left the embassy, but waited for him instead at his apartment building. Giant flakes of snow were drifting down and settling on the small Fiat in a soft white blanket that seemed to warm and protect the two occupants huddled inside. Rodzenko's Skoda pulled up in front of his door at six-thirty. The chauffeur checked the lobby, then held the door open for Rodzenko, who dashed from the car to the building with his head bent against the snow. Under his arm he carried a long, thin white cardboard box.

As soon as the lights in the fourth-floor apartment came on, Heller turned to Elizabeth. "Okay, let's go," he instructed her.

She switched on the motor, cleaned the windshield with the wipers, eased slowly out and, rounding one corner and then another, came up the street that ran parallel to Rodzenko's. There she found a parking space behind an old American Ford with enormous tail lights. Heller cracked his window; he could see the rear of Rodzenko's building looming over the smaller apartment house across the street. "I tried it this afternoon," he told Elizabeth. "He could easily go down to the boiler room using the fire stairs. The door is locked on the inside with a hook. He crosses the courtyard, where the garbage cans are stacked, to the other building. The door there has a regular lock, but it shouldn't be too difficult for the KGB *résident* to get a key. He goes to the basement garage. There was one car with diplomatic plates—a brown Volvo."

Twenty minutes later they heard the basement garage door across the street being cranked open. A brown Volvo, with only its parking lights on, eased up the ramp. Heller and Elizabeth slumped into their seats as the Volvo's headlights came on and played across their snow-covered windows. As the Volvo pulled past, Heller opened his window to take a look at the driver. It was Rodzenko.

Elizabeth let him get to the corner before she pulled out after him. The streets of Prague were muted by the cushion of snow that had fallen. What traffic there was moved slowly on the slippery pavement, and Elizabeth had no trouble following the Volvo as it headed south on Kvetna, a wide boulevard with tracks and small groups of people huddled every few blocks waiting for the next trolley. After a while Kvetna became Budejovicka. At Antala Staska, the Volvo turned right, and then left on Percharova. Halfway down Percharova, a block full of prewar apartment houses with enormous windows and peeling facades, Rodzenko pulled into the underground parking lot of the only modern apartment building in sight.

Heller signaled for Elizabeth to keep going. As they passed the ramp, the Volvo's tail lights were just disappearing.

"How are you going to find out which apartment she's in?" asked Elizabeth.

"*You'll* find out for me tomorrow," Heller told her. "Don't worry. It'll be like taking candy from a baby."

They waited down the street from the Soviet embassy the next morning until Rodzenko arrived, then threaded their way through heavy morning traffic to the modern apartment building on Percharova. Heller let Elizabeth off at the corner. He rolled down his window, and she came around to say goodbye. "You don't happen to possess a cigarette?" he asked nervously; he was suddenly uneasy at the prospect of sending her into the lion's den.

Elizabeth leaned down to the open window. "I don't smoke," she reminded him. "You don't smoke. Neither one of us smokes. Relax. It'll be like taking carrots from a baby." And she kissed him lightly on the lips and left.

A clipboard in hand, pen poised, Elizabeth started on the top floor. "I'm taking a survey for the State Housing Cooperative," she informed the housewife with her hair up in plastic curlers who opened the first door she came to. She explained what she wanted. The woman, immediately on her guard at the idea of dealing with any bureaucracy, let Elizabeth in and followed her from room to room as she took notes on her clipboard. At the next apartment, a ten-year-old girl with a runny nose announced in a high-pitched voice that she was alone and had been instructed not to let anyone in. Elizabeth saw enough from the partly open door to eliminate that apartment too.

And so it went from door to door: a nasal woman who peered at Elizabeth through the top of her bifocals; a retired man who stepped back gallantly to let her in; a scrubbed young mother who could barely hear what Elizabeth said over the wails of her twin babies.

One floor down there was a lady dentist who had broken her arm skiing; an old grandmother baby-sitting for a daughter-in-law she obviously didn't like; then two doors where no one answered. And then Elizabeth came to an apartment which, curiously, had a peephole installed in the door. Over the door a small plaque read "405." Elizabeth put her forefinger on the bell and pressed. When no one answered, she rang a second time. She had the distinct impression that she was being sized up through the fish-eye lens of the peephole. Finally the door opened a crack and a heavy-set man dressed in a blue warm-up suit stared out at her.

Elizabeth smiled as brightly as she could bring herself to. "I'm taking a survey," she said sweetly, "for the State Housing Cooperative."

The heavy-set man eyed her suspiciously. "This is not a convenient time." He spoke Czech with what Elizabeth took to be a Russian accent.

"It won't take long," Elizabeth tried to persuade him. "If I don't get the information now, they'll only send me back again. I need to count the rooms, and mark how many full-time residents there are." She looked at the man with wide, innocent eyes.

He considered it for a moment. "I suppose it will be all right," he said reluctantly.

193

He opened the door, glanced up and down the corridor, let her in and closed the door after her.

Heller played the devil's advocate. "How can you be sure?" he demanded.

"*Eight* rooms for *three* people! Only someone very important gets that kind of space. And the man who answered the door— he spoke Czech with a Russian accent!"

"Did you see anyone else in the apartment?"

"There was another man drinking coffee in the kitchen," Elizabeth reported.

"Russian?"

She shrugged. "He never said a word."

"What about the girl?" Heller squeezed Elizabeth's wrist in his eagerness to hear what she had to say. "What about Gretchen?"

"When I tried one of the bedroom doors," she recounted, "it was locked. I thought I heard a faint coughing sound coming from inside. But I couldn't be sure if it was a man or a woman who was doing the coughing."

A snow plow with a blinking red light rumbled past, pushing the snow onto the curb across the street. Heller leaned back in his seat in the parked Fiat. He felt as if a great weight were pressing against his rib cage, and he breathed deeply several times to control the pain. "It must have been Gretchen," he said softly.

"If it was," Elizabeth said brightly, "I know where she's going to be at eighty-thirty tomorrow morning!"

"How?"

"As I was leaving, I rested my clipboard on a hall table to write on it. I made believe my pen had gone dry—I shook it several times—and hunted in my handbag for another one. All the while I was looking at the objects in a pewter plate on the table. There was a matchbook, some cleaning receipts, several sets of keys, and one of those printed appointment cards that doctors give out."

"You remember what it said?" Heller demanded.

"I remember," Elizabeth assured him. "It read, 'Dr. Vratislav

Havelka, Radiologist.' Underneath in ink it said, 'Tuesday, eight-thirty.' "

Driving back toward the nest, Heller rested a hand on Elizabeth's thigh. "Thank you," he said simply, "for your help."

"You don't have to thank me," she replied, though it was easy to see she was pleased. "You're giving the concert. I'm just turning the pages."

The man who had been drinking coffee in the kitchen waited downstairs in the car. The heavy-set man who spoke Czech with a Russian accent took up a position in the hallway just outside the door with the bronze plaque that read, VRATISLAV HAVELKA, RADIOLOGIST. Inside in the tiny waiting room Gretchen leafed absently through some fashion magazines, sneering at the thin models with their sucked-in cheeks. Every few minutes her body was convulsed by a hacking cough.

Elizabeth, barely recognizable with her hair piled on top of her head in a bun, appeared at the door of the waiting room. She was dressed in a nurse's uniform. "If you'll come with me . . ." she said in Czech.

"I'm sorry, I don't speak Czech," Gretchen replied in English.

Elizabeth smiled thinly and repeated in English, "If you will come with me . . ."

Gretchen tossed aside the magazine and followed Elizabeth through the office to a door marked DANGER—X-RAYS. Elizabeth instructed her to remove her sweater and blouse and brassiere (which looked as if it hadn't been washed in months). She laid the clothes on a chair and left. Gretchen, naked from the waist up, stretched out on the examination table.

Heller, wearing a white smock over his suit, slid into the seat before a console in the control room, which looked out onto the X-ray room through a thick pane of glass. He studied the console panel. The X-ray machine had been imported from London; all the switches and dials and knobs and meters were labeled in English. He depressed one lever and the large gray X-ray machine above Gretchen came into life and slanted down toward her chest. Heller leaned toward a small microphone and flicked on the switch that activated it.

"Can you hear me?" he asked.

Gretchen turned her head toward the control booth. "You're not Dr. Havelka," she said. "Where is Dr. Havelka?"

"I'm taking his place today," Heller said. "What do you know about X rays?"

"I know what everyone knows," Gretchen replied. She coughed into her hand for a moment, then wiped her lips on the back of her wrist. "It's not a good idea to get too many of them."

Heller said, "An overdose will make you vomit. A very heavy dose will make your hair fall out, give you skin cancer. It will even kill you."

The first alarm bells went off in Gretchen's head. She sat bolt upright and covered her heavy breasts with one arm. "You speak English very well! Why are you telling me this?"

"Where is Juan Antonio? Where is Horst Schiller?"

The questions hung in the air. Gretchen, thoroughly alarmed, stared at Heller through the thick glass pane. "Who are you?" she whispered.

Heller flicked a switch on the console. Above Gretchen's head, the X-ray machine emitted a soft zzzzzzzzz for five long seconds.

Gretchen's eyes widened in panic. She stared at the black nozzle of the X-ray machine in terror, then bolted for the door and pulled on the handle. It was locked.

"Where is Juan Antonio?" Heller repeated the question. "Where is Horst Schiller?" He played with the remote-control lever that positioned the X-ray machine; it swiveled relentlessly and advanced toward Gretchen, who stood with her back to the door. Again the soft zzzzzzzzz came from the nozzle.

Gretchen raced for another corner of the room. She pressed herself against the wall and started to scream, but the scream gave way to a spasm of coughing, and she sank to the floor weakly gasping for breath. In German she sobbed, "You can't do this to me."

Across the room, the X-ray nozzle swiveled and started toward her.

Speaking into the microphone, Heller said, "Remember the girl you killed in Munich?"

"I didn't kill her," Gretchen screamed. "Schiller killed her."

"Schiller pulled the trigger," Heller taunted her. "You picked out her passport. Where is Juan Antonio? Where is Schiller?"

The X-ray nozzle pointed down toward the figure of Gretchen. She crawled away from it, but it followed her. Inside the control booth, Heller closed his eyes and summoned up the image of Sarah—her face angled to a sun that wasn't shining, her eyes pleading for help that wasn't forthcoming—and he pushed the switch activating the nozzle. Once again the distinctive zzzzzzzz bombarded Gretchen's body.

"Please, I beg you—" Again Gretchen was convulsed by a fit of coughing. When it subsided, she cried out, "Oh my God, what's happening to me?" She looked over her shoulder and saw the nozzle advancing on her and crawled toward the pane of glass separating her from Heller and pushed herself up until her face was only inches from his. "I can't tell you," she gasped. "They'll kill me if I tell you."

"I'll kill you if you don't," Heller coldly informed her.

He flicked the switch. The soft zzzzzzzz bombarded Gretchen's back.

Gretchen's teeth were chattering uncontrollably; she had bitten into her lip and blood ran down her chin. "Juan Antonio . . . Juan Antonio has an apartment in the Hotel Flora . . . in Prague . . . Schiller lives in Karlovy Vary . . . in one of the small hotels next to the spa . . . Hotel Balkan." And she coughed and then collapsed in a heap on the floor.

In the control booth Heller played with the lever, positioning the nozzle over Gretchen's body, then pressed the switch activating it.

Gretchen became aware of the soft steady zzzzzzzz filling the room. She stirred and with an effort turned her head and focused on the nozzle and opened her mouth to scream.

Heller, watching from behind the pane of glass, turned off the microphone; he could see Gretchen's mouth working, but he couldn't hear her. He removed the white smock and threw it over the back of the seat and walked shakily out of the control booth.

Elizabeth was waiting for him outside. She motioned with her head toward the front door of the office, which she had locked; the heavy-set man was banging on it with the butt of a pistol and shouting in Russian.

"Let's go," Heller told her.

"Did you get what you wanted?" Elizabeth asked.

Heller nodded grimly. "I got just what I wanted."

With Elizabeth in tow, Heller raced through the narrow laboratory, past Dr. Havelka and his nurse bound and gagged with surgical tape, out the back door. From behind them came the sound of a pistol going off as the Russian bodyguard shot out the lock and burst into the office.

CHAPTER FOURTEEN

THE Professor watched through the observation window of the operating room. Several doctors were hovering over the naked body stretched out on the table. One was pumping away with the heel of his hand on her heart. Another was giving her an injection in her neck. Karol, wearing a white doctor's coat and a surgical mask, waited nearby to catch anything she might say if she regained consciousness. A lady doctor felt for a pulse, then turned tiredly away. The doctor pumping on her heart straightened. Karol looked at the Professor through the observation window and shook his head.

The Professor wandered down the well-lit corridor toward the emergency entrance. His hands were clasped behind his back, his brow furrowed in thought. He was trying to figure out what Francis Bacon had to do with the American cipher expert and the Czech girl who raised guinea fowl and the fat man who had been shot in the back of his knee.

Rodzenko, looking as if most of the blood had been drained

from his face, came running down the corridor. "I just found out," he said, gasping for breath. He looked genuinely shaken. It occurred to the Professor for the first time that the love affair between Rodzenko and Gretchen may have involved more than operational convenience.

"I'm afraid it is no use," the Professor said as gently as he could. He linked his arm through Rodzenko's and drew him back toward the door.

"Who did this thing?" Rodzenko demanded.

The Professor put on a mask of confused concern. "We don't have the slightest idea," he said. Behind the professionally blank look in his eyes, the Professor was diligently following a trail of inquiry. It led from the Bulgarian who sold a piece of information to a windmill on the frontier to an art deco nest on the edge of the Vltava to the fat man to Rodzenko to Gretchen. There was no reason to think it would stop there. Gretchen was a steppingstone to Juan Antonio, and Juan Antonio was just a notch down the ladder from Horst Schiller. And Horst Schiller . . . Horst Schiller was the single person in the world who interested the Professor more than Francis Bacon.

The Director, gracious to a fault, accompanied the two senators whom he had lunched with to the main entrance. Rutledge waited a discreet step or two behind.

"Mighty nice of you to have us over," said Senator Barton, a heavy man whose scalp glistened with perspiration. He pumped the Director's hand as if television cameras were trained on them. "Reckon you strained the Company budget a tiny bit with that there Lafite-Rothschild, but what the hell, it was in a good cause."

Senator Rodgers, who talked in the clipped accents of the Eastern Establishment, offered his hand to the Director. "I appreciate the briefing as much as the wine," he said.

"Anytime, gentlemen," said the Director. "We like to think we're serving the country. Our people, our files, are open to you whenever and wherever you want."

When the senators had left, the Director started back toward the bank of elevators with Rutledge. The friendly, relaxed expression of a moment before had been replaced by cold fury. "What in Christ's name is going on with Heller?" he demanded.

Rutledge blanched uncomfortably. "You know the old saying, 'If something can go wrong, it will.' Well, it has. The doctors in Germany managed to save Yaneff's leg; he'll walk again, but not very fast. As for the German girl, she was found in a radiologist's office. Apparently Heller got to her too. The X-ray machine had been turned on and left on. She picked up a lot of radiation, but that wasn't what killed her. She died of heart failure." And very pointedly Rutledge added, "We don't have any idea what Heller got out of her."

Rutledge followed the Director into the elevator and pressed seven. The doors slid closed. "We've got to consider the possibility that he may get as far as Schiller," the Director said.

"If he gets to Schiller," Rutledge said, "chances are one of them will kill the other without discussing it first."

The Director shook his head. "I want Heller terminated. I don't want him anywhere near Schiller."

"The colonel said he was tagging around with Inquiline," Rutledge said. "We may lose her along with Heller."

The Director waved a hand. "That's a loss we'll just have to live with."

The elevator arrived at the seventh floor. Rutledge said, "I know someone who'll be delighted to take on the assignment."

The elevator was out of another world, another century even. It was large and carpeted and lined with quilted leather and mahogany paneling. There was a banquette along the back wall and a stained-glass dome overhead. The elevator rose on its greased cables without a sound. The gruff old gentleman who operated it pulled the brass and wood control handle back to the center slot; the elevator eased to a stop at the ninth floor. The operator, who wore a frayed blue uniform with gold piping and had the name "Martin" sewn in gold thread over the breast pocket, reached with a white-gloved hand to slide back the grill, then stepped out and held the outer door open for his passengers.

The two Russians got out first. One had a face like a prune. The other carried a woman's umbrella. They stood a moment looking up and down the empty hallway. Then one of them called to the third man in the elevator.

Horst Schiller, drawn, preoccupied, stared at the floor and had to be summoned a second time by his Russian bodyguards. He politely nodded his thanks to the operator and followed the two Russians down the hall and knocked once on a door. It opened almost immediately. Schiller went in. The two Russians waited in the hallway.

Inside, Schiller burst into the bedroom and switched on the overhead light. Juan Antonio, in bed with a very shapely bleached blonde, lunged for the pistol he always kept under his pillow. When he saw who it was, he burst out laughing and slapped the girl on the rump. She darted naked from the bed and disappeared into the bathroom. Juan Antonio reached for a cigarette on his night table and lit up. Then he leaned against the wall, his back to the Che Guevara poster he had taped up behind the bed.

"You look worried," Juan Antonio said. He spoke in Spanish.

Schiller answered in German. "Someone got to Gretchen. They shot her full of X rays when she went to her radiologist."

The muscles in Juan Antonio's neck contorted. "Did she talk?"

Schiller paced back and forth near the foot of the bed. He stopped to pick up one of Juan Antonio's weights, hefted it to see how heavy it was and set it down again. "How would I know if she talked. She was unconscious when they found her. She died in the hospital. They said it was heart failure." Schiller shook his head like a schoolteacher dismissing an outdated theory. "She was frightened to death."

Juan Antonio regarded Schiller uneasily. "Maybe it's the Israelis. Or one of the radical factions—"

"It's the Americans," Schiller said. "It's the CIA. They sent in a professional killer. The Czechs almost got him when he came across the frontier."

He went over to the window and opened the Venetian blind

the width of a finger and looked down at the street. A furniture van had blocked traffic to off-load some chairs and tables, and the drivers stuck behind it were furious. Schiller kept his back turned to Juan Antonio so he wouldn't see how confused he was. "It's the CIA that's after us," he repeated.

CHAPTER
FIFTEEN

OUTSIDE the nest a driving hailstorm had reduced visibility to almost zero, obliging planes to come in even lower than usual. For Heller and Elizabeth, it was like living at the center of sound; while it lasted, nothing else existed. He pressed his mouth over hers and pinched her nipple between his thumb and forefinger. Elizabeth cried into his mouth, or thought she did. If there was a cry, it was lost in the roar of the jet hurtling through the storm overhead. She shook her head violently to free herself, and gasped for air, but his mouth was instantly clamped back over hers. Another plane was approaching, and the world, what there was of it inside the room, disintegrated into isolated sensations. And then the plane was past and Heller rolled off her and lay next to her panting.

When still another plane had gone by, she turned her head toward him and spoke into the darkness. Her voice trembled. "That was not lovemaking in the usual sense of the phrase. Admit it, your mind was somewhere else. You didn't even know who I was. Please. Don't do it again. Not like that." After a while she propped herself up on an elbow. "When you make love like that, what is it you want?"

"To lose myself," said Heller. "To almost but not quite die." Heller reached for her in the darkness. "Also to give you pleasure."

"You make it sound like a professional obligation," remarked Elizabeth.

This brought a bitter laugh from Heller. "It's an amateur obligation. I'm an amateur."

"What is the difference between a professional and an amateur?" challenged Elizabeth.

Heller thought for a moment. "An amateur is someone who suspects that enough isn't really as good as a feast."

Elizabeth didn't smile. "Seriously?"

"Seriously," Heller said, "it's someone who thinks that if something is worth doing, it may be worth doing badly."

"Ah"—Elizabeth seemed very pleased with the answer— "that is very original." She ran her finger tips over his lips. "You are very original. There are moments—only moments—when I am almost in love with you. But they quickly pass, and I later think it was just curiosity and . . ."

"And?"

Elizabeth's voice turned husky. "And . . . desire."

They slept for several hours, Elizabeth (soundly) with the Italian plugs in her ears, Heller (fitfully) with a pillow jammed over his head. Around midnight the planes thinned out and then stopped altogether, and the silence woke Heller. He wound the bed quilt around him and searched in the darkness for the cognac bottle he had left on the desk in the alcove library.

Which is when he heard the guinea fowl start up. One moment they were quiet; the next they were chattering away with a kind of intensive panic. Heller listened for a moment and shrugged and turned back toward the bedroom with the bottle of cognac in his hand. Then from somewhere downstairs he heard the faint, vaguely musical tinkling of falling glass, and his skin crawled with fear. He padded over to the door and put his ear to it. Nothing. He thought about getting his pistol from his overcoat pocket, but that would mean flicking on the light,

which would seep under the door and give away the one advantage he had: whoever was there didn't know that he was
awake! So Heller gripped the cognac bottle by its throat and
shrank back against the wall until he felt he was part of it, and
waited.

It was a long time in coming, so long that Heller began to
wonder whether the intruder existed only in his imagination.
Then suddenly he knew as a matter of absolute fact that someone
was on the other side of the door. No sound reached his ears, and
still he *knew!* He rested his finger tips lightly against the door and
felt the first faint pressure against them as it opened with infinite
slowness. Heller, breathing silently through his wide-open mouth,
carefully raised the bottle over his head. A shadow, walking on
rubber soles, stepped into the room and appeared to sink into a
crouch. Heller thought he caught the gleam of a metallic object
thrust out in front. He took one short step forward and brought
the bottle down hard on the head of the figure.

The bottle shattered in Heller's hands. Cognac spattered
over his arms and legs. The figure slumped against the bed and
fell to the floor. Elizabeth bolted upright. "Who's there?" she
cried and lunged for the chain on the bed lamp. It overturned
and fell to the floor. With little frightened gasps she traced the
electric cord until she found the lamp and managed to turn on
the light.

In the yellowish glow from the fallen lamp, Heller stood over
the figure sprawling at his feet. Heller was clutching what was left
of the bottle and shaking like a leaf. Elizabeth came over in bare
feet and held him until he stopped shaking. Then she reached
down and tossed away the pistol on the floor, and she pulled on
the shoulder of the unconscious figure until the intruder lay on
his back.

Heller stared down at the face. "Colonel Henderson!"

"You know him?" Elizabeth demanded.

"I know him," Heller acknowledged.

"Whose side is he on?" Elizabeth asked. She stood up and
looked Heller in the eyes. "Whose side are *we* on?" she asked
softly.

Heller realized for the first time that she was naked. He

grabbed her arm and pushed her toward the bathroom. "We've got to get out of here," he told her.

Elizabeth resisted. "Why?"

Heller went back to Henderson and knelt down beside him. He felt for his pulse and found it, though he wasn't sure if he was relieved or disappointed. "Certain people are trying to keep me from doing what I came to do," he explained. "Somewhere along the way they must have spotted us together."

"If they spotted me, and knew who I was, that means . . ."

Heller motioned toward the bathroom with his head. "That means you'd better get dressed," he told her. "And fast."

She was ready ten minutes later. "Will I be coming back here?" she asked.

Heller shook his head.

She tossed some clothes and toilet articles in a small sack, removed a pillowcase and wrapped her wedding photo in it and put it on top of her other things. "And my birds? Who will feed my birds?"

Heller snapped, "The hell with your birds." He drew his pistol, checked to see the pin was protruding from the slide and started down the stairs; there was always the possibility that Henderson had not been alone. Outside, an incredible stillness—the kind that comes only after a storm—filled the air. Heller ducked into the Fiat, reached under the seat for the keys and started the engine. Elizabeth ran up to the driver's side. She seemed very determined. "It'll only take a minute," she yelled. Before he could reply, she raced off toward the long low buildings that housed the guinea fowl. As she approached, they set up their howling again. Elizabeth threw open the door, and then ran over and did the same at the second building. Several birds stuck their bony heads outside, took in the world, seemed to like what they saw and carried their oversized bodies out into the night to peck with staccato jerks of their necks at the wet ground. By the time Elizabeth got back to the car, several hundred birds, chattering madly, were milling uncertainly around the driveway, as if their new-found freedom had complicated their lives. Heller threw the Fiat into first and crawled away from the nest; the birds scattered out of his path and closed in behind them like a sea. Elizabeth never looked back; true to her word, she didn't want happy endings, only endings. Her eyes set dead ahead, her face expressionless, her hands folded in her lap, she allowed Heller to lead her away from a place she had dearly loved.

Driving along badly lighted streets that threw back yellowish reflections from their moist surfaces, Heller headed in the general direction of Prague. The rain started again and thickened until the windshield wipers couldn't clear the flow, and then it let up suddenly. The inside of the car smelled of wet wool. At one intersection the light was stuck on red. Heller waited several minutes and then crossed and pulled up near a dark church with high twin spires that jutted up like needles.

Elizabeth stirred in her seat; she seemed chilled by thoughts more than the weather. "Colonel Henderson works for the same people you work for?" she asked.

"Yes."

She accepted this cautiously. "That means the people you work for are not pleased with your services."

"I have the same impression," Heller agreed.

"You didn't really come here to teach me ciphers."

"No."

"You came here to find the German girl?"

"The German girl and two others."

"They did something to you, these three people?"

Heller nodded.

"Where are the scars?"

He looked at her in surprise. "Where are the scars?"

"The scars, yes. Where are they?"

"Where yours are," Heller said.

Elizabeth's mouth opened slightly. She started to say something and changed her mind.

Heller said, "Look, is there someplace we can go—some friend who will put us up until I figure something out?"

Elizabeth considered the problem. "I have an old uncle—"

"If he's your uncle," Heller said, "they'll know all about him."

"He's not really my uncle," she said. "He was engaged to my mother's sister, but she died before they could marry. I used to see him when I was a child. There's not much chance anyone would think of looking for us there."

"Where is this uncle who isn't really an uncle?"

Elizabeth said, "He works as a night watchman in a factory. He lives in the center of Prague, in a tiny apartment near all the big tourist hotels."

"Near the Hotel Flora?"

"You know the Flora?"

Heller nodded grimly. "One of the men I'm looking for lives in the Hotel Flora."

Elizabeth smiled thinly. "Then we can kill two birds with one rock."

"One stone," Heller said. "Two birds are generally killed with one stone."

Elizabeth shrugged. "Rock. Stone. What's the difference?" A faraway look came into her eyes. "The birds are just the same dead."

"I see your point," conceded Heller.

They huddled in the car until Elizabeth's uncle returned to his apartment after the night shift at the factory. The sky was thick with rain clouds; an occasional ray of light seeped through, but they looked for the most part impenetrable. It was possible to imagine that the sun would never be seen again.

Elizabeth pointed him out as he came down the street, his head high, his thick glasses fogged by the moisture that hung in the early morning air. He walked with an inner calm, and an unassailable sense of his own dignity.

After he had passed, they abandoned the car on a side street half a dozen blocks away—if Henderson knew the identity of Inquiline, he knew the identity of Inquiline's car—and walked back to the uncle's apartment.

Heller lingered in the shadows on the landing beneath the top floor of the old prewar building. One flight up, Elizabeth rapped softly on the door. "Uncle Ludvik, are you there?" she called quietly in Czech. "It's me, Elizabeth."

The darkness of the landing where Heller was waiting was

cut by a shaft of light from Ludvik's partly open door. He could hear Elizabeth talking urgently in undertones to her uncle. Then she leaned over the railing. "It's all right to come up," she told Heller.

Heller climbed the stairs to the low-ceilinged apartment. Elizabeth made the introductions. "This is my Uncle Ludvik. Uncle Ludvik, this is my American friend I told you about."

Heller offered his hand, and the frail man took it. He studied Heller through his thick lenses. "I am honored," he said in a very formal, if halting, English, "to make your acquaintanceship. A friend of Elizabeth's is a welcome guest here."

Heller looked around. Uncle Ludvik's attic apartment—two rooms with slanting ceilings and tiny windows—was a study in old-world dignity. The furniture and carpets, prewar relics, were salvaged from a much larger apartment where they had been more in proportion to the surroundings. There was an old Gramophone on a table and a collection of 78-rpm classical records. On one wall next to an enormous gilt-edged mirror were several small oil paintings, the kind an old man like Ludvik would sell off, one every year or so, to make ends meet. Scotch-taped to the mirror was a newspaper photograph, its edges curling with age, of Eduard Benes being sworn in as President of Czechoslovakia in 1946.

Ludvik slipped into a minuscule bathroom and changed into a double-breasted suit jacket and trousers, and then prepared tea on the hotplate in the corner of the room that had been transformed into a kitchen. Heller could hear the saucers and cups and spoons being laid out in a tray behind the partition, a silk screen that had been mended dozens of times. Ludvik served the tea in a fragile prewar pot with a broken spout that leaked when he poured.

Balancing the teacup and saucer awkwardly on his knees, helping himself to three lumps of sugar from a bowl on the small table with delicate legs, accepting a buttered cracker from Ludvik, Heller explained in very general terms why he had come to Prague. "The one who lives in the Hotel Flora is named Juan Antonio," Heller wound up. "He is a terrorist, a killer."

Uncle Ludvik nodded as he listened to Heller's account. Then he sipped his tea and studied the worn carpet underfoot for a long moment, weighing his words before he spoke them. Elizabeth and Heller exchanged looks. Finally Uncle Ludvik raised his eyes. "My very young friend," he told Heller, "I was ready to fight in the First World War against the Russians, but they said I was too young. I was ready to fight against the Germans in the second war, but they said I was too old." He took another sip of tea. "I was ready to fight against the Bolshevists when they took over Czechoslovakia in 1948, but they said it was no use." He smiled with radiant dignity. "I am still ready for the good fight. It is only a matter of instructing me."

They talked most of the morning, with the conversation roaming back and forth across a wide spectrum of subjects—poetry, philosophy, fly casting, blind chess, medicine, the differences between centuries, systems, sexes. Ludvik played some scratchy 78-rpm Mozart sonatas, absently humming parts in a falsetto voice slightly off pitch. At one point Heller said something, and Ludvik got up and paced the room excitedly, removing and polishing his eyeglasses and gesturing with them in his hand. "Not at all, not at all!" he exclaimed. "The heart of the matter is that we are accomplices—we all contribute to our own destruction. Jews rounded up Jews for Herr Eichmann. Blacks helped white slave traders capture blacks. Impressed seamen formed gangs to impress other seamen."

"Where does it stop?" demanded Elizabeth.

Ludvik slipped his glasses back onto his nose and focused on his two visitors. "It stops with me," he declared, his eyes flashing, his thin hair lifting as he tossed his head in emphasis. "I don't contribute to my own annihilation."

Ludvik waved his hand by way of apology—he hadn't intended to get excited—and settled into a seat. Heller cleared his throat and asked for a cigarette. Ludvik produced one from a silver case, and he made absolutely no comment as Heller went through the ritual of testing himself and then calmly returning it to the old man. Toward noon Ludvik left for half an hour, without saying where he was going, and returned with a small package under his arm, which turned out to be three slices of salmon he had scavenged from some mysterious source. He served it simply, on buttered toast, and produced from the depths of a crowded closet a bottle of 1939 Château Lafite, which he asked Heller to uncork. "I have been saving this for an occasion," he said with contained pride, rubbing his hands together in anticipation. "This smells to me like an occasion!"

He poured out a small amount for himself, rolled it around in a plain kitchen tumbler and tasted it. "It is definitely not vinegar," he said happily. "A bit watery, but there is no mistaking the bouquet"—he stuck his long nose into the glass and sniffed—"reminiscent of a field of faded violets, if you ask me." He carefully poured some for Heller and Elizabeth, and then half filled his own glass. "My father gave this bottle of wine to me when I announced to him my impending marriage. My future wife, which is to say your aunt, Elizabeth, decided we would open it on the birth of our first child." The old man smiled; there was no trace of self-pity in his expression or his tone. "Unfortunately, we never had the chance to open the wine."

Elizabeth explained to Heller: "My aunt was killed at the time of the Anschluss in Austria—a stray bullet during one of the demonstrations."

The old man, afraid that Heller would be embarrassed, quickly changed the subject. "What do you think of my wine?" he asked politely.

Heller dutifully sipped some. "It is the best wine I've ever tasted in my life," he said sincerely.

Later, Ludvik waved aside Elizabeth's protests and fixed a bed for himself in the second room, which had originally been used to store skis when the house belonged to one family. That night, dressed again in his coveralls, he joined them for a late dinner, and toward midnight he went off to work.

Elizabeth took off her clothes and climbed into Ludvik's narrow wooden bed alongside Heller. "The night shift was the only one he could get," she explained when Heller asked why Ludvik worked odd hours. "He never made a secret of what he thought of the Communists. He's lucky to have work at all."

They listened to some of Ludvik's old 78s on the Gramophone. Near the end of one record the needle got stuck in the grooves. Elizabeth drew the quilt around her body and padded over to put on a new record. The sound of "Valse Triste" filled the attic. When Elizabeth turned back to the bed, she found Heller—looking slightly ridiculous wrapped in his blanket—barring the way. He held out his arms, inviting her to waltz. She hesitated, then folded herself into them and the two of them, wrapped in their covers, waltzed slowly around the cold room. The record ended, but Elizabeth and Heller, their breath vaporizing, continued to waltz. Then suddenly she stopped and stared at him in a peculiar way.

"What is it?" Heller demanded.

She offered it as a formula: "It has been my experience that every time you get something in life, you give up something."

She seemed to be speaking in a private code, but Heller—to his own surprise—sensed what she meant. "If you were to get me"—he spelled out the thing that was worrying her—"you would lose what went before—you would lose *him.*"

Elizabeth thought about it a moment. "Not so much him," she said. "But the absolute conviction I had then that it was special, unique; that the love we had for each other came from another time and another place and could not again be found in this world"—she looked around the attic in frustration—"this world that puts someone like Uncle Ludvik into overalls and sends him off to watch nights." She leaned forward and rested her forehead on Heller's chest for a long moment. When she looked up again, she was smiling as if she knew something he didn't know, something important, something that would change lives. Behind her smile was a secret!

Heller nervously asked, "Why do you smile?"

The smile disappeared from Elizabeth's face. "If cats can have nine lives," she said seriously, "what is to prevent humans from having two?"

Ludvik buttonholed the man as he came out of the service entrance and he took him to a coffee bar around the corner.

"What's new?" Ludvik demanded, counting out coins from his change purse and placing them in a neat row on the counter.

"What's new is you are buying me a coffee for the first time in fifteen years," the other man answered. He opened his overcoat and took off a thick woolen scarf. Underneath he had on a frayed blue uniform with gold piping and the name "Martin" sewn in gold thread over the breast pocket. "Not that I'm complaining," he quickly added, "not that at all." He eyed Ludvik for a moment, then blew noisily on his scalding coffee. "What is it you need, Ludvik?"

Ludvik put an index finger to his lips and considered the question. "What makes you think I need anything?"

The man named Martin snorted through his nostrils.

"What I need," Ludvik finally admitted, "is information."

Ludvik let himself in without a sound and found Heller and Elizabeth sleeping back to back in his old wooden bed. Heller rolled over and opened his eyes. Ludvik put a finger to his lips and motioned for him to dress and join him at the small table with fragile legs. By the time Heller was dressed, Ludvik had prepared tea. They talked in whispers.

"I have an acquaintance who runs an elevator in the Hotel Flora," Ludvik reported, obviously proud of what he had accomplished. "His name is Martin. I saw him when he came off duty this morning. I asked him about your Juan Antonio." Ludvik checked to make sure Elizabeth was still asleep. "He's there all right, just as you said. He has a suite of rooms on the ninth floor. There are always one or two bodyguards around his door. The bodyguards are Russian. Everyone thought he was Russian too. But Martin says he heard him curse in Spanish in his elevator once. Juan Antonio was going down for his morning swim—"

Heller perked up. "He swims in the morning? Where?"

Ludvik dipped a single lump of sugar into his teacup and watched the moisture climb up until the lump dissolved between his fingers. "Martin says it is the only time Juan Antonio leaves his suite," Ludvik explained. "Food is brought to him. Women are brought to him. But every morning, before the hotel pool opens for the guests, he descends with his bodyguards and goes for a swim."

"He swims every morning," Heller repeated excitedly.

"Before the pool opens, yes. At eight. Just as Martin goes off duty. He is often the last person Martin carries in his elevator." Ludvik understood what Heller was thinking. "His bodyguards are with him every moment. You will not be able to get near to him. You can see him if you want to: There is an underwater window in the basement bar."

Across the room Elizabeth rolled onto her back and stretched and lifted her head off the pillow. "Up already?" she asked.

"Ludvik's back," Heller said.

"Good morning, dear Elizabeth," said Ludvik.

Elizabeth propped herself up against the backboard, the quilt tucked up to her chin. "I had a nightmare," she announced calmly. "I dreamed I was trapped in a room that was getting smaller and smaller. The only way out was through a door locked with a combination lock. I kept trying different combinations, but none of them seemed to work. At the last possible second I got the number right. The door snapped open and I slid down a ramp just as the walls closed in." She laughed nervously. "I escaped by the enamel of my teeth."

Heller, preoccupied with thoughts of his own, didn't correct her.

Elizabeth was reluctant to let him leave. "Allow me at least to go with you," she begged. "They say two hearts are better than one."

"Two heads are what's better than one," Heller said. He kissed her on the lips and looked into her eyes and called a second goodbye to Ludvik and turned abruptly and started down the stairs. At the front door of the building he glanced around cautiously. The world, as far as he could make out, appeared to be in order. Stores had long since closed for the night; the one restaurant he could see was full of couples lingering over coffee. A group of teenagers, several carrying guitars, stood bunched on the corner waiting for a break in traffic. When it came, they laughingly surged across the street. Melting into the evening flow of pedestrians, Heller turned up his collar and started off in the general direction of the Hotel Flora.

Half an hour later an ancient silver taxi pulled up at the curb in front of the building. One man climbed out, signaled for the two others in the front to stay where they were and entered the building. He looked up the stairs, listened for a long moment, then started to climb toward the top floor. There he drew an automatic pistol from his pocket, checked to make sure it was loaded and rapped softly on Uncle Ludvik's door.

"I'll get it," Ludvik called as he started to unlock the door.

For the better part of an hour Heller huddled in the side entranceway to a department store directly across the street from the Flora, an old building that was the latest word in hotels when it first opened its ornate revolving door between the great crash and the great war. As far as Heller could make out, everything was normal. He watched as tourists, traveling salesmen and an occasional hooker made their way into or out of the brightly lit lobby. A giant doorman wearing an Army greatcoat over his uniform blew shrilly on a whistle to summon a taxi. Several women Heller took for tourist guides chatted on the sidewalk for a moment, then pecked each other on the cheek and headed off in different directions.

Heller's opportunity came when a busload of German tourists, back from an evening at the ballet, pulled up at the door. As the members of the group filed into the hotel through the revolving door, Heller hurried across the street and casually slipped in with them.

Inside, he looked around uncertainly. The carpeting was thick underfoot and muffled every sound. Spots of yellowish light, cast from the thousands of faces of cut glass on an enormous overhead chandelier, danced across the walls like nervous butterflies. Behind a high, polished reception desk a gaunt man in a worn tuxedo slapped his palm down on a bell and motioned for the young boy in a tight uniform and round cap to take away two valises belonging to a heavily veiled woman. The lobby crawled with English tourists. For an instant Heller thought he recognized one! And a second! And a third! To his horror, he realized he had wandered into the midst of the English group that had been on the bus that brought him to Prague. He quickly turned away to study a poster advertising a Chopin piano recital.

Across the lobby, a rail-thin man was collecting his key from the night clerk. Plucking at his wife's elbow, he asked, "Isn't that the chap who was on the bus with us?"

The wife tugged at his sleeve. "Come along to bed," she ordered. "It's none of our affair."

The rail-thin man allowed himself to be drawn off. "I could have sworn . . ." He cast a puzzled glance over his shoulder, shook his head and disappeared into the elevator.

Heller spotted the discreet sign advising clients of the presence on the premises of a nightclub, and indicating by a bright red arrow where it could be found. He descended a long staircase with a tarnished brass banister on either side, pushed through a set of swinging doors and then a second set and found himself in the nightclub.

It was a socialist imitation of the capitalist model. And a bad imitation at that. The lighting was neon, the hard kind that makes skin look bluish and at times almost metallic. A middle-aged Czech singer wearing a tight sequin gown, and a tired-looking four-man combo provided what passed for entertainment—fifteen-year-old American songs sung in barely recognizable English. On top of everything, the acoustics were bad.

Thirty or so customers, men mostly, were huddled around a dozen round tables, drinking noisily, paying no attention to the music. A waiter scurried between the tables and the bar bringing refills and making change when someone wanted to pay a bill. Heller hung his overcoat on a peg in a small cloakroom. He noticed an unmarked door on the far side of the cloakroom, wondered vaguely what it led to, decided he would find out later and headed for a free stool at the bar.

"I'll have a cognac," Heller told the bartender, and watched as he meticulously measured a shot of three-star Bulgarian Pliska into a snifter, rang up the bill on his cash register and planted both the cognac and the bill on the bar.

Sipping his cognac, Heller swiveled on his stool and surveyed the nightclub. Across the room, behind the singer and the four-man combo on the bandstand, was a door marked FIRE EXIT in Czech, French and English. It was the type that could only be opened by a brass push bar from the inside. To Heller's left, one of the bartenders disappeared into the cloakroom and emerged a moment later carrying a case of Schweppes, which meant that the unmarked door in the cloakroom led to a storage room.

Heller turned back to study the thick picture window behind

the bar that provided an underwater view of the hotel's swimming pool. A girl with long hair, wearing a one-piece tank suit, swam past. A second girl, in a bikini, dove straight for the picture window, grabbed a handrail and began blowing bubbles.

An Englishman on the bar stool next to Heller swayed in his general direction. "We're being watched, you know," he announced in an undertone.

Heller tensed.

The Englishman nodded. "She's checking"—he hiccupped —"checking up on me."

Heller asked, "Who's checking up on you?"

The Englishman inclined his head toward the girl in the bikini. "My wife. Wants to make sure I don't drink too much. She's got fantastic breath control, don't"—he hiccupped again—"don't you think? Can stay under water two minutes. What?"

In a burst of bubbles, the girl quit the picture window and headed for the surface. The Englishman waved goodbye. Swiveling back to Heller, speaking confidentially, he said, "Made love under water once. Damn near drowned. Had to give me mouth to mouth during *and* after." He laughed at his own joke and took another gulp of scotch.

The Englishman sucked in great amounts of air and held his breath until he figured the hiccups were gone. The long-haired girl in the one-piece suit appeared at the picture window. The Englishman blew her a kiss. Leaning toward Heller again, he announced, "I want to pose a delicate question. Are you ready?"

"I'm as ready as I'm ever going to be."

The Englishman sized up Heller for the first time. "You don't look ready. Never mind, here it is. Who, in your opinion, is on the inside looking out—her, or us?"

The girl rose toward the surface. The Englishman hiccupped again, and held his breath again. After a while, he leaned toward Heller, his elbow on the bar, his chin supported by his palm. "You're American, aren't you? I can tell by your accent. Tell the truth, what do you think of all this?" He waved his hand to take in the nightclub, the city, the country.

"All this?"

"What do you think of the *system?*"

The last thing in the world Heller wanted was to be drawn

into a discussion on the merits of socialism. "I don't know much about it," he replied vaguely. "I'm only passing through. I haven't seen enough to form an opinion."

"Well, I have," the Englishman said. Heller could smell his breath as he leaned even closer and lowered his voice. "I have formed an opinion. Orwell had it all wrong. It isn't big brother that's watching you. It's *father*. They treat everyone as if they're bloody *children*. They pat you on the head if you're a good little boy. They slap you on the knuckles if you make waves. You won't believe this, but yesterday a copper stopped me for jaywalking. *Jaywalking!* You know what the bugger did? What the bugger did was make me jaywalk back the way I came and come around the right way!"

Eventually the Englishman's wife joined them at the bar. Heller offered a made-up name and shook her hand. "The pool is the nicest thing in Prague," the girl said. She ran her fingers through her hair, which was still wet.

"And the sexiest," added the Englishman.

"It's a hell of a country," sighed the girl. "You can buy the pill in any chemist's, but the directions on the box mention everything it's good for *except* birth control."

Toward 1 A.M. the nightclub began to empty out. Heller waited until almost everyone had gone, then thanked his neighbors for a pleasant evening and made his way to the cloakroom. A quick look over his shoulder convinced him that nobody was paying the slightest attention to him. He retrieved his coat, tried the handle on the unmarked door, found it open and ducked into the room.

It was, as he had surmised, a storage room. It was filled with spare chairs and tables and dozens of cartons of beer and liquor and Schweppes. Working quickly, Heller rearranged some of the cartons against the back wall to create a small cave behind them, then crawled in, spread his coat on the floor and curled up on it.

Twenty minutes went by. The door opened. Heller could hear a burst of music from the combo. A waiter carried in a case of empties and returned a moment later with a second. The door slammed shut and the music faded. When the door opened again, the music had ceased entirely. From his hiding place behind the cartons, Heller heard cases of empties being stacked near the door. The waiters and barmen seemed to be trading quips in Czech. Then the light was switched off and the door to the storage room slammed shut. Heller could hear a key turning in the lock. He waited a long while, and when he heard nothing more he crawled out from behind the cartons and felt along the wall for the light switch. He found it and turned on the naked overhead bulb. He put his ear against the door and listened. There was no sound from the nightclub. He looked around the storage room and spotted a broken metal dolly. From it he retrieved a long flat piece of metal and began to force the lock. After a few minutes of working the metal back and forth between the lock and the door jamb, it gave, and the door opened.

Heller cautiously put his head into the cloakroom and listened. Satisfied there was no one around, he stepped through the cloakroom into the darkened nightclub. The only illumination came from the picture window of the lighted swimming pool; it cast undulating bands on the wall and gave Heller the eerie sensation of being under water himself. He looked at the clock on the wall. It read two-ten. Every time the minute hand moved a notch, it made a distinct sound, like a lock snapping shut. Heller threw his overcoat over the back of a chair, drew another up for his feet and took up a position facing the picture window and the pool. And waited. And thought: of Sarah drowning him with desire; of her father patiently packing obscure manuals into manila envelopes; of the long trek that had taken him to Prague; of the erstwhile Viscount St. Albans, Francis Bacon, who had planted a message in an epilogue; and most of all, of Elizabeth, who was ready for endings as long as they weren't happy and she could first liberate her guinea fowl!

Eventually Heller dozed, his head against the back of the chair. Several times he shook himself awake and peered at the wall clock, but each time it was hours until his rendezvous with Juan Antonio and he slumped back against the chair and dozed again.

One of the bodyguards rang for the elevator. When it arrived, he nodded at Martin and signaled to his colleague at the door of the room. Juan Antonio, wearing a white terrycloth bathrobe supplied by the hotel to its special clients, entered the elevator. The second bodyguard brought up the rear. The elevator operator manipulated the controls. Slowly the elevator descended to the level below the main lobby. One of the Russians peeked through the round porthole in the locked door leading to the pool, confirmed that it was empty and opened the door with a large key. He locked it again as soon as Juan Antonio had entered.

Juan Antonio stripped off the bathrobe and handed it to one of the bodyguards, who frowned unhappily. He didn't appreciate the way Juan Antonio had of treating him like a servant. He flung the bathrobe over the back of a chair and fished in his pocket for a cigarette.

Juan Antonio prided himself on his swimming style. The son of a Bolivian brain surgeon, raised in the capital of La Paz, he had been the star sprinter on his high school team, and there had been talk of grooming him for international competitions—talk that was interrupted by his first arrest (for distributing leaflets), his escape (financed by his father) and his subsequent full-time devotion to political activities. But Juan Antonio never lost his love of swimming; it was, in fact, the availability of the pool that had attracted him to the Flora "between missions."

Now he did a series of knee bends and body twists to limber up his muscles, and he climbed onto the diving board anticipating the first exhilarating contact with the water.

Heller came awake with a start. It took him an instant to remember where he was and why he had come; the sight of the window in the pool brought it all back in a rush. He checked the wall clock. It was almost eight. Stiffly, his neck aching, he slipped into his overcoat, reached into the pocket and came out with his large German pistol. He checked to make sure a round was in the chamber and retreated until his back was against the handle of the fire door behind the bandstand. Then Heller sank into the distinctive crouching position that he had not quite mastered on the Farm in Virginia, his legs spread, the weight on the balls of his feet, the pistol thrust out in front and gripped with both hands. He sighted on the picture window of the swimming pool.

Juan Antonio came into view doing a perfect swan dive toward the center of the pool. His long hair flowed back away from his head. His eyes were wide open. Heller squeezed the trigger. The boom of the shot echoed through the nightclub. A small puncture hole appeared in the picture window. Instantly a jet stream of water arced out from the hole under enormous pressure. Cracks appeared in the thick glass, spreading outward from the puncture hole. And then, just as Heller had calculated, the dam broke; the window disintegrated under the weight of the water, which burst like a torrent into the nightclub.

Heller turned and raced out the fire door and up the steps to the back alley and safety.

Behind him, Juan Antonio was smashed against the side of the pool, then was sucked through the opening into the nightclub, where his broken body drifted face down amid the splinters of furniture and drums and bottles that washed back and forth with increasing gentleness as the force of the storm abated.

CHAPTER SIXTEEN

THE firemen had finished pumping out most of the water, and the male nurses, their trousers rolled up to their knees, their feet bare, were loading the corpse onto a stretcher. Juan Antonio was unrecognizable. His face had collapsed like a deflated balloon. One leg was folded straight back at the hip, giving to the body a grotesque shape that made the few people standing around turn away.

The Professor, his hands clasped firmly behind his back, watched the proceedings with a clinical eye for detail. Juan Antonio (according to his Russian bodyguards) had come down for his morning swim. The window in the side of the pool had given way. The water had flooded the bar. Juan Antonio had been sucked through along with the water.

The two co-managers of the hotel were claiming that the whole thing was an unfortunate accident. They were obliged to; their insurance, provided by a West German group, only covered accidents, and specifically excepted "acts of war."

The male nurses drew a white sheet over the body on the stretcher and waded toward their shoes and socks lined up in neat rows on the steps. Karol, tramping through the debris in fisherman's hip boots he had somehow acquired, came up to the Professor, who stood high and dry on a righted chair just inside the door. The young assistant held out a tray on which he had collected broken pieces of the window that once held back the water in the pool. The Professor sorted through the glass with his gloved fingers, and came up with one small shard that had a sixteenth of a circle on one edge. He held it up to the emergency light that had been rigged overhead.

"Bullet hole?" inquired Karol.

"I don't think anyone poked a finger through the glass," replied the Professor. Suddenly he was sorry for the sarcastic answer; but the closer the trail got to Schiller, the more edgy he felt. And he knew what Karol didn't know: The trail was specific now. Schiller was running scared. Somewhere in Prague he had left a calling card—and an invitation.

It only remained to attend the denouement.

He should have been elated. Two down, one to go. He should have felt as if he was saving his own life. But he didn't. If he felt anything, it was tiredness and emptiness; a sense of having wasted part of himself. Revenge wasn't sweet; it was bitter-sweet. And then he knew that his heart was no longer in it. The manhunt was over. The hell with the third man, the hell with the whole thing. He thought of Elizabeth and the clichés she somehow managed to get slightly wrong. Maybe she knew something—something important—that other people didn't know. Maybe the bending of the cliché was really an original way of looking at the world; a kind of poetic distortion. In the end, two hearts were better than one!

He would have to get Elizabeth out of what he had gotten her into; it was within the realm of possibility that once out, they would be able to construct something between them—Elizabeth with her bent clichés tossed like straws to the wind, and Heller with his penchant for hunting between the lines for the real text.

Overhead fresh gusts from the east had swept the sky clear

of clouds; the few that remained raced past high over the city. The sunlight was bright but not warm..The streets were crowded with shoppers; it was the day before a national holiday, and people hurried about their business with the thought of the three-day weekend looming ahead.

Heller wandered back in the general direction of Uncle Ludvik's flat, sticking to side streets whenever he could, moving with the flow of people when he couldn't. At one corner a preoccupied woman grabbed his arm and asked him something; Heller assumed she wanted directions. He pulled free and smiled and hurried off without saying a word. At Ludvik's building a young mother was trying to wrestle a heavy Russian baby carriage up the few steps to the lobby. Heller bent and lifted one end and helped her, and she thanked him profusely.

He took the steps to the attic two at a time. As he approached the door, he slowed down. The door was open a crack!

Heller flattened himself against the wall and drew his pistol. "Elizabeth?" he called softly. "Ludvik?"

There was no answer.

Heller looked around uncertainly. Overhead, an electric bulb cast long shadows on the wooden floor. He used his handkerchief to unscrew the bulb, throwing the hallway into pitch darkness. Then, his back to the wall, he eased open the door with his toe.

Inside, it was deathly quiet. Heller reached out and lobbed the light bulb into the apartment. As it struck the far wall and shattered, he flung himself through the door onto the floor. The room was in total darkness. Thick drapes, a relic from wartime blackouts, had been drawn across the windows. Flat on Ludvik's old carpet, his pistol gripped in both hands, Heller lay without moving a muscle, without breathing. And he stared into the blackness and listened with his eyes as well as his ears, listened as he had never listened in his life.

Except for the distant rumble of traffic, no sound reached his eyes or his ears.

Slowly, silently, Heller inched to his knees, and then to his feet, and began feeling along the wall for the light switch. The fingers of his left hand came to it, a smooth metal plate with many coats of paint on it. He flicked on the switch. The room was suddenly bathed in light from a globe overhead. Heller wheeled, his pistol out in front. Something across the room caught his eye; his pistol was pointing straight at it, his trigger finger was contracting—when his brain sorted out what it was.

It was Uncle Ludvik, wearing his coveralls, hanging by the neck from a piano wire attached to the hook on the wall that had held the heavy gilt mirror. The mirror had been taken down and leaned against the wall and shattered with a kick.

The apartment had been searched by someone who was angry—or frightened. Drawers had been yanked out and thrown along with their contents into a corner. Cushions had been ripped open. Books had been pulled from their bindings. Ludvik's precious oil paintings had been torn from their frames. The old narrow wooden bed had been demolished.

Stunned, unable to swallow, unable for a long moment to breathe or close his eyes, Heller turned as if in a dream toward the bathroom door. It had been locked and then had been kicked in. Now it hung on its hinges, ajar; obscene.

Gingerly Heller pushed aside the broken door with finger tips numb with fear. He had no doubt what he would find inside, and relief literally surged through him like an electric current when he discovered she was *not* in the bathroom. The small medicine chest was wide open. Heller ran his fingers over the items on the glass shelves—dental floss, smelling salts, eyedrops, half a dozen vials of homeopathic pills. Absently he reached down and turned off the cold water faucet, which had been dripping, and closed the door of the medicine chest.

Written on the outside mirror in lipstick was a message of sorts: "Ho   Sc."

If it had been the police, Heller reasoned, they'd still be here. So it wasn't the police. He picked up a lipstick on the sink and filled in the missing letters as if he were breaking a cipher back in his Company workroom: "Ho*rst* S*c*hiller."

"Schiller!" Heller turned back to survey the wrecked room and the corpse of Uncle Ludvik. "Schiller!"

He found the telephone directory buried under a stack of books that had been thrown into a corner. The embassy was listed under "United States." It gave three numbers. Heller tore out the page, traced the wire until he came across the telephone under the ruins of the bed, and carefully dialed the number.

A woman answered. Heller asked to speak to the military attaché. He was put through to another extension. After seven or eight rings, a man answered. Speaking carefully, measuring each word, Heller said, "I want to speak to Colonel Henderson, please."

The man on the other end seemed genuinely puzzled. "There is no Colonel Henderson here," he said.

"Colonel is not his real rank," Heller whispered fiercely into the phone. He felt his self-control slipping through his fingers. "Henderson is not his real name. It is a matter of someone's life or death. I must speak to him."

The man at the embassy said a few words to a secretary in the office, which Heller couldn't make out. Then he came back on the line. "You must be making a mistake," he said. "This is the American Embassy you're talking with. Who is it you were trying to reach? Hello? Hello?"

Heller never hung up. He just dropped the phone on the floor and left.

Unrelated details. Fragments. Figments (of despair?): the crowded old station full of peasants carrying back to the country-side whatever had tempted them in the city—East German radios, sweaters, long-playing records, a child's tricycle; the loudspeaker announcement of arrivals and departures echoing through the high dome with missing panes of glass; the train compartment with the tall, thin, awkward man wearing an astrakhan and ga-loshes, twin sisters in their fifties, a mother and son who never said a word to each other and their dog that farted; the conductor who punched the ticket and then recovered the tiny circle of paper from his puncher and deposited it in his jacket pocket; the fields full of winter cabbages stretching away to the horizon; the horizon, sharp as a razor's edge, perfect for celestial navigation.

The twin sisters got off first; and at a modern station soon after, the mother and son departed (still without a word to each other) along with their dog. Which left the tall, thin, awkward man, who was obviously relieved that the dog was no longer with them. Glancing up at Heller, adjusting his spectacles to better see what he was dealing with, he said in meticulous English, "I am not at all certain I would have survived another minute." He leaned toward Heller—they were sitting across from each other, their knees almost touching—and reflected, "What is so interesting, if you were to ask me, is the psychological environment. Here we are, six adults trapped for one reason or another in a train compartment. The dog lies at our feet blowing out a cloud of noxious gas, and nobody utters a word, as if the subject is too delicate to mention, as if the failure to mention it will somehow make it go away."

The man smiled, revealing two stainless steel incisors. "Permit me to introduce myself. I am Professor Emeritus Jozef Lako at your beck and call. I am going to Karlovy Vary for my annual fifteen-day mud-bath and spring-water cure, to which I attribute the longevity that I hope to enjoy."

Heller accepted the offered hand—he had no choice—and then he saw it again: the faded bluish numbers tattooed on the inside of the wrist! Heller studied the Professor's face, which looked naggingly familiar. "How did you know to speak to me in English?" he inquired.

The Professor blew his nose into a colorful handkerchief and carefully folded it away in his pocket. "I pride myself on my ability to recognize people by their nationality," he explained. "You are not Czech, of that one can be certain. There is no dentist in Prague to my knowledge who uses gold for inlays. Gold teeth, yes. But inlays, never." He apologized with a cautious toss of his head. "I spotted yours when you yawned. To go on: You are not Scandinavian, that much is clear from the overall look of you. You could have been German, but your lips aren't heavy enough. You could have been English, but your cheekbones aren't high enough. Which more or less reduced it to France, Spain or the United States of America. You are not at all Latin enough in the eyes to be Spanish, and not at all latent enough in the eyes to be French. Which"—Professor Emeritus Lako shrugged modestly—"left the United States of America."

Heller recognized the Professor now, as much by his manner of speaking as by his physical appearance. What a coincidence to find himself sharing a compartment with the very same man who had been lecturing on Francis Bacon at the university!

The talkative Professor was just what the doctor ordered; Heller was bone-tired and frightened that he had started something he couldn't finish, and he needed someone to *listen* to. It took his mind off his troubles. The Professor was one of those people who loved the sound of his own voice. To keep him going, all you had to do was interject an occasional "How right you are" or "I see your point." Or simply nod. Once launched, he seemed to plunge along out of inertia, leaping from subject to subject with transitions that would not have withstood any reasonable academic test.

"Of course, he made a big point of telling everyone he came from a fine old family," the Professor was saying of someone Heller had never heard of. Outside, the starless darkness closed in on the speeding train like a tunnel. "If I told him once, I told him a thousand times: All families are old families. Some just kept better records than others. His central thesis, if I understood him correctly, was the essential absence of subtlety in all language. The acid test—which none of the fourteen languages he spoke fluently, or the twelve others he could read, met—seemed to be whether it had words to differentiate between the love of someone for, say, a mother, a brother, a friend, a sexual partner, a dog, a flower, love of life, love that consisted mostly of physical desire, love that was made up of patience and habit, puppy loves, first loves, second loves, and so on and so forth." The Professor snorted and tossed his head in admiration. "He was never to my knowledge translated, which is why his work is generally not known outside of my native Slovakia. The one edition that exists was printed privately. In it, he succumbed to the common temptation we all of us have."

"Which temptation is that?" Heller asked politely.

The Professor seemed surprised at the question. "Why, the temptation to assume a morally superior tone, of course. He himself couldn't resist. He had a strange attitude toward death too. When he married, his father-in-law obliged him to draw up a will. It was a point of pride with him that he didn't use the common expression 'When I die,' but rather 'If I die.' He is buried in

Banska Bystrica. Strange man. Died of syphilis. Remarkable tomb. On it you will find the words 'Death is a debt one owes to nature. I've paid'! " Professor Emeritus Lako smiled philosophically. " 'I've paid'! Sets one to thinking, doesn't it?"

The Professor fished a gold Patek Philippe from the pocket of his vest and snapped it open. "We should be getting there in a moment or two. A car from my hotel is due to meet me. Will you give me the pleasure of dropping you somewhere?"

Heller declined politely. He had no idea what he would do when he arrived, but whatever it was, he would do it alone. The train lost speed. The brakes gripped the wheels, sparks flew and the train pulled to a stop in the station. Heller climbed down, then reached up to take the Professor's small plastic valise. He handed it back to him on the platform.

"Thank you," said the Professor, and then, oddly, he hurried off without a word.

Heller looked up at the well-lit sign over the entrance to the station—KARLOVY VARY—printed in heavy black letters. In smaller letters underneath was the name the spa was known by in the West—"Karlsbad." The few people who had gotten off the train walked quickly through the station to the street, where they disappeared in taxis or cars. Heller glanced around uncertainly. The train was starting out of the station. Steam swirled around his feet. At the far end of the platform, just beyond the station building, he could make out the dim figures of two men in raincoats and fedoras. Heller looked back over his shoulder and spotted two more at the other end of the platform behind him. He turned and walked briskly into the station, which was empty except for an old man behind the ticket grill and a peasant woman mopping the floor. Heller made his way through the damp-smelling waiting room to the front door of the station and stepped out into the cold night.

An ancient silver taxi, the kind that was in vogue before what the socialist countries call the Great Patriotic War, was waiting at the curb, its motor idling, a jet of exhaust coming quietly out of its tail pipe. The back door of the taxi was invitingly ajar. A man sat behind the wheel looking straight ahead. Heller hesitated. To his left the two men in raincoats and fedoras were coming around the end of the station building. To his right the other two were also coming into view.

Heller descended the wide marble stairs of the station and circled the taxi, examining the driver, who looked like a mortician. He was middle-aged, dressed in a neat black suit, and he wore a hearing aid. He avoided all eye contact and stared straight ahead.

With a last glance at the four figures closing in on him, Heller ducked into the back of the taxi. The driver, with a professional gesture, reached back and pulled the door closed, pushed down the flag starting the meter, then carefully threw the car into gear. Moving with tired elegance, the taxi crawled across the cobblestones of the square in front of the station and turned into a wide boulevard that ran the length of a deep valley. Above, on the slopes towering over the valley, stood the hotels and pensions and villas of the spa, their lights twinkling in place of stars in the moist air.

Heller heard the taxi meter clicking away. Every so often a new number dropped into view. "Nice night," Heller commented. When the driver said nothing, he tapped him on the shoulder. "What does this mean, fifteen?" he asked, pointing to the meter. "Fifteen what? Rupees? Stodinki? Or maybe pence? That must be it, fifteen pence."

The driver, his two hands fixed firmly on the large steering wheel, remained impassive.

Heller looked up at the famous Imperial Sanatorium on one slope, with its two distinctive towers illuminated by floodlights. It was so high it was linked to the spa by cable car. "How do you feel about taking carrots from babies?" Heller asked the driver. The sound of his own voice reassured him, reminded him he was alive, though how long this state of grace would last was anybody's guess. "What's your position on threads in haystacks?" Heller leaned forward until his mouth almost touched the driver's hearing aid. "In your opinion," he yelled, "who plays when the mouse is away? The dog? The cat? All of the above? While you're at it, which is better than one, two hearts or two heads?"

The driver ignored his passenger. They passed the huge glass-covered arcade where in season hordes of people holding mugs strolled around as if they didn't have a care in the world, sucking up through bent-glass straws the purging water of the spa. Turning left, the taxi climbed along a narrower street lined with run-down prewar hotels boarded up during the off-season. Heller pivoted in his seat to look out the narrow rear window; as far as he could make out, nobody appeared to be following him. He shrugged with a certain fatefulness. Nobody had to follow him; he didn't know where he was going, but they did. They had even sent a car around.

Once across the valley, the taxi turned into a manufacturing district—porcelain and glassware factories, a modern light bulb plant, several stores and warehouses, then an entire block where the buildings had been torn down to make way for an industrial complex. Ahead, Heller could make out the outlines of an enormous old warehouse standing off by itself, set back from the street. The taxi headed directly for it and pulled up before a small side door. A bright bulb gleamed over the door. The driver stopped the meter and reached back to open the passenger door for Heller.

Heller looked at the open door without much appetite. "Don't you want me to pay you?" He laughed nervously. "After all, a bird in the pocket is worth two in the bush." He studied the driver's expressionless face for some hint of the fate that awaited him. "Then again, maybe it isn't," he said, and he jumped out of the taxi. Behind him, the door immediately slammed closed and the mortician drove off without so much as a look over his shoulder.

Heller approached the door, which was open a crack, and peeked in. The interior was pitch black. Standing off to one side, his back against the building, he slid the finger tips of his right hand in the crack and eased the door open the width of his foot. He waited for a long moment, and then peered in again. Nothing. No light. No sound. Only a dense, frightening stillness.

He flattened himself against the outside of the building. His heart was pounding against his rib cage; suddenly it mattered a great deal whether he was on the giving end or the receiving end of the violence! For a moment he thought how ironic it would be to have a heart attack now. The world would never learn who really wrote Shakespeare's plays! He drew in several long, measured breaths, restoring some semblance of calm to his body; to his mind also.

Heller made a last effort to think things through. He had followed the trail like a schoolboy on a picnic—Karlovy Vary, the taxi, the warehouse, the open door. He had done exactly what he was supposed to do. But he knew that if he stepped through the door he would never come out alive; and more than ever, he wanted to save his life. Yet he had to go in—because he wanted to save her life too. Her life and his life were two sides of the same life.

He tried to imagine what a professional like Henderson would do. He would weigh the odds and turn his back on the warehouse and leave, that's what Henderson would do. Heller looked up and down the length of the building. A dozen or so paces farther along the wall to his left he could make out an office window.

He took off his overcoat, removed the pistol from its pocket and rolled the coat into a ball. With his right hand he gripped the edge of the open door. Then he flung it open against its hinges and in the same instant pitched the rolled-up overcoat as far into the warehouse as he could. Then he made his way to the office window along the wall.

In another incarnation, Heller—then a simple cipher clerk, palindrome inventor, impeccably shabby Company man, lover of Sarah—had felt that mere hurrying would solve most problems; now he had an instinctive feeling that he must do whatever he did slowly, painstakingly. It was what Solzhenitsyn called work in the final inch. He raised his eyes above the sill and looked through the window. All he saw was his own gaunt face staring back. He reached up and tried the window. It opened smoothly under the pressure of his fingers. Was this a good omen or a bad one? Heller wished that someone could tell him, could help him. He was tired of going around in ones. He slid a leg over the sill, climbed into the warehouse, dropped to the floor in a crouch and listened.

After a while his night vision started to come to him and he began to make out objects: a desk, a wooden filing cabinet, a bookcase, another door. Rising cautiously to his feet, he inched his way toward it. He felt around carefully. There was a window in the door, but it was covered with a shade. Behind the shade the panes of glass seemed exceptionally thin. And cold. With infinite slowness Heller turned the knob and eased open the door. There was a very faint squeal of hinges, like some sound an insect would make. Heller listened for a moment, then let himself into the warehouse proper and gently closed the door behind him. The click it made when it snapped shut seemed to resound through the enormous space that Heller sensed opening before him.

Holding his pistol in his right hand, the barrel pointing toward the floor, Heller started forward. One step. Then another. Specks of light seemed to dance along ice walls on either side of him. The cement floor was cold underfoot as he advanced along it, between the curious corridors that seemed to fold themselves around him.

Off to one side there was the distinct sound of a master switch being thrown, and an instant later the electricity reached the naked bulbs hanging on long electric cords from the high roof. Each bulb had over it an old-fashioned round reflector, which cast pools of light on the cement floor, surrounded by shadows and darkness.

As the lights came on, Heller tensed, then slowly sank into his firing crouch, the pistol gripped in both hands out in front, his head swiveling from side to side in search of a target. He saw now why he thought the walls on either side of him were made of ice. He was in a kind of crystal palace, a storage house for giant slabs of glass and mirror, which were leaning upright on wooden racks placed in endless rows. Whichever way he looked he saw reflected pools of light and several versions of himself bent over his pistol, his mouth open, listening with darting eyes.

Sticking to the shadows between the pools of light, dwarfed by the giant slabs of glass and mirror, walking upright, his pistol dangling from his right hand, breathing only occasionally, Heller made his way down the corridors of crystal. Again and again he caught glimpses of a figure moving off to one side, or just ahead; but it was an image of himself in one of the mirrors. His eyes searched the heights and then the side alleys that angled off at intersections. He peered through several layers of glass to the mirrors in the alley parallel to the one he was in.

Suddenly, at a crossroad of alleys, with mirrors and glass

slabs casting back half a dozen reflections of himself, he stopped in his tracks. Directly ahead, seemingly suspended in air, was Colonel Henderson. His hair was matted with dried blood. He crouched in the prescribed Company firing position, legs spread, arms extended, both hands holding a pistol which was pointing directly at Heller.

Colonel Henderson tossed his head to clear the hair away from his eyes. In another place, in another time, the gesture would have captured Henderson's sense of bravado. But here and now it seemed almost like a nervous tic. The effect was pathetic, almost demented.

For an endless moment Henderson sighted on Heller's stomach, and Heller unconsciously sucked in his breath to receive the bullet. Then Henderson's mouth began to work, but it took a moment for any sound to emerge. His voice, when Heller finally heard it, was distorted with hate and almost unrecognizable.

"I'm Colonel Henderson," he snarled. His eyes bulged behind his National Health spectacles. His tongue darted out to moisten his lips. "Henderson isn't my real name. Colonel isn't my real rank. No matter." He blinked several times, as if clearing his clouded vision. "No matter. Even if you do precisely as I tell you, there is no chance you will come out of this alive."

"Where is she?" Heller demanded. To his own ear his words sounded hollow and distant, as if they were not the original but the echo.

The barrel of Henderson's pistol described a small circle. "Tell him," Henderson commanded in a high-pitched voice. "Tell him it's you who's trying to kill him, not us."

Heller looked around. All he saw were reflections of Henderson and himself. "Tell whom?"

"Schiller," Henderson exploded. He sank more deeply into his firing crouch. "Tell Schiller. Tell him about the girl in Munich."

"Schiller's here?"

"Tell him how you blackmailed us into sending you," Henderson shouted. He was ranting now, the phrases slipping out disjointed, barely coherent. Saliva trickled from one corner of his mouth.

Heller turned and called into the crystal alleys: "Schiller!"

The name echoed through the warehouse.

Henderson was rapidly losing what control he had left. His words came out in great husky sobs. "Tell him, goddamnit . . . the messages you stole . . . the Farm . . . the girl in Munich. Tell him it was your idea . . . the frontier . . ." Henderson was screaming now. "You should have shot me at the frontier. You had no right . . ." He brought the pistol up and tossed the hair away from his eyes and was about to jerk, not squeeze, the trigger when a single shot echoed through the corridors of glass and mirror.

Henderson's pistol slipped from his fingers and clattered to the cement. His eyes widened (in surprise? in relief?). Suddenly calm, he sank to his knees. The muscles in his face began to relax. When he spoke, he was able to recapture some of his old bravado. "We're the good guys," he taunted Heller. His body was racked by a fit of coughing. Blood spilled from his mouth. "Wait till you see the—"

He pitched forward, his face slamming into the cement, dead.

Heller finished the sentence for him: "—bad guys." And somehow he knew exactly where to look. He raised his eyes and turned to the right; and there he was, floating in several layers of glass, suspended in the crystal palace, obscenely close to her, his right hand gripping her tightly around the chest, his left hand holding an Egyptian nine-millimeter Parabellum pressed to her skull.

Elizabeth raised her face as she would have to the sun, if there had been a sun. Around them there was a stillness so profound it felt as if time were standing still. She tried to smile. Silent tears streamed down her cheeks. She shut her eyes.

Heller waited in the stillness for the shot to ring out, the shot that would end all life for him a second time.

Speaking in English, his pronunciation correct, his voice cold, Schiller demanded, "Tell me what? What are you supposed to tell me?"

The voice didn't seem to come from the image, but rather from *behind* Heller. He turned quickly. There was *another* Schiller, floating in several layers of glass, suspended, obscenely close to Elizabeth. Off to the right there was a third image! And to the left a fourth!

"I'm supposed to tell you that if things go according to plan, it's the early bird who generally catches the worm," Heller called.

Schiller yelled, "Don't play games with me." His voice echoed from image to image. "You know I'm not bluffing. I will pull the trigger if I have to. The girl is CIA. Henderson was CIA. You are CIA. Why is the CIA trying to kill me?" He took a step forward, pushing Elizabeth along with him, and screamed out the question a second time. "Why is the Company trying to eliminate me? The killing in Munich wiped out the last shred of doubt about me in anybody's mind."

"The killing in Munich wiped out doubt?" Heller wasn't sure he had heard correctly.

"I was in a position to perform services for your Central Intelligence Agency no one ever dreamed of," Schiller burst out. "We could have infiltrated every terrorist movement in the world. We could have used them . . ."

As Schiller ranted on, Heller once again had the uncomfortable sense of being both the participant and the observer at the same time. The participant was stunned at the implications of what Schiller was saying. The observer, coolly detached, was vaguely aware that something was not quite right, some detail that he couldn't identify. The voice of Schiller didn't appear to be coming from the image of Schiller he was looking at; but with all the echoes, Heller couldn't be sure exactly where it was coming from. And then it dawned on him. The Schiller he was looking at had his *right* hand around Elizabeth and his *left* hand holding the gun to her head. Heller closed his eyes and recalled the film clip taken in front of the consulate in Munich. He could see it clearly. That Schiller had his *left* hand around Sarah and his *right* hand holding the pistol to her head. Schiller was right-handed! Heller looked again at Schiller's image—and realized it was a mirror image! He looked over his shoulder. Of the four Schillers he could see, two held the pistol in their right hand.

He had to keep him talking.

"You thought you were working for the Company?" challenged Heller.

"I *was* working for the Company," cried Schiller. "We planned the raid together. We picked the American consulate so nobody would suspect the CIA. The Germans were supposed to give in to us. Your people tried to make them give in. But the Chancellor turned out to be more stubborn than we calculated. The killing of the girl—that was my idea." He said it with unconcealed pride. "A soldier in the field has to innovate. I did what had to be done. I improved on the original plan. We could have had the world in the palm of our hands."

"We?" sneered Heller.

A twisted, ironic smile appeared on Elizabeth's face. "We are them," she said.

Schiller, shouting in frustration, cried, "Terrorism is a sickness. I am the cure. All those years wasted!" He struggled to control himself. "All those years." And then he screamed, *"Years!"* The word echoed through the warehouse. "Y-e-a-r-s . . . e-a-r-s."

Heller thought he had it now. His eyes darted from one mirror to another, calculating angles, estimating distances, following the voice to its origin, to Schiller, the real Schiller, standing behind a giant pane of glass.

"The CIA doesn't want to kill you," Heller called out. His mind was working fast. "I want to kill you. I was going to marry the girl you murdered in Munich."

Elizabeth's eyes opened. A lot of things were falling into place.

"I blackmailed the Company into sending me," Heller plunged on. "I wanted revenge."

"Revenge!" Schiller's body rocked with wild laughter. He released his grip on Elizabeth and stepped past her, his fingers clutching the front of her shirt. "Henderson was telling the truth. It's not the CIA. It's only you!"

Elizabeth wrenched herself out of Schiller's grasp and dashed away. Schiller spun around toward her, dropped into the classic Company firing crouch, thrust forward his pistol in both hands and aimed carefully at her back as she darted between mirrors.

Heller wheeled and sighted on the image of Schiller he had decided was the real one. He breathed in and let half the breath out and started to squeeze, not jerk, the trigger, thinking all the while that to hit something you have to want to hit it. And he wanted to hit it, he wanted it so badly he could taste blood on his tongue. He didn't so much aim at Schiller as *connect* himself to him. He cast out in his mind's eye a line from the business end of his pistol to the target and willed the bullet to travel along it.

Heller's pistol exploded and recoiled. The giant pane of glass between him and Schiller, shattered by the impact of the bullet, turned opaque. From behind what had now become a screen, a shot rang out, and then a second. Off to one side, half a dozen mirrors splintered. Shards of glass flew off in all directions, landing on the cement with a distinctly musical sound.

Bleeding profusely from a bullet through his neck, his eyes wide open and totally sightless, Schiller staggered out from behind the opaque pane of glass and sank to the ground. What life there was left in him ebbed quietly. The small pool of blood collecting around his body grew larger. A finger twitched, then was still. There was a soft gurgling from his throat, and then no sound at all.

Elizabeth came up to Heller. The Mona Lisa–like smile began to creep over his features as he realized that it was over, all over. Then he remembered what might have happened, and the smile froze and ebbed like a tide going out. He put an arm over Elizabeth's shoulder and drew her close, and she leaned tiredly against him. He could feel her trembling.

"It's finished," Heller comforted her.

"You are wrong," she told him quietly. "It is only just beginning!"

Something in her tone made him look at her. She was staring past his shoulder, tears welling in her ash-colored eyes. Heller followed her gaze and saw what she had seen and knew she was right; it was only just beginning.

In the aisle behind them a dozen Czech soldiers armed with submachine pistols were advancing toward them. Heller glanced to his right and then to his left, knowing all the while what he would see. The soldiers were coming toward them from every direction.

Leading one of the groups, his hands folded behind his back, his galoshes pounding heavily on the cement floor, his head cocked inquisitively to one side, was Professor Emeritus Lako. He walked directly up to Schiller's body, stirred it with his toe and muttered something in German (a line of poetry? a curse?). He continued to stare for a moment at Schiller, then abruptly turned and planted himself in front of Heller, cleared his throat and politely held out a gloved hand, palm up.

At first Heller wasn't sure what he wanted. Then he understood. He placed his P-38, butt first, in the Professor's palm. The Professor passed it to Karol and turned back to Heller.

"Am I permitted to ask you a question?" Heller inquired.

"You can always ask," Professor Emeritus Lako informed him.

"Exactly what is it you are Professor Emeritus of?"

Lako smiled grimly. "The human comedy," he said. "On that subject, I am the world's living expert."

CHAPTER
SEVENTEEN

HELLER and Elizabeth were sitting side by side on a bench in the back of the covered military truck. They were obviously taking back roads, because the ride was a rough one. A baby-faced soldier, his submachine pistol resting across his knees, sat on one side of them. Karol sat on the other. Professor Emeritus Lako sat across from them. He was holding on to the edge of his bench with both hands. His galoshes were planted flat on the floor of the truck. The bouncing around had caused his socks to fall to his ankles, but he restrained the impulse to pull them up again; he considered it would be undignified.

Heller called across, "Could I trouble you for a cigarette?"

"No trouble." Professor Emeritus Lako handed Heller a cigarette, then took one himself. He limited himself to three cigarettes a day, and had already used up his ration, but he decided he deserved a bonus. He lit up and tossed his cigarette lighter to Heller, who started to light his, had second thoughts, extinguished the lighter and tossed it back. Then he handed back the cigarette. Professor Emeritus Lako took it without comment, as if what had transpired was the most natural thing in the world. He pulled his gold watch from his vest pocket and clicked it open. "We should be there quite soon," he assured Heller.

"Where are we going?" Elizabeth asked.

Professor Emeritus Lako smiled encouragingly. "You will know that, dear lady, when we get there."

Heller asked, "How did you first get onto me?"

That brought a short laugh from the Professor. "I got onto you, as you put it, as soon as you set a foot across our frontier." When Heller looked puzzled, the Professor elaborated. "What do you think, Karol? There is no harm in telling him. We were tipped off that an American agent was coming across. He was said to be on a mission of assassination. This in itself was very unusual. The Americans are adept as anyone at this sort of thing, but they usually leave the dirty work to mercenaries—to people hired for the occasion. Generally East Europeans who speak the language and can melt away once the mission is accomplished. But the detail that made the tip-off really intriguing was that it came from the Americans themselves!" The Professor raised a palm in protest. "It goes without saying, they didn't know I knew this. It was Karol here who put his talented nose to the ground and tracked it down. The information was given to us by the Bulgarians, who got it from a Pole who specializes in tidbits of this kind. This particular Pole not only passed on the information, but for a little extra consideration he let us have the source, which turned out to be your Central Intelligence Agency's station chief in Prague, a very fat man now recuperating in a German hospital from a rather nasty knee wound."

Professor Emeritus Lako sucked thoughtfully on his cigarette —he had a peculiar way of holding it tucked between his thumb and third finger—and then burst into a fit of coughing. "Foul things," he managed to say, holding out his cigarette. "Bulgarian tobacco. Very strong. I keep trying . . . give them up."

"It is one of my pet projects too," admitted Heller.

"Where was I?" Professor Emeritus Lako continued.

"You were up to the fat man recuperating from a knee wound," Karol prompted him.

"Just so. Consider the situation from my point of view: I

242

knew where I could find an American agent who had crossed our border illegally—an old shed near a windmill—"

Heller's brain was racing ahead. "You surrounded the windmill, not the shed!" he exclaimed. "You let me slip through your fingers on purpose!"

Professor Emeritus Lako spread his hands apologetically. "You have a logical head on your shoulders. You see the contours of my problem. I had to do something, or the Americans would have been suspicious about my failure to act on the information I had received. But I was curious to know why the Americans had denounced one of their own agents. The part of me that is a serious student of the human comedy suspected that he had come to kill someone whom the Americans didn't want dead. Now someone the Americans want alive, as opposed to dead, is of great interest to a man unfortunate enough to be in my line of work."

The driver pulled back the flap separating the cab from the rest of the truck and asked the Professor something in Czech. "He wants to know how close to bring the truck," Elizabeth whispered to Heller. "The Professor told him, Within walking distance, but far enough away so as not to be seen."

Professor Emeritus Lako's cigarette was burning dangerously close to his lips, but he continued to puff away at it without alarm. "When all is said and done, we only made one relatively minor miscalculation, isn't that so, Karol? We were told someone was coming over on an assassination mission. And we naturally assumed he would be a professional."

"How do you know I'm not?" challenged Heller.

Professor Emeritus Lako's eyes widened innocently. "Why, you're still alive, that's how. You succeeded because you are an amateur. A professional would have failed."

Heller accepted this with a philosophical smile. "How long did it take you to find me in Prague?"

The Professor averted his eyes in embarrassment. "We found you," he replied, "when you found her." Heller glanced quickly at Elizabeth. "No, no, it's not at all what you are thinking," the Professor added hurriedly. "She is not working for us. Though in all modesty I must tell you that she eventually would have. You see, we were keeping close track of the fat man when he recruited her. We planted microphones in the very unusual nest that she lived in and in her car, and we waited for her to establish herself firmly with the Americans before attempting to turn her. Her little operation was relatively harmless. Obviously the Americans were just testing her. She would ultimately have been given more important things to do."

"You soon knew whom I had come to kill." Heller frowned. "But you didn't try to stop me."

The Professor became aware of his cigarette, reluctantly dropped it to the floor and ground it out underfoot. He looked up and tapped his forefinger against his skull. "Remember, I am a Professor Emeritus of the human comedy! You weren't after the German girl Gretchen. You weren't after Juan Antonio. Neither one of them was . . . significant." The Professor repeated the word with emphasis. "*Significant.*" His eyes took on a distant look, and he said in a low voice, "Horst Schiller *was* significant—to our Russian friends, to the Palestinians, to *me*. As a matter of absolute routine, a man with access to as many people and groups as Schiller has to be closely watched. There was never anything to make us suspect him—until I discovered that you wanted to kill him and the Americans didn't want you to! That they were in fact prepared to shoot you down in the street to prevent you from even getting near him!" The Professor's expression softened. "I must tell you"—he spoke directly to Elizabeth—"that I am not without feelings. I play the game because the game is fascinating to play. But I would have stopped Schiller from killing Ludvik if I could have. We were following Schiller. We came on the scene *after* he had left." He shrugged philosophically. "Death is a debt one owes to nature, isn't that so? Ludvik's paid."

Heller said, "You realized Schiller was trying to lure me to Karlovy Vary, to the warehouse?"

Professor Emeritus Lako said tiredly. "He obviously had something important to ask you. It only remained for us to hear the question—and your answer."

"And then you knew," Heller said.

"And then we knew. Schiller worked for your CIA. He was infiltrating the various terrorist groups, not to mention the Soviet KGB, and reporting to Washington. And to establish his bona fides beyond all doubt, he had to commit a murder. Any murder would do. Which brings us to you. He killed a young lady, your young lady, and you went after him for revenge."

The truck slowed down and stopped. The driver cut the motor. Professor Emeritus Lako squinted at Heller. "You told Schiller you had blackmailed the CIA into sending you." His manner was casual, too casual. "I don't mean to be indelicate, but with what did you blackmail them?"

Heller's eyes danced with excitement. "Some cables that will ruin them if they ever get into print."

The Professor accepted this with a nod. "And will they?"

When Heller didn't immediately answer, he repeated the question. "Will they ever get into print?"

Heller saw where this was leading; used correctly, it was a ticket out of the country. "Not while we're in Czechoslovakia, they won't."

The Professor folded his hands in his lap and stared at the canvas roof of the truck for several minutes. Then he looked at Heller. Then at the roof again. Finally he said, "The CIA went along with you after you blackmailed them, so you obviously did have your hands on some incriminating material." He spoke very carefully, as if words were mines and he didn't want to step on one by accident. "I gather from conversations we overheard at the nest that you are something of an expert on one-time ciphers. This would suggest that the material you had came from messages you deciphered for them. After you left America, the CIA tried several times to eliminate you. That in turn would suggest that they had recovered the incriminating material and no longer considered your blackmail threat valid. You are an intelligent man, you must be as aware of this as I am."

Heller said, "They may have recovered the material, yes. But I hid a second set!"

"How can I know you are telling the truth?" asked the Professor.

"What do you have to lose?" argued Heller. "Horst Schiller killed my lady in Munich. Horst Schiller worked for the CIA. If I have the material, as I say, I have every reason to want to use it. Even if I'm lying, the least I'll do is go back and tell everyone who will listen that the CIA employed the terrorist who led the raid in Munich."

245

"Just so." Professor Emeritus Lako glanced again at his gold watch. "I assume she is part of the bargain we are concocting?"

Heller nodded. "I'll need proof—a witness."

Elizabeth looked inquiringly at Heller. "He's letting us go?"

Heller reached for her hand. "He's letting us go," he told her.

Karol helped the Professor down from the back of the truck. Heller and Elizabeth followed him out. The morning was cloudy and bitterly cold, but no one seemed to notice it. The Professor linked his arm through Heller's and walked with him to within sight of the bus. Karol and Elizabeth lagged behind. "Tell me," said the Professor, his voice conspiratorially low, "do you really think Bacon wrote the plays?" He smiled apologetically. "Our microphones . . ."

"There's absolutely no doubt about it."

"And you can prove it, once and for all?"

"I broke the cipher," Heller said. "Nobody will be able to ignore it."

"And you will publicize this when you return?"

"Of course."

"Ah"—Professor Emeritus Lako sighed—"just so."

Heller could make out the frontier post now, and the tourists peering impatiently out of bus windows. Several border guards stood next to the crossing gate, smoking and talking in undertones. Professor Emeritus Lako stopped almost reluctantly. "It is better if I leave you here," he told Heller.

Heller asked, "How long have you been on the trail of Schiller?"

The Professor pursed his lips; there was more than a hint of bitterness to his expression. "So you read between the lines. I have been following the career of Horst Schiller ever since he turned up at Patrice Lumumba University in Moscow." The Professor understood that he had raised more questions than he had answered. He clasped his hands behind his back, elevated his chin and sniffed at the cold morning air. "During the war I was betrayed into the hands of the Gestapo by a man I considered to be a good friend. I trusted him with my life, and as a result I almost lost it. The man's name was Karl Schiller. Horst Schiller was his son."

Heller pushed his eyeglasses back up along his nose with a forefinger. "You were after revenge too?"

"Just so."

"Was it worth it?" Heller asked.

The Professor's eyes seemed to cloud over. "It was . . . very satisfying. And you?"

Heller glanced at Elizabeth, who was waiting for him a few paces away. "I wouldn't do it again," he confessed, "but it was just as advertised. It brought me back from the dead."

The tourists in the bus were grumbling with annoyance, but not too loudly; they were, after all, still *inside* a Communist country. They had been held at the frontier for two hours. "Believe me, it is merely a formality," the harassed customs officer had explained, but he never specified what the formality was, and nobody dared ask. When the doors to the bus finally swung open and a man and woman climbed aboard, the English tourists, now twenty-six days out of London and counting, understood that this was what they had been held at the border for. Then the rail-thin schoolteacher with the ruddy cheeks and the hairpiece recognized Heller. "Good God," he cried. "It's *him* again!"

Heller couldn't resist. Speaking in a loud voice to Elizabeth, he said in perfect English, "That jacket of his must have been in its prime in the forties. And with the wig on, he doesn't look all that fresh either."

Heller and Elizabeth settled into seats in the back of the bus. The motor started. The soldiers cranked up the crossing gate. The English tourists, glued to their places, never said a word as the bus crept toward the Austrian side of the frontier.

Professor Emeritus Lako stood with his hands clasped behind his back, staring after the disappearing bus. Karol, off to one side, stamped his feet on the ground and blew onto his finger tips, which were numb with cold. "Do you really think he has it?" he asked the Professor. His voice sounded brittle in the thin morning air.

The professor seemed to *absorb* the question. His lids half closed and a faraway look occupied the territory in and around his eyes, almost as if he were following a trail of inquiry to another country, or another century.

"He has it," Professor Emeritus Lako said confidently. He permitted the barest trace of a smile to lurk on his blue lips.

Karol, who thought he knew all of the Professor's moods, found himself in the presence of a new one. The half smile of smug satisfaction seemed to transform the Professor's face. And then he recognized the smile! It was the same one that was frozen on the lips of the woman painted by Leonardo da Vinci and called the Mona Lisa!

CHAPTER
EIGHTEEN

THE bus pulled into the parking lot just as the cars on the highway were starting to turn on their headlights. The air brakes took hold, the bus stopped and the doors swung open. The passengers filed out and headed for the diner. "Three-quarters of an hour," the driver called over his shoulder.

Heller and Elizabeth found a booth next to the window. The waitress wrote their order on her pad and returned a few minutes later with two number four club specials, one with mayo, one without. Later they ordered two teas, one with cream, one without. Absently stirring his tea, Heller asked Elizabeth if she happened to have a cigarette.

"You don't smoke," she reminded him.

"You're right," Heller agreed. "I don't smoke." He turned to a man in the next booth. "Can I bum a cigarette from you?"

The man held out a pack. Heller pulled a cigarette from it, accepted matches and turned back to Elizabeth, the cigarette dangling from his lips. He struck the match and held it just out of reach of the end of the cigarette, seemingly mesmerized by the flame. Then he muttered, "The hell with it," and lit up. He dragged on the cigarette and held the smoke in his lungs and then slowly exhaled through his nose.

Elizabeth said, "You *didn't* smoke." She leaned toward him across the table. "When are you going to tell me?"

Heller, caught up in the luxury of smoking again, played innocent. "Tell you what?"

Elizabeth gestured with her eyes toward the dinner. "Tell me why we've come all this way to eat in this particular restaurant in the middle of someplace called New Jersey. To say it frankly, the food isn't that good."

"I wanted to see my horoscope," Heller explained. He slid out of the booth and motioned her to follow him. The young manager with apple-red cheeks looked up from his cash register as Heller was passing. "It's you again. You've come back for your Astro-Flash?" He laughed.

"As a matter of fact, yes," admitted Heller.

He led Elizabeth to the Astro-Flash computer in the alcove near the front door. He fished in his pocket for some loose change, picked out two quarters and inserted them in the slot, then punched in his birth year, day and hour. "I was born on the eighth day of the first month of 1943, at three-thirty in the afternoon. Leo was ascendant."

The computer digested the information, buzzed for a long moment, then began to spew out Heller's horoscope. A Mona Lisa–like smile spread across his face as the printout slipped through his fingers. It read:

FROM STATION CHIEF MEXICO CITY FOR DIRECTOR'S EYES ONLY STOP COMMUNIST PARTY SECRETARY'S DEATH RULED ACCIDENTAL STOP FORENSIC STUDY FAILED DISCOVER EITHER PELLET OR TRACE OF POISON STOP REQUEST YOU DEPOSIT HUNDRED THOUSAND SWISS FRANCS IN ZURICH ACCOUNT OF LOCAL MEDICAL EXAMINER ANOTHER HUNDRED THOUSAND TO ATTORNEY GENERAL WHO AC- CEPTED ACCIDENTAL DEATH RULING AND CLOSED CASE.

FROM STATION CHIEF ROME FOR DIRECTOR'S EYES ONLY
STOP MONEY DEPOSITED IN GENEVA. ·. . .

Elizabeth was all for striking while the iron was heavy. "Hot," Heller corrected her. "You strike while the iron is hot. Not heavy." But he took her point and put the call through as soon as they arrived in New York. Frank Molton, the journalist who had once phoned him in Washington, came on the line after a few moments. Heller told Molton who he was. He could hear a quick intake of breath at the other end of the line. "There are a lot of rumors around town about you," Molton said.

"I'll come by and confirm them," Heller said.

They met in the managing editor's office on the sixth floor. Molton was there, the managing editor, one of the editorial writers, a secretary who recorded in shorthand everything that was said, and (on Heller's insistence) the literary page editor, who sat off in a corner not at all sure why he had been invited.

"My God, my God," Molton kept murmuring as he scanned the printout Heller had given him. His eyes darted hungrily from paragraph to paragraph. The managing editor, reading over his shoulder, whistled through his teeth. "The Director specifically denied that one under oath," he exclaimed, tapping his finger on the message headed FROM STATION CHIEF MANILA.

Heller wandered over to the literary page editor in the corner. "My name's Heller," he introduced himself. He pulled up a seat. "I used to work for the CIA. I don't work for them anymore. I never actually quit. But I'm going to. I'm a professional cryptologist—something of an expert on ciphers."

The literary page editor, a mild man in an old Harris tweed jacket with Ivy League–issue patches on the elbows, nodded politely. Molton, the managing editor and the editorial writer were already talking about how they would break the story. The managing editor said they would have to put together a team—typesetters, secretaries, researchers—to keep the thing secret even inside the house until the piece ran. Molton saw the story in three parts and started outlining them off the top of his head. "We'll lead off with a piece on Horst Schiller—how he worked for the CIA at the time he committed murder in Munich. We'll follow that with a piece, based on the messages, on the CIA's dirty tricks . . ."

Heller turned back to the literary page editor and asked earnestly, "When's the last time you read the epilogue to Bacon's *Tempest?*"